Nothing Gold Can Stay

by

Mary J. Carter

Nothing Gold Can Stay

COPYRIGHT © 2023 by Mary J. Carter

Cover Art by *Kristian Norris*

The Wild Rose Press, Inc.
PO Box 708
Adams Basin, NY 14410-0708
Visit us at www.thewildrosepress.com

Publishing History
First Edition, 2023
Trade Paperback ISBN 978-1-5092-5065-3
Digital ISBN 978-1-5092-5066-0

Published in the United States of America

"Who are you, really?" she asked as if this were all a dream.

"I am the one destined for you," he assured her.

His words, indeed, his very presence here against Nature's brooding but magnificent sky, seemed torn from the page of a romantic novel. He lured her in such a way Civette could feel the depths of her being drifting willingly to his. She spoke with the voice of her body.

"When you smile at me, I exist," she said.

"This is the world and the heavens themselves when you are near me," he replied.

Civette lifted her face up to his, and in her eyes, there was a wonderment he knew was his to discover. The reawakened wind moved around them. Yet all was soundless—soundless as the moments that hold a sky captive before a storm. Civette took Adrian's heavenly face into her hands and kissed him.

He did not kiss her back.

Civette, being wise, broke away. Behaving as if nothing had happened, she took Adrian's hand and led him to a bench that overlooked the sweeping gardens. They watched and listened as the treetops ceased to sway and the autumn winds returned to the west. It was as if Nature realized her powers of persuasion had failed and was now summoning them back to her core.

Still holding his hand, Civette spoke. "I have a question for you, Adrian. Do you believe in magic spells?"

"With all my heart," he said.

Dedication

For my daughters,
Shelby and Jamie,
in honor of that road trip
when we passed a grove of spooky birch trees,
and you asked me to tell you a story.
Here's another, for all the Halloweens to come.

*A reimagining of
Nathaniel Hawthorne's masterful legend
"Feathertop"
and the subsequent 1911 Broadway play
"The Scarecrow or The Glass of Truth"
written by poet & dramatist, Percy MacKaye*

Chapter One: You've Come Back

One night when half my life behind me lay, I wandered from the straight lost path afar.
~Dante Alighieri—Inferno

Summer 1947

On the northern edge of Fairwell, beneath the ever-flowing clouds, lay a ruin known as Cairy Hollow.

Locals shunned the place. Stories were told, though, whispered tales that grew darker with each retelling. Even those who'd never witnessed the house could picture it in their minds. Cairy Hollow was a haven of restless energy where, it was rumored, the forces of Nature had their day.

What fascination Nature held for this particular territory was any mortal's guess. After all, one rarely gets a straight answer from the wind or the driving rain. It may have been due to the fact that New Englanders could be cold, even in the raging depths of summer. Perhaps it was that the heedless Cairys built their mansion on Nature's sacred ground. Still, there were those who insisted it all came down to a reckless wish whispered in the wrong ear. Whatever the true cause, Nature weighed her judgment with a fierce and unforgiving hand.

A stranger ambling along the river's edge might not,

at first, notice the shell of that once-envied estate. Instead, one would sense the churning mist. Nowhere else but in this vale would it gather. Within that mist, overgrown grass rippled in currents, luring one's gaze up toward the unexpected monument of smoldered wood, pummeled bricks, and shattered glass. At an initial glance, and particularly under a caravan of clouds, Cairy Hollow might appear as the proud jewel of its past. However, with but a sweep of her silvery glance, an emerging moon easily dispelled whatever illusions the deserted manor had clung to. The beauty Cairy Hollow claimed in bygone days would never be realized again.

On a blustery summer night, far below that lonely wreckage, a trespasser appeared. There was no vehicle nearby, no means of transport. It was as if this trespasser had been blown in by the wind. With resolute strides, the man made his way toward the house. The hour was late. Twilight crept in with the fog. The hill ahead was strewn with indistinct rubble. Along the ascent, a faint glimmer rose from the gloom. Kneeling, the man scraped away the sludge. The trampled ground was resentful at first. It held fast to its garments of mud and stones. Beneath the sediment were the remains of a jeweled pin. The clasp was badly crushed. A portion of its golden coil had snapped away.

He held it up, and the whimsical moon winked at the piece. Within that waxy glow, the face of a beautiful woman appeared. Her unusual eyes smiled at him. The man watched until her lovely countenance faded into moonshadow. It troubled him to see her go.

The man considered keeping his treasure. But then a voice inside his head—an alluring voice he cherished from his past—urged him not to. This ornament was meant to rest. Holding it tightly for a moment, he tossed the pin onto a mound of rocks. It rang with a light, metallic noise as it skipped across the rubble. A low wind curled through that forlorn monument and left. The man paused at the sounds.

Before him was a bluff buried deep in wildflowers. The man didn't expect to find such beauty in this desolate stretch. It had the jarring effect of a bright shawl draped over a battered corpse. Crossing the ridge, he brushed their petals with his fingertips. Murmurs from the garden seemed to say:

"You've come back.

We knew you would.

Do you remember this place?

You should.

You were the master of it for an entire day.

One never sees the heavens from the woods.

Stay with us now and forever, if you'd like.

We have stories to tell.

And songs to sing from years gone by, such as—

The winter's passed and the leaves are green. The time has passed that we have seen."

The windswept song echoed about his ears. He had no desire to hear it, and walked on. Over his shoulder, the hushed messages continued.

"No, no, don't leave.

We'd adore the company.

Besides, isn't there something you should tell us?

Something we've been terribly curious about."

Consumed by the sight before him, the trespasser heard no more. A tree lay impaled on the entrance gate. Within a knot of that skewered oak was an entombed crest of gold. The letters *C* and *H* were pressed together and suffocated in bark. Years of vengeful weather had corroded the iron beneath. Scarce little of its varnish remained. Forged arrow rails pointed up toward a salvation that no longer cared.

The man did not turn away. If anything, he was more determined. He put his hand to that once majestic oak and then to his heart before forging on.

What had been a well-groomed road was now a gully of boulders, lifeless tree limbs, leaves, and decay. Only the wild roses thrived in the debris. Their jagged heads and thorns bobbing, they cast wraithlike shadows across the drive. *Come here, come here,* they seemed to chant in the breath of night. *We won't hurt you.*

Guided by the moon's shimmer in a gashed-out stream, the man left the course of the road. He entered an overgrown maze of rhododendrons. Their blossoms were large and facelike in the murky gloom. The ground was blanketed with pink and white petals. He crushed them beneath his feet, misting his path with a fragrance of cloves.

At the heart of this labyrinth stood a statue of an angel. The guardian was kneeling, her pretty head bowed, upon a chipped pedestal. It appeared that her prayers, much like those of the mangled gate, were of no use. The angel's extended arm had been severed, and her crumbled wings tethered by vines. It wasn't just the neglected gardens. There was an unmistakable essence of doom about the place. It was bitter and rank coming after the sugary balm of the flowers, and it engulfed the intruder's lungs with foreboding.

In a notch between the hills were the last vestiges of the house. The man moved closer and, as he did, the place seemed to come alive. Along the winding drive, he swore he could see a steady progression of fine vehicles. The leading car's hood ornament, a gold-plated *Spirit of Ecstasy*, flickered like bright coins through the brume. As the phantom Rolls pulled in beneath the portico, the grand hall beyond burst with light. Strains of music and laughter rose on the breeze, and dancers swirled about as if cradled on clouds. The man knew the lyrics to the old tune. He murmured along, "*It was there I kissed my love a sad goodbye…*"

The light, the music, and the ethereal dancers faded, and waves of fog obliterated the stagelight of the sky. With that motion, all the man's imaginings were swept away. It wasn't that his mind was weak. Indeed, he possessed a mind full of airy notions and fancies. The prankish mist had played tricks on his senses. What remained of the house was silent and still and friendless. No warming smoke curled from the stone-faced chimneys. Even the wrens had long abandoned their nests.

A legion of nameless shrubs and vines had clawed their way through the veranda. Choking the walls, they scaled to where a willful moss conquered the last traces of roofline. The few windowpanes that survived were glazed with neglect, reflecting nothing. There was sadness in the air. It crept in murmurs about the gaping casements and the eroded rails. The desolate house was weeping.

Suddenly, from a half-clad casement, a tiny spark flared. The candlelight grew, casting a hideous form against the wall within. It was the shadow of an old woman, magnifying as she made her way toward the buckled front door. She was reciting a poem in a broken rhythm with her steps. Her breathy prose floated through the ruptured walls.

"The birds have less to say for themselves
In the wood-world's torn despair
Than now these numberless years the elves,
Although they are no less there.
All song of the woods is crushed like some
Wild, easily shattered rose.
Come, be my love in the wet woods; come,
Where the boughs rain when it blows."

With a tug, the door wrenched open. An echo of scraping wood escaped down the halls. The sound frightened the birds from the shadowy trees. Upward they flew, threshing the fog with their wings. Silence returned. The man at the door could have been a demon, it mattered not. The old woman barely raised her hunched form. "Come in," she said.

The trespasser stepped inside. His face reflected the awe he felt as he looked around. Where elegant wallpaper once reigned, years of mold had formed sinister outlines of flying creatures, phantoms, and elongated faces locked in torment. Ravens had gathered on the musty furniture and atop the scat-stained sculptures. A few had even perched themselves on the gilded portrait frames. With tilted heads and emotionless stares, the birds studied their unexpected guest.

"I saw you walking up the hill," the old woman said.

The visitor nodded as if he couldn't quite remember. "This house, is it yours now?" he asked.

"I fly in from time to time," she replied. "This was the Cairy mansion in years past. John Cairy was the last to reside in this fool's palace. His mortal remains are buried somewhere around these parts. Only the crickets know where. It might be comforting to know that his soul fared better."

"Does anyone ever—visit?" the man asked.

The old woman scoffed. "Curious children, mostly. Many don't make it past the essence of the woods. Only the boldest aren't frightened by felled branches and warnings murmured in the wind. Some intrepid adults, such as yourself, make it all the way to this door. Adults can sense the anguish here. For the young, it's mostly a dare, or a chilling adventure. Still, no one cares much about the Cairys. It's this house everyone comes to gape at and hear tell of—this house, the power that destroyed it, and the wild souls that possess it now."

Hearing this, the ravens ruffled their feathers and called out with pride.

"I am eager to hear that story," the visitor confessed.

"Are you certain? You may have little interest in stories about hobgoblins and wraiths and the ghastly fiends of Nature."

A trail of air whipped around an outside wall and left with a piercing howl. The man went to the window half expecting to see something, or someone, there.

"'Tis the wind," said his host, "and nothing more."

"For a moment there, I thought—"

"Even thoughts here are nothing more than fleeting ghosts." Picking up a gnarled and solitary candle, the old woman motioned at her guest to follow. "So, it's the demise of Cairy Hollow you wish to hear about? For that, we must roll back the hands of time, and open with the tale of a broken man."

They settled themselves upon the skeletal staircase that swept toward the open roofline and on to the stars. The old woman drew a deep breath. The ravens leaned in and listened.

"It all began on a restless night," she told them. "A hooded figure entered Ravenswood Forest. With that first step, everything changed. Darkness rose from the damp places.

"A sensation of being followed caused the hooded figure to whirl about and look. There was no one there. Not even a sound. Only a vast meadow could be seen beyond the hem of the woods. Its waist-high grass swayed with the rhythm of a moonlit ocean. Despite the surrounding gloom, it was a vision of peacefulness and comfort. However, here, within this fortress of trees, shadows were preferred. Arched branches twisted and curved and happily distorted any hope of light.

"The hooded figure moved on with cautious steps. It was apparent that Lady Nature cared nothing about offering direction. Every turn mirrored a path taken before. The farther into the woods this figure fled, the heavier the night air fashioned its clouds above the cold and listless earth.

"Leaning against a moss-covered boulder, the intruder paused. A chilled wind swept by, billowing the intruder's hood and revealing the face of a troubled young woman. With hesitation, she uttered a hello. Something beneath last year's leaves rustled by. Not far ahead, the movement and the noises ceased. Nothing appeared. No one was there. All around, a weighted silence fell. Even the untamed wind held its breath. Taking its cue from the fading horizon, the forest shuttered its last beacons of light.

"The woman said hello once again. Her voice startled two ravens out of a stark birch tree. With a smooth circle and a taunting *ca-caw*, the sleek birds flew off toward the east. Without questioning why, the woman followed.

"At long last, a tiny glow beckoned over the gnarled roots and knotted banks of vine. In the clearing ahead stood a cottage. An outpost dwelling on the Cairy estate, the place had fallen into disrepair. Storm gusts rattled the frail windowpanes, and even the house itself seemed to shudder. The harbinger ravens settled themselves on the moss-covered roof. One uttered a low and desolate sound, prompting the other to laugh. Hiding behind a half-starved elm, the woman waited and watched. She knew that Olen Devereux would soon appear.

"Within minutes, he emerged from a woodland path. Sturdy of muscle, Olen Devereux was surprisingly graceful. A smooth-talking man, he was known for his scent of warm leather and his reckless, ice-blue eyes. For all his counterfeits, women adored him. Some would say, with a blush, that Olen Devereux was like a wayward and naughty child.

"Moving through the slate gray shadows and past the ghostly lilacs, Olen stepped up onto the porch. The boards were sagging and barren but for the busy spiders weaving their webs between the rails. Olen knocked on the door, and Bess Dalby answered.

"Bess was a lovely being, exhilarating as the wind and bright as a summer sun. She lived among the wild souls of the forest and was not afraid. Bess was a seamstress. Working by needle, thread, and lamplight, she lived alone. But Bess was not entirely lonely. She smiled up at Olen. He stepped inside.

"The woman watched Olen and Bess through the window glass. How comfortable they were together, how natural. Bess began to laugh. The glow on her face made her truly beautiful. Bess then drew the shade, leaving her intruder to imagine what only the shadows could see.

"Fretful moments passed. The woman sighed. As if to mock her, the breath of her sigh lingered in the late October air. She could see her glum reflection in its cloud. The woman turned toward the inky outline of the woods. Gaunt branches, bowed by the wind, creaked with an echoing laughter. Hearing this, the ravens on the roof joined in.

" 'What a cursed place this is,' the woman muttered.

"Fog painted in the spaces between the trees. Something with a texture of bristled fur crept by her heels. The woman looked down, only to discover that she was ensnared in thorns. One tenacious snarl had, somehow, wound itself around her ankle. The young woman could feel the nettles burn. Trying not to scream, she wrenched her foot out of their grasp. The spiky quills surrendered with a snap. Recoiling, they slithered away. She watched the groundcover tremble in its wake. Gone, gone, she hoped. Gone, but where? The woman hugged herself in an effort to steady her breathing.

"It was then she realized something. Waves of fog were draining from the trees. Tumbling toward her, they banked around her coat. As the woman waved it away, the brume settled in the form of a shrouded specter. Hovering, it tilted its head as if to ask her a question. *Why is your tortured face so pale?*

"She raced through the pasture, the defiant Indian grass lashing at her heels. 'What have I done to you?' she begged of the grievous Nature around her.

"A cluster of moss flew with a fiendish shriek into her face. It stung her eyes and filled her gasping mouth with the sour medicine of moldy earth. Back through the starless woods the young woman stumbled and ran, while the burgeoning skies howled and leaves dropped like tears from the trees.

"The woman didn't stop until she reached the lawn of Cairy Hollow. Encased in a pool of gray light, she searched through the windows until she found John Cairy. Entering a side door, she joined him in his study.

" 'Leona,' he said. John knew by the look on his sister's face that she had disturbing news to share.

"His head bowed, John Cairy listened while, all about the house, servants moved from room to room extinguishing the bone-white candles one by one."

Chapter Two: Before a Mirror

October 31st, 1925

"You have to witness this with your own eyes."

With prancing steps, Civette Middleton led her beau across the marble hall of Cairy Hollow and into the semi-darkness of the ballroom. A section of wall was adorned with dusky green drapes fringed with tassels of gold. The young man, Richard Marlow by name, seemed entirely unimpressed.

"You dragged me in here to look at curtains?" he said.

"Don't you like them?" Civette asked.

Richard shrugged. "Not particularly," he confessed.

Civette set him before the drapes. "Forget all that. I want to test you," she said.

Richard glanced about. "By way of the furnishings? I'm an accountant, Civette, not a designer."

"No, silly man, within this mirror. I want to be assured that you truly love me."

"There's a mirror back there?" he asked her.

Civette explained that it wasn't just any mirror. It was found tucked away in one of the estate barns. Mrs. Beals, the housekeeper, knew all about this special looking-glass. It once belonged to a sorceress living deep within Ravenswood Forest. The mirror was called the Glass of Truth. It reflected viewers as they truly were. It was an amazing piece of magic, really. Not a misstep in motive or character could be shielded from its sight.

"Your mirror sounds more like a parlor game to me," said Richard. "Something to drag out when the champagne is gone and the women are bored. Now tell me, did your uncle actually approve adding such a waste of space to his ballroom?"

"Again, it's called the Glass of Truth, and there is nothing wasteful about it. Honestly, Richard, how can you not appreciate something as unique and mysterious as this?"

Richard made a face. It did matter. He asked her again how such a questionable piece ended up in the ballroom. Civette avoided Richard's question by staring at his feet.

"What have you been doing? Your shoes are dusty," she said.

"I went for a walk," he replied.

"You went for a walk before breakfast?" she said. "How unlike you."

Civette was smiling. Still, her questions annoyed him. "So, I'm here in front of your monster mirror," Richard said over his true thoughts. "What next?"

"When I open the drapes, you must look directly within," she said.

"Can't you see in my eyes the love I feel for you?"

"Clever eyes can lie." Civette leaned into his side. "You and I have been thrown together since we were snotty-nosed children. You're like an older brother to me. Other men gaze at me with far different looks— looks, I will confess, that make me go all weak and fluttery inside."

"Is that a fact?" Richard replied. Civette did not

answer, nor did she blush, not even in the slightest. "And here I thought I was special," he complained.

His gentle plea did not sway her. The only response Richard received was a playful toss of her glistening hair. He found this hurtful, especially on top of the other slights he'd just endured. Richard looked at Civette, truly looked at her, with wounded curiosity. She was such a compelling creature. It really didn't matter that Civette had a mindset fixed on the make-believe. In fact, her whimsical notions typically humored him. So, why this abrupt change? It was maddening to allow a simple looking-glass to shatter their charming world. Richard changed his tactics.

"Consider the risks, my darling," he said. "What if this mirror proves I'm no better than a stage villain?"

"I will leave you for the first attractive man I see," she replied.

"And what if you end up being false?"

"It's likely you'll stay with me and try to change my mind."

"Consider it done."

A sudden noise interrupted their jests. A goldfinch, menaced by two ravens, had been forced into the window glass. Civette and Richard rushed over to look. The delicate bird lay dead on the lawn.

"It's an omen," said Civette.

"Don't be foolish," said Richard. "Such things happen every day."

Civette remained at the window. The death of that innocent creature held her there. She found herself mourning that lost little bird and its lost little life. Its glasslike eyes, wide and glaring, reflected such horror.

Richard pulled at her hand. Returning to the mirror,

Civette tied back the lush velvet drapes. Sprites of dust danced on pale cylinders of morning light. The Glass of Truth, with all its fine gilt edging, was unveiled. However, the cast of a sullen day played cruel tricks at first. Richard was blinded by the silver light. His hair appeared deathly white. Civette could not see her reflection from her sparkling eyes to her heart. Being the superstitious girl that she was, Civette began to fuss. Fortunately, a passing cloud blocked Nature's sleight, and all seemed well again.

"It appears that you do love me," said Civette.

"What a goose you are. Of course I love you," he replied.

Civette looked back to the glass with rapture. "There we both are, as we have always appeared to one another."

"How amazing that a mirror belonging to some moonstruck woman in the woods should actually turn out to be—a mirror," Richard replied.

It was then that Civette's uncle emerged from the cooler regions of the back hall. At close inspection, John Cairy was a commonplace specimen of middle manners and middle years. Had he been a stranger alongside his fellow man at a roadside tavern, no one would have suspected the wealth that propelled his younger self. No barmaid would ever again witness the light of love and happiness that once enlivened his face. His features and complexion were now trained to perform as a mask of polite behavior and little else.

"Are you rehearsing your Romeo and Juliet scene for your highly anticipated entrance tonight?" he jested.

"I was showing Richard the latest addition to our ballroom," said Civette.

"Your imaginative niece claims this looking-glass

was once the charmed property of a witch," said Richard.

John inspected the mirror. A shadow of painful recognition swept over him. "Where did this come from?" he asked.

Alarmed by her uncle's reaction, Civette attempted to sound nonchalant. "Evan and Phoebe brought it in from the barn where it has been stored all these years. It was terribly neglected. I had them clean it and place it here. I think it looks ever so lovely, don't you?"

John Cairy was not listening. Instead, he continued to stare, fixated, at his own reflection. An aura the color of jaded smoke hovered, strange and misgiving, about his weary head. He looked behind him. Nothing was there—not even an explainable column of morning light. Yet, when he turned back to the mirror, the portending wisp remained. John wondered why no one else noticed. Even though the ballroom was cold, John went to a window and opened it. "I imagine your mother won't be thrilled by the presence of this mirror, either."

"Did I hear myself being mentioned?"

Civette's mother entered and paused at the doorway. Although she'd been of fair interest in her youth, years of suspicion and loneliness had dulled her to the core. John barely looked at his sister. Leona's existence was something John quietly lamented.

"We were discussing this mirror," said Civette.

"Why, it's an exact copy of a mirror we once owned," said Leona. "I remember thinking as a child that this gold carving on top was the hat of a whimsical court jester."

"Do you mean the mirror you gave Bess Dalby?" asked John.

Leona flinched at the mention of Bess's name. "I

loaned it to that creature," Leona declared. "I never gave it to her. Why would I have done such a thing?"

"Who is Bess Dalby?" asked Richard.

"Was," Leona corrected. "Bess Dalby was an ungifted seamstress who freeloaded on this estate. Not at all pretty, I tell you, and highly dramatic, to boot. She claimed to commune with the spirits of Nature, or some such thing. I remember her boasting that she could move clouds from the sun, revive dead flowers, and even turn her scarecrow into a living man, if she cared to. Can you imagine such rubbish? There was no lack of stories from her, or about her. Bess Dalby ended up nothing but trouble for anyone who was foolish enough to cross her path. Thank goodness she's gone."

"Oh, do stop," said John. The bitterness of wasted years flowed with every word.

Leona wasn't listening. Patting her hair, Leona looked into the mirror. Her hand paused mid-air. Her image was as lackluster as old china that had been shoved to the back of the pantry. The moment enraged her. This was not how Leona Cairy Middleton envisioned herself. Not in the least. There had to be something wrong with that accursed glass.

Without a further word, Leona dropped the curtain and left the room. A menacing wind whipped in from the east. Two ravens rode its crest past the window.

Chapter Three: Ne'er-Do-Wells in the Woods

The workmen stared at the cottage.

Mrs. Middleton was correct in saying the cottage had to come down. There were gaping holes in the moss-covered roof, and hornets' towers rooted everywhere. The porch boards were bone-colored and snapped away in places. The dried-out front door had buckled. Taking it all in, the taller man said to the other that the cottage was an eyesore.

They went inside and were horrified by what they saw. Ravens had taken over the place. What furniture remained had been torn up for nesting. One raven had settled herself on the hood of an old wooden cradle and was rocking it while she crooned. It was a startling sight, and cold. It was colder even than the grip of late autumn outside.

Their assessment completed, the men walked away. Their conversation was volleyed about by the trees. The two men never looked back. If they had, they would have witnessed a sight more haunting than the derelict cottage itself.

A pair of ravens flew down from the cottage roof. Barely had their talons touched earth when they materialized as two ladies, sleek and dark and astonishingly beautiful. Atop their heads were serpentine snoods capped with atifets cresting in the form of beaks. Instead of customary gowns, they wore form-fitting suits of satin black beneath their flowing yet jagged capes. Bejeweled from their heads to their high-set heels, their attire seemed a mysterious blend of medieval and visionary.

The Raven Ladies let out a cry. The wind captured their sound, sending it upward in a booming spiral. The fury of it caused the weathervane on the cottage roof to spin.

That weathervane was a unique piece, a bold grasshopper struck in bronze. As it spun it inhaled the Raven Ladies' lament. Dazzling sparks, the hue of river lightning, danced above the roofline. A wave of smoke rushed over the tip of the cottage, gray, piqued, and impatient. Lingering over the weathervane, it caught itself up in the maelstrom, only to vanish, revealing a bizarre little man balancing on the pitched roof where the grasshopper had been. Dressed as a strolling player from days of old, this airborne being had a horned head with wiry wisps of hair, two coal-like eyes, a crooked nose, and a devilish grin. Without so much as a hello, he began to sing:

"With a host of furious fancies,
Whereof I am commander,
With a burning spear and a horse of air,
To the wilderness I wander.
By a knight of ghosts and shadows,
I summoned am to tourney,
Ten leagues beyond the wild world's end,
Methinks my final journey."

"Gad Zeus, what noise," said the raven known as Mirth.

With a laugh and an effortless leap, the man settled to the ground upon his small, clasping feet.

"Why are you always singing the same tired song, Balefire?" complained the raven known as Sorrow.

"*Captain* Balefire," he corrected. His remark was met with icy stares. "As you wish," he said. "I saw, and heard, what just happened. An eyesore, indeed. I understand your frustration."

"That's putting it mildly," Sorrow replied. "Because of a stupid woman's memories, we'll all have to find another place to shelter. And that includes you, Balefire."

"Noted," he said. "But we have time to change that. And perhaps our move could end up for the better."

The Raven Ladies tilted their pretty heads in question.

"What do you say to having Cairy Hollow all to ourselves?" Balefire asked.

"Impossible," said Sorrow.

"John Cairy has a niece. Even though she's his sister's child, she'll likely end up with the place," said Mirth.

"What if we get rid of the niece?" said Balefire.

"Could we corner her and peck her eyes out?" asked Sorrow. She sounded hopeful.

"Let's execute such intentions with an air of romance," said Balefire. Glancing over a field, he noticed an odd sculpture of vegetation, utensils, flails, and sticks. "What have we here?" he asked.

"Bess Dalby's long abandoned scarecrow," said Mirth.

"That, I knew," said Balefire.

"For a garden that no longer serves purpose," Sorrow concluded.

"Now, now, ladies. In Nature's world, we are rarely

hasty. But when we are, we are magnificent." His odd face quite merry, Balefire moved toward the scarecrow. "See here, he has a puffed-up chest, a stick up his backside, and not an ounce of brains to balance it all. Yes, he'll do nicely as a man."

With lightning-fast movements, the Raven Ladies hopped forward and, with bobbing heads, they studied Bess's forgotten scarecrow. Their faces reflected contempt.

"He's nothing but bones."

"And reeking rot."

"He has no beauty."

"He has no heart."

From the trees, the lingering leaves began to rustle. To those on the ground, it seemed as if they whispered, *He could be divinely handsome and true.*

Balefire groaned. "Don't listen to them," he said. "They are autumn's last leaves, and far too sentimental. Now, on to our true mission."

"Which is?" questioned Mirth.

"To somehow spark this pile of rubbish into marriage material for the illustrious Miss Middleton," said Balefire.

Sorrow made a face. "You poor, delusional man," she said. Sorrow felt for Balefire in the sense that anything doomed possessed the ability to impassion her.

"You could make it so, Captain," hinted Mirth. "You could make him resemble a real man."

"I could," agreed the imp.

"Shall our dandy puppet be saucy and cruel?" said Sorrow.

"With a joyfully conniving mind?" added Mirth.

"What mind?" said Sorrow. "There's no place to put

one."

Plucking a fallen leaf from the ground, Balefire tapped it rhythmically against his chin. "Our conqueror should have a lively face, even if he's solely meant to rule over a barren field."

"Let's skip past the looks and the royal duties," said Sorrow. "We are about to lose our home."

Balefire did not appear to have a care. Spotting a broken ladderback chair on the cottage porch, he settled it within the scarecrow as a strong set of ribs. Balefire then filled its chest with corn stalks for lungs, and straw to hold it all together. Next, came a pumpkin head. It was a bit bumpy and rough on one side, and sadly rumpled on the other. But it was the best choice from the field. Last, but not least, Balefire gifted him a blood-red beet root for a heart.

"What a sharp lad you are," he said.

"Sharp," began Sorrow.

"And naked," concluded Mirth.

Balefire had an idea. They could see it glowing on his metallic face. "Let us rely on She-who-knows-all-about-adornment," he said. Stepping back, Balefire held out his hands. "Lady Nature, work thy wonders."

The forest around them swept into action. A nearby bank of clover spun a dress shirt and stockings as fine and as soft as spring petals. From the hayfield came a golden waistcoat with acorn buttons set so handsome no one would guess their humble origins. The laughing shrubs wove a pair of trousers as good as any that could be tailored in a big city. Meanwhile, the wind and the leaves fashioned their scarecrow with an autumn jacket that reigned beyond comparison.

Balefire neatened the scarecrow's attire. As he

worked, storm clouds crept higher over the horizon, and the air was rich with the promise of rain. Its warning breeze was welcomed. A stubborn drought had ruled for far too long. In the distance, thunder rolled. The Raven Ladies flinched, poised for flight. Balefire, however, paid no heed. He even appeared to delight in the threat of an oncoming gale.

"I say we model our puppet after Prince Charming," he said. "What a delightful innocent he would be."

"Princes are dull," declared Mirth.

"He'd be better off as a wolf," said Sorrow.

"A wolf?" echoed Mirth.

Sorrow shrugged. "Certainly, a wolf. What woman doesn't love one?"

"Better to be a wolf in sheep's clothing," said Balefire. "So, the true plan is this: Our prince of sticks will capture the niece's heart, thus luring her away from that mansion high above it all. With that, it's only a matter of time until we woodland creatures take it over shingle by shingle, and room by room. Simple, yes?"

"There is one catch," said Mirth.

"Only one?" asked Balefire.

"Civette Middleton is in love with a man named Richard Marlow," said Sorrow.

"We saw him. As humans go, he's not entirely revolting," said Mirth.

"Bah," said Balefire. "Her new suitor here will be leagues ahead of that Marlow man." Balefire stood aside and pointed at his creation. "He'll have good looks tempered with a dash of imagination, a pinch of satire, and a brimming dose of charm. What else might a gentleman caller require?"

"A conscience," Sorrow said quietly. This made

them all pause—if but for the briefest of moments.

"Let that come after the luring, and thus too late," said Mirth.

Balefire nodded in agreement. "Our dandy will need a nouveau British accent, and an air of old money. Oh, and a pair of shoes."

All at once, the grape arbor vines began to sway, and orchestrated whispers brushed the air. Before anyone could question what was going on, a fine pair of leather-like shoes were catapulted out of the stalks. Balefire bowed in thanks.

"One last thing. Do forgive me." Taking up a handful of raven feathers from the patchy dirt, Balefire pierced them, one by one, about the sagging pumpkin head. "From the sable scalps of your adversaries, a plumage guaranteed to render you as enchanting as the darkest secrets of night. Yes, we are all charming artists, to be sure."

"His hair is quite fine," admitted Mirth.

"But what about those hands? Must they be flails?" asked Sorrow.

"Indeed," said Balefire. "One for satire and one for wit, just like you ladies."

"How you flatter us," the Raven Ladies replied together.

"I knew you'd see it that way," Balefire murmured. He then lifted his arms and his face toward the sky. "May I have your attention, please. I bring you an extraordinary rogue, a man of good fortune, and a master of grace. He is a paragon of devotion, quick with compliments both false and true, to woo—and win—his ladylove. He's as handsome as a god, blessed with the grace of angels, and a subtle dash of 'devil may care,' affectionate, honorable, and merry. May I present Nature's most loyal and trusted servant, Monsieur Pumpkinhead."

The scarecrow had not changed a wink but for its stuffed chest, its artful attire, and the band of feathers poked through its dismal pumpkin skull.

"What hoax is this?" asked Sorrow.

Mirth agreed. "He appears to be more of a *Monsieur Pumpkinrot*."

Balefire placed his crooked fingers upon his temples. "It pains me to weave my spells in the wilds of New England. The citizens here are so skeptical, so quick to condemn and yell such nasty things as 'demon' and 'warlock.' It jars me."

"It's true," said Sorrow. "You haven't been yourself since you swarmed London in 1748."

"Can you really bring this pitiful creation to life?" asked Mirth.

"I—can try," Balefire mumbled.

"And we can help," echoed the Raven Ladies and the leaves in the trees.

"In the beginning—" Balefire began. He stopped and peered intently at the scarecrow. "In the beginning was—" he hesitated again.

"The gourd," jested Mirth.

"It shall have to do," said Balefire. "From these modest ingredients, may thy spirit rise."

The Raven Ladies backed away as Balefire began to spin about the scarecrow. The dust at Balefire's feet rose in charged clouds, whirling above the meadow and covering the swaying grass in a lavender hue. As Balefire circled, he called out compelling phrases to the wonders of Nature around him. The Raven Ladies threw back their heads and uttered rattling cries. Beneath their chants, a hollow chorus rumbled from the trees. The skies went dark, and a second coil of thunder crawled up from the earth. Its rumble bore through every living creature.

With the hook of his hand, Balefire gashed an opening across the scarecrow's lower face. "Speak, Pumpkin Jack, speak and conquer!" he ordered. The restless wind and the pulsating earth ceased with a violent roar.

Nothing happened.

Balefire became angered. "By the dog! Have I lost the hang of it? Zeus propelled the lightning, and all were amazed. Ra championed the sun, and all were warmed. But what does Balefire do? Ah, the devil—that's it! Our matrix requires a blaze of hellfire."

Balefire turned an intent gaze upon the Raven Ladies. "Go to the cottage," he said. "On the inside frame of the bedroom closet door rests a golden pin. It was given to Bess by John Cairy as a pledge of his gentlemanly admiration. Bring it here, or all is lost. Our defender must have it as the drive of revenge within him."

Balefire's command reeked of evil. Sorrow shivered. "Perhaps what we're doing is all wrong," she said.

"It's too late," Balefire replied. "There was a slight pulse from his heart. I felt it. Would you crush a baby starling doing its best to break free from its shell? Prevent Nature from setting forth such beauty upon this eager earth? Surely, you wouldn't. So bring me that talisman. You will thank me for it."

Mirth practically flew inside the cottage and

returned with the pin. The centerpiece of it was a diamond snake wrapped around a shining coil of gold. The snake's eyes were emeralds, and a bright ruby rested like a large apple in its mouth. After a moment's hesitation, Mirth gave the pin to Balefire. He held it in his open hand.

"John Cairy. That man admired Bess Dalby so." Balefire sighed. "They would sit there together, upon those plain and dusty steps, and smile and talk and laugh about everything and yet nothing at all. For so many, however, time runs its course. Smiles dim, talk fades to silence, and laughter flows into tears. That which is passionately called young love often dies within the lyrics of sad, old songs."

Mirth, being young and headstrong, cared nothing about the death of things. She only knew what she wanted now. Mirth indicated with a wave of her hands that Balefire should get on with it. Balefire obliged, fastening the pin within the scarecrow's golden vest. The jewels atop the golden coil radiated with a stark and merciless light.

"Brighten stone, brighten soul, 'tis the realm upon us. Torch the light within his eyes, nearer now, Adonis," he chanted. Balefire's utterance rang with a static hum.

The emerald eyes in the pin flared once more, and as they did, the scarecrow lurched on its rickety frame. Balefire was ecstatic. He held out his hands to the Raven Ladies. "Come, we must dance in celebration of this new life," he said.

Balefire drew the ladies in. An unearthly cry blew through the trees, the very crests of which began to arc and weave against the violet streaks in the sky. With raised heads, the dancing trio chanted:

"Flails flip, broom sweep
Think deep
Sic itur ad astra.
Cornstalk and beetroot talk
Nunc aut nunquam.
Corn cob and raven feather
End the spell all together
Vivo et vincam."

The hollow wind carried itself into a cyclone around the scarecrow. The scarecrow abruptly raised his head. He was not attractive in the least. He was unyielding and dark and cold. The whirlwind about him splintered into hundreds of tiny feather-like curls, and died away.

"I've done all I can," Balefire told Mirth. "It's up to you now."

"What do you mean?" she asked.

"You must give him the breath of promise. Only then will ignorant people see the beauty in him." Balefire paused. "All I ask, all I humbly beg, is that you grant our gentleman prince a kiss. With that single kiss, he will live one day."

Mirth was astonished. All this magic and expectation for just one day? No sane woman would fall for a man she'd known for less than a day.

"Fine, then. I'm a player. Let's up the ante," said Balefire. "If this fanciful slop pile is granted the gift of honest love, he will become a true, living man. But he has only one day for that to happen. One day."

"And at the end of this one day, what else happens?" asked Sorrow.

"Ah," Balefire replied, "I forgot to reveal the resolution to our theatrical masterpiece. This handsome rogue meets and seduces Civette Middleton. Act One, he lures her away. Act Two, he lures her away to this very cottage where you ladies and your kin get to gouge her eyes out, just for fun, as the grand finale."

"I like this plan," said Sorrow.

"Noted," said Balefire. He swung toward Mirth. "And now, for that kiss."

"Why me and not her?" asked Mirth.

"For the simple reason that you embody the joy of first love, and Sorrow here represents the end results of it."

Sorrow smirked. She was proud of her truths. Mirth sighed and stood before the scarecrow. There was such emptiness in his carved-out eyes. It was as if the solitude of night sheltered there. Closing her own eyes, she put her lips to his cold, hard face.

" 'What were thy lips the worse for one poor kiss,' " quoted Sorrow.

The scarecrow drew a deep and rasping breath. Mirth staggered back. The scarecrow's features were frenzied, and he began to writhe. The paltry boards of his framework snapped away as easily as dried twigs. The crumpled scarecrow uttered a low and mournful wail. He reeked of mildewed hay and incinerated flesh, and his eyes blazed with despair.

Sorrow panicked. Could not the rest of them see that this tragic creature was begging for death? Sorrow felt an overwhelming desire, born of pity and of fear, to have their hasty creation destroyed. She picked up a large stone, but Mirth held her back.

Mirth pointed. The scarecrow was struggling to stand. With each rattled breath he drew, the rancid air about him cleared. With each arduous lift of his head, his face colored with beauty. His neck grew stately and strong, his chin chiseled. Prominent cheekbones shaped beneath the blossoming bronze of his skin. Even his nose was nobly fitting to his expression. But his eyes were best. The Raven Ladies considered them, for lack of a more poetic word, eloquent. In moments, the once despicable scarecrow was calm and magnificent. Not a man in one's most secretive dreams could ever compare.

"He's as alluring as a golden light in the cradle of the universe," exclaimed Sorrow.

"All this beauty thrust upon an unsuspecting beast," said Balefire. "Do you think it's wasted?"

"No," said Mirth.

"His eyes possess the blaze of a hunter's moon," said Sorrow.

"They are windows of wonder," observed Mirth.

"He was but born today," said Balefire. "Now, take a step, Prince Scarecrow."

Their creation did as he was told. His first pace was ungainly and tentative, resulting in him collapsing against Balefire.

"Distress not, my festered friend, 'twas well attempted," said the captain.

With a laboring breath that crackled like straw, the scarecrow stood tall. Raising his trembling arm, he arched it in an awkward salute.

"See how he hails," said Balefire.

"And with such—grace," said Mirth.

Sorrow was mystified. "He grows more handsome by the minute."

Balefire smiled at the transformed scarecrow. "We shall name you Sir Adrian Bramwell for as long as the sentiment and your celebrated day of reign shall last. Across the sea on broomstick legs to sweep the gullible

Miss Middleton away for our benefit. Sir Adrian Bramwell. It does have a treacherous fairytale-gone-wrong ring to it."

"I would simply call him George," said Sorrow, to which no one paid the least bit of mind.

Balefire placed the scarecrow's hand on his own shoulder to steady him. "Are you ready to receive an audience? The first of what shall be several eager young ladies begs to present herself."

With a wondrous grin, Mirth curtseyed low. Her silken cape rustled the dust of the field. "My lord," she said with unaccustomed seriousness.

The scarecrow struggled to speak. "My la-dy," he managed to say, which caused the Raven Ladies to shriek with surprise.

"He called me 'my lady,' " said Mirth. "I shall die with delight."

"Say it again, Master Bramwell," commanded Sorrow.

Look within your heart. The words will come, whispered the leaves.

"From—the depths—of—my—heart, dear la-dy." The elegant scarecrow attempted to say more, but he could not form a single thought. He trembled in frustration.

"He is crippled by the violence of his emotions," exclaimed Sorrow.

"He is merely going to fall," said Mirth.

"Master Bramwell requires a walking stick," said the captain.

Balefire faced Bess's dilapidated cottage and raised his left arm slowly toward the roof. The base of the weathervane upon which Balefire had been tethered as a grasshopper began to sway. With a snap, it broke away from the buckled slates. Floating down against the lavender sky, it nestled within Balefire's waiting grasp. Balefire moved his hand over the pedestal cap, causing it to glow like a kindled ruby. Its gleam was answered with a shudder of lightning across the sky. They all looked up in wonderment and then back to the radiating gem.

Balefire placed his palm upon the ruby and, within a mirage of air, Balefire was attired in a fine frock coat with a low-cut vest. His white shirt was topped with a small bowtie, the ends of which were pointed fashionably down. Balefire's tousled hair was neatened, and a stylish mustache sprouted above his sly grin.

Mirth was astonished. "Captain Balefire, you have no idea the respect I have for you right now," she said.

"Respect is fallow praise meant to cover where no true feelings exist. Be in awe of me, dear Mirth. It's a far better tribute, and one I'm sure you'll recall with passion over time." He turned to the scarecrow. "Attend, Sir Adrian Bramwell. I am Captain Balefire, your mentor, and I am ready to accompany you. Are you prepared for your task?"

The scarecrow nodded as the words flowed less haltingly from his lips. "I go—with my mentor—Captain Balefire—to pay my respects to Mr. John—Cairy—and conquer the heart of his—niece—Civette." The scarecrow bowed to Mirth once again, this time with a tad more elegance. "Permit me, my lady," he concluded.

"Permit you?" Mirth exclaimed. "God speed."

"Uh, uh, uh," cautioned Sorrow. "We dare not call upon that Being at such a time."

"How true, sister," agreed Mirth. "Captain Balefire,

you must teach him his tricks along the way. Do not let him fail."

Balefire grinned. "Trust me. Between here and Cairy Hollow, I will be the wind about his head and the devil glued to his ear. It is a task for which I am well prepared."

The Raven Ladies were beside themselves with wonder. They beheld their scarecrow's face, and especially his eyes. Black as night they were, but the light within them shone of molten gold. They were compelling eyes, but there seemed to be no substance beyond their brush of beauty. It was as if he were looking without seeing and seeing without feeling. If eyes were indeed the mirror to the soul, it was evident he did not possess one. But then again, did their scarecrow require a soul? A soul was but a reservoir for all the things one has been. Their newly created champion had yet to be. Perhaps an emissary sent to destroy an unsuspecting person's life was better off without scruples. How welcomed it would be, Sorrow told herself, to commit evil against an enemy and not suffer a care.

From the splayed oak limbs above, their fellow ravens began to call.

"Listen," said Sorrow.

"Your legion heralds your arrival," said Mirth.

"Long reign Sir Adrian Bramwell," the Raven Ladies chanted together.

"Count them," said Sorrow. "There's one for sorrow."

"Two for mirth," said the lady herself.

Balefire trailed his arm across the unsettled horizon. "There's three, flying straightaway to Cairy Hollow. Three for a wedding as the treasured verses claim. If events go as we've planned them, my patriarch of the corn, that doomed wedding will be yours."

"Flight of the crows," said Mirth.

"Tells how the wind blows," said Sorrow.

The Raven Ladies arched their sleek backs and threw back their heads. The burnish of their splendid jewels melted away, and their sleek costumes formed into feathers. With a shrill call, the glossy ravens spiraled upward, becoming one with the stormy sky.

"Go on your way," they called to Balefire from the air. "Dazzle the girl and bring us all our reward."

With halting motions, Bramwell looked upward. "My distinguished ladies—believe me to be—your most devoted—and obedient—servant."

Hail, Sir Adrian Bramwell, the voices of Nature rejoiced. The scarecrow marveled at his praise. Balefire did notice a change within his puppet's glance. It was a light of reckoning. Balefire was pleased. Fully prepared, they walked away. As they did, the anxious skies splintered with light, and the crows cawed triumphantly from the trees.

Chapter Four: Arrival

A steady stream of florists carried arrangements into the ballroom of Cairy Hollow. Richard Marlow eyed the overblown bouquets and laughed.

"Who died or is about to?" he asked through the haze of his fourth cigarette that morning.

Leona scurried in. Her sullen mood from the prior hour had mostly dissipated. No one particularly noticed. "Why are you lounging about when we have our Halloween Ball happening here tonight?" she asked.

Observing the profusion of flowers, John shook his head. "More to the point, why are we going through such an expense for people who are here merely for free food and drink?"

"And to witness Richard and Civette's touching rendition of *Romeo and Juliet*," reminded his sister.

"Looks more like their funeral, to me," John mumbled.

Tall, gangly, and attired in clothing yet to fit him, a young man named Evan appeared at the door. His father was the groundskeeper on the estate. Evan was a gardener. However, Evan had been coerced into playing a footman for the evening's festivities. The young man's face demonstrated his lack of enthusiasm over the prospect.

"There's a visitor," Evan reported. He shuffled as he spoke.

"This early? Who is it?" John asked. He found it necessary to speak in a raised voice because the family's hounds had begun to bark.

"A stranger, sir, but a gentleman, I'm guessing. He's got a manservant of sorts. An odd one, with weird, pointy ears."

As she was long accustomed to doing, Leona Middleton dashed to the window to see what kind of vehicle their caller owned. Leona was always one to judge any guest's importance by the conveyances they owned and the clothing they wore.

"I see no car," she said. Her tone, as it could be in such cases, was dismissive. What Leona did notice against the unsettled morning was a pair of luminous ravens. They heckled at her from the juniper tree. Leona glared. They glared back.

"His vehicle was left in town," Evan was saying. "They walked."

"Walked? We're quite far," John observed.

"Perhaps he's perspiring and should remain outside," said Richard.

"Don't keep our guest waiting," John told Evan. "Have Alice bring him here while you get the hounds to hush. What could possibly be wrong? They're howling in such an ungodly way."

"Sorry, sir, but Alice ran straightaway to her room. When she saw your guest, Alice mumbled something about having to comb her hair."

Evan left, shaking his head. Leona leaned toward her brother.

"Who do you think this is?" she practically hissed. "It can't be anyone I know. If it were, they'd simply walk in. My friends are perfectly at ease here."

Her weary brother and his depleted bank account couldn't agree more.

"Oh, dear God," Richard whispered to Civette. "I despise socializing."

"And I adore it," Civette replied. "Oh, Richard, have no fears. Merely say the word, and I will smooth down your rough edges in no time. You'll see."

Richard bristled with caution. What edges Richard possessed, he considered to be marks of character. He did not fear them, and he saw no reason to change them.

Evan returned and stood at the inner side of the doorway. He'd never before announced anyone like true footmen do. His face locked in nervous concentration, Evan raised his awkward voice and said, "Sir Adrian Bramwell, son of the Marchioness of Guileford, nephew of the Baron of Wittenberg, and cousin to the Count of Charmbord." Having concluded without a flaw, Evan congratulated himself with a balled fist. "Oh, and Captain Balefire."

Adrian Bramwell appeared, paling everything in the room with his dark beauty. Off to his side stood a triumphant Balefire.

John Cairy stepped forward. "You are more than welcome, Sir Adrian."

"Sir Adrian Bramwell of the Rookeries," advised the captain.

"Say again?" asked John.

"The Rookeries, good sir. It's a unique colony of the British Isles," Balefire explained.

Although John had never heard of the place, he pretended to. "I am honored," he said.

"Honored," Adrian echoed with a voice that effortlessly caressed the soul.

"And you are?" John asked Balefire.

"Sir Bramwell's steadfast companion and mentor, Captain Balefire," he claimed. "You are John Cairy, I presume?"

"I am. And this is my sister, Leona Middleton."

Leona was too spellbound by the young man's looks to speak. John moved on. "And Richard Marlow."

"I am the son, nephew, and cousin to no one in particular," Richard said in jest.

"No one," Adrian repeated with a superior nod.

"With your permission, gentlemen, may I present my niece, Miss Civette Middleton," said John.

"Miss Civette," said Adrian. He made the sound of her name shimmer. Bowing, Adrian kissed Civette's hand. He smelled of October leaves and sunshine.

Never having witnessed the pulchritude of his own self, Adrian had no idea what to expect from others. While she was alluring, Adrian sensed that there was something rather weak and artificial about Miss Middleton. She would never be welcomed by Nature. Of this, he was certain. She would never survive.

More was made in the way of introductions and pleasantries. However, the words were muted under the pulses of the ladies' hearts. They could fathom nothing but their newly arrived guest. This man, this exquisite creation, was the face of a romantic song, a theater idol, or the prince one envisioned within the heart-wrenching realm of a fairytale. They'd never seen anyone so attractive. His ebony hair was lustrous, and his skin glistened like copper in candlelight. A bewitching glow burned in his eyes, and his smile, so honest, yet so shy— why, it was almost as though he were smiling for the first time.

"You have—ahem—recently arrived at our village?" John was saying.

"We have circled this vast and wondrous globe," said the captain.

Richard scoffed. "Only to end up in this remote and colorless pocket of New England?"

"If it were not for the drought, our trees and gardens would offer unrivaled color at present," said Civette.

"That's not what I meant by colorless," Richard said under his breath.

"Begging pardon, your name again?" Leona asked the captain.

"Balefire, madam, a name inspired by the sacrificial flame evoked by hell-bent ritualists. Or, if your delicate nature prefers, in more romantic circles it is a bonfire where lovers gather to dance and—revel. My mother was a Caelifera, and my father a lightning bolt. Sparks were bound to happen."

"Your mother's name is Italian, I take it?" asked Leona.

"Latin. My mother was insanely devoted to the opera. Handel's *Agrippina* was a favorite. You are familiar with the story, are you not?" asked Balefire.

Leona hesitated. "She was a goddess of the earth or some such thing. Am I right?"

"Distantly related, perhaps," Balefire replied. "Agrippina plotted the downfall of poor, innocent Claudius so that her own ill-begotten bloodline would remain in power. She's not the only shameless, self-absorbed schemer in the tale. Nearly everyone is downright ruthless. It's about deception, rotten people, and all manners of delectable evils set to music, just as such things should be."

Leona appeared momentarily puzzled. However, the comedic look upon Balefire's face made her laugh. "Oh, good sir, you are quite the devil," she professed.

"You doubly flatter me," Balefire replied.

Taking Sir Bramwell by the arm, Civette crossed the room on the pretense of showing him the scope of Cairy Hollow's lawns. Richard was astonished by her actions. He obviously did not know Civette as well as he believed. John sighed and stood by Richard because he did.

"You never told us what brought you here," John said to the captain.

"Sir Adrian's father visited, oh, some twenty-odd years ago. He was a houseguest of Governor Haile's. Sir Bramwell called upon a business associate in your village, and it was here that he found himself unexpectedly and most passionately in love."

"With a village girl of Fairwell?" Leona exclaimed. "Who might this rarity of beauty be?"

Being the self-absorbed woman that she was, Leona indulged a notion that this rarity might have been her. A rousing blush of possibility was painted upon her face. Seeing this, Balefire could barely disguise his grin or his willingness to answer.

"That particular beauty was Miss Elizabeth Dalby. You knew her, of course," he said.

Neither John nor Leona spoke, although the language of their individual thoughts could easily be surmised.

"The elder Sir Bramwell begged Bess to leave with him. But it was to no avail. It seems Bess was in love with another," said Balefire.

This brought about another reflective pause, which

Balefire delighted in creating. He spoke on. "The elder Sir Bramwell returned to England a broken man. He married, but he never forgot his dear Bess. Now a widower, he sent his only son to see her. It will destroy him to hear that Bess Dalby is gone—destroy him beyond measure."

While there was much to think about, there was nothing left to say. The group looked to where Adrian and Civette stood by the vestal white curtains. Adrian was holding Civette's palm and looking upon it tenderly. Civette was nothing short of enraptured.

"Can you really tell fortunes?" Civette whispered.

"More than that, I can bestow them," he claimed.

"You amaze me."

"Yes," Adrian replied. He then frowned.

"What is it?"

"Miss Middleton, you are cruel. Your hand confirms it. See this line? Rejection. You will reject someone who loves you with untold passion."

"That's hardly possible," Civette began until she realized she wasn't quite certain what she was saying. With a delicate touch, Civette took Adrian's hand. She was surprised to find no wear. His face and his hands were locked in youthful beauty. "Sir Bramwell," she said, "the print of your palm is unusual. See this line here? It's supposed to be the path of life."

"Life," Adrian repeated, and his tone emanated such warmth for the word.

"How nicely you said that. But your lifeline begins away from the edge of your palm and abruptly breaks. The same goes for this line, the indicator of—love."

"It breaks?" Adrian asked.

"I can't be sure. There's this other faint line below

it. Perhaps you lose love but regain it after time."

"Then that is the path to my heart," he professed.

"Your pulse," said Civette. "I swear I cannot feel your heartbeat at all."

"That is because I have lost it."

Civette assumed he was joking. "Lost it? But where?" She looked up with laughing eyes, only to discover his dulled in pain. "Sir Bramwell, are you ill?"

Balefire rushed over and placed the ruby gem of the walking stick beneath Adrian's left hand. "Pardon, Miss Middleton, but I must confide to you that Sir Adrian's heart is responsive to his emotions. When he feels ardently, it altogether stops."

"Captain Balefire, you're frightening me," said Civette.

"My charge is sensitive. But with care, and the gift of a true and honest love, he will endure."

Adrian drew a grateful breath. "Oh, miss, you have given it back to me. Why did you not keep it?"

"Keep what?" she asked.

His gaze drew strength from hers. "My heart."

A bell chimed faintly through the humid air. Balefire looked about. "Judas," he said, "are we receiving a message from the other side?"

"It's merely the doorbell," said John.

All eyes drifted toward the hall. Meanwhile, Balefire deftly covered the ruby crest of his puppet's walking stick. The stone had begun to pulse in a cold and most calculating way.

Chapter Five: Fair Iris

Yet another caller arrived on the doorstep of Cairy Hollow. It was a friend of Civette and Richard's, a certain Miss Iris Owen. The family went to the foyer to greet her.

An engaging and accomplished young woman in her own right, Iris had nonetheless lived her life in Civette Middleton's shadow. On this particular morning, Iris was attired in wool tweed knickers and a sporting jacket. Tossing her scarf and pulled-down beret upon a chair, Iris went directly to Civette and took her hands within her own.

"You can't imagine my outrage, Civ. My costume for your Ball didn't arrive."

Adrian Bramwell appeared in the doorway. Any further complaints from Iris's lips were halted at the sight of him. Iris was fully aware she was staring, but she couldn't prevent herself. It was as if the air surrounding this visitor possessed texture and sound—that it was hailing the magnificence of this perfect creature.

"Oh, I could just die," she said.

"May you perish with pleasure, young miss," said Adrian.

Everyone laughed. Everyone, that was, except Richard. Richard was thoroughly annoyed and cared little who noticed. A handsome man was one thing. A handsome man with wit and charm was entirely another.

"Do introduce us," Balefire pleaded in an ingratiating manner.

"Sir Bramwell, Captain Balefire, allow me to introduce you to Miss Iris Owen," said John.

Adrian bowed. "Miss Iris Owen—a no one," he said.

"Pardon?" she murmured.

"It's something of a joke Mr. Marlow started," said Balefire.

"Unintentionally, I assure you," said Richard.

"Life never gives you what you intend. It only grants what you strive for," said Adrian.

Balefire was surprised by his puppet's impromptu burst of wisdom. Adrian took Iris's hand and kissed it. Pushing at her unruly hair, Iris cursed her luck for appearing tomboyish in front of such a man.

"How clever, sir, how profound," she said.

"He gets that from me," bragged the captain.

"Sir Bramwell has such a pretty way with words," Civette whispered to Richard.

"Don't flatter the man," Richard grumbled. "His head is big enough."

"I'm merely being gracious to our guest," Civette said.

"Evidently, you have forgotten there are more than just one," replied Richard.

"Iris? Iris is a longtime friend. If it's the captain you speak of, he's a servant. He doesn't count. Sir Bramwell is our sole and honored guest."

"I'll wager you're infatuated with your 'sole and honored guest'—that lopsided fool, pretending to be the titled peerage of some imaginary place. The Rookeries, indeed."

Civette offered hasty claims to the contrary.

Regardless, whatever assurances she gave Richard meant nothing. Her promises were feeble, and the passion in her eyes sadly betrayed each and every word.

Leona suggested that they all have tea in the formal parlor. Rarely utilized by day, the formal parlor was a tomb of relics, trinkets, and baubles once cherished and now, like their stories, long forgotten. The same went for the portraits on the walls. These were the framed remembrances of the men and women who had forged the family's fortunes. The descendants they looked down upon possessed no such drive. These present-day Cairys preferred to dine and dance upon that teetering foundation of wealth with little thought for the morrow. They were, for the most part, blind to it all, even to the pervading scent of decline in this room—the touchstones of a family on their way to ruin.

It was, in summary, an austere parlor. However, with his presence, Adrian Bramwell brought a sense of life to the place, an unparalleled radiance that splashed the walls and colored the room with an unforeseen and welcome promise.

The ladies gathered closest to Adrian. John grudgingly sat beside his sister. He knew without a glance that Leona was insistent on his pretending to be attentive. Richard was the wisest of them all. He retired to a window seat where he might display any genuine manner of expression without the fear of getting caught.

Iris noticed Sir Bramwell staring at Civette. What a lovely look he had in his eyes. Iris uttered a tiny sigh of despair. She knew she was rather boisterous and plain. No one ever said to her, "How beautiful you are," as they would time and time again to Civette. No, some would simply mutter comments such as, "Those pearls are quite nice on you, dear," when she chose to dress for formal occasions, or, "That color suits you." Lazy phrases like these meant nothing. Pearls were always pleasant, and for every person alive there was at least one color that didn't make them look hideously near death.

How unfair it was that females like Civette were praised at every turn. For Iris, one kind and even half-meaningful compliment would fill her heart with joy. Iris looked around in aimless frustration. Sir Bramwell was still regarding Civette with unmistakable admiration. What Iris wouldn't give to tear one tribute away from Civette. Just one. The indifferent Civette, with her long string of trophies, would never miss it.

"A Steinway rococo grand?" she heard that strange Captain Balefire exclaim. "Do allow me to perform something for you."

"But sir, it is morning," cautioned Leona.

"You New Englanders and the sacred morning. I'm surprised any of you were even born before noon." Balefire strode to the piano and seated himself like a maestro. "I shall perform a precocious old tune in honor of Miss Iris Owen," he announced.

Suspicion crawled through Iris's head. It couldn't be possible, but had that eerie little man read her thoughts? It seemed more than evident in the tone of his voice. Iris sat bolt upright, her round face coloring with fear. Meanwhile, Balefire bawdily began to play and sing:

"Fair Iris I love and hourly I die,
But not for a lip nor a languishing eye:
She's fickle and false, and there I agree;
For I am as false and as fickle as she:
We neither believe what either can say;
And neither believing, we neither betray.

'Tis civil to swear and say things, of course;
We mean not the taking for better or worse.
When present we love, when absent agree;
I think not of Iris, nor Iris of me:
The legend of love no couple can find
So easy to part, or so equally joined."

Balefire concluded by madly laughing and applauding for himself. From the others, his performance was met with silence and confusion, particularly, it was noted, from Miss Iris Owen herself.

"Perhaps another song?" Balefire asked.

"Perhaps another time," Leona replied.

"With pleasure," said Balefire. He always insisted on having the last word, no matter the setting. Balefire then went to the window, for the darkened day had relented, and a thin gray rain began to fall.

"At last," uttered Leona, as if Nature had been disobeying her direct orders for far too long.

"At last," Balefire murmured, and he studied the rainswept scenario with appreciation.

Chapter Six: Nature

Bess Dalby's field seemed barren and forlorn without her scarecrow there.

In their feathered bird forms, Sorrow and Mirth stared at the rows of wilted stalks. The corn's frayed edges, which only weeks before had flowed like silken hair, were rotted, and the once golden kernels were now blanched and drained. A barrette glimmered in the crusty earth. It had gone unnoticed where the scarecrow stood for years.

A shadow, much like a rolling wave, swept across the field. Sorrow and Mirth watched with fascination as it crept by them. Nature's breath grew cold and damp. The duo listened as a hollow breeze crept down the tree trunk. It chattered without words. A faint electrical smell filled their lungs. They shivered.

How peculiar the morning light was, violet and gray, with glowing borders of burnt orange. The last of the autumn leaves appeared to be moving without wind. It was then that woodland creatures began to appear at the fringes of the forest. Not a step closer did they take. In their motionless stances, they too stared at the ungoverned field.

The light lost its tinges of gold. The wind found its voice. Nature changed her mind and her mood and allowed it to rain. It drummed on the ancient roof of Bess Dalby's cottage. A crevice in the porch ceiling groaned and gave way, the water making a *drip, drip, drip* sound on the slanted and parched wooden floor.

Chapter Seven: What They Would Give

The sound of the door getting kicked by a thick and dull shoe was heard. Scullery maid Phoebe entered the parlor. Her coal-dusted chin was tucked as she attempted to balance the delicate tea things on a wide silver tray. Leona was embarrassed beyond words. Alice was the one who was clean, dressed properly, and trained to deliver tea. Leona wondered where Alice might be.

As Phoebe set down her burden with a disturbing clatter, she caught sight of Mr. Cairy's guest. Giggling with awe, Phoebe skittered out of the room. A wincing odor of kitchen grease and sweat trailed in her wake. Leona considered reprimanding Phoebe but changed her mind. Leona had far more engaging goals at present. While her daughter dutifully poured tea, Leona turned to her beguiling guest.

"Sir Bramwell, tell us what you do to occupy yourself," she asked. "When you're not traveling the world, that is."

"I govern the land," he replied.

"Where might that be?" Richard asked. His hope was that it was far, far away.

"Oh, you wouldn't know it. It's a realm of mystical fields and the hushed secrets of the forest."

Leona found Adrian's answer odd, but continued. "What is it you govern?"

"Pumpkins, mostly. Fruits of gold, round like the

rising sun."

Civette giggled before realizing she shouldn't have. She glanced at Adrian and was relieved, indeed even astonished, to see that he was delighted by her response.

Balefire chimed in. "Sir Adrian is an artist with words. In whatever country he is visiting, he tinges his vocabulary with the local idiom. He means, of course, not pumpkins but rare pomegranates."

"And we, of course, applaud him," Civette replied. The warmth of her tone tore through Richard's heart. Civette leaned toward her mother. "Have you noticed his regal bearing, Mama? He is every bit a titled gentleman," she said.

He may be titled, but he walks as though he's balancing on broomsticks, Richard assured himself.

John cleared his throat. "Tell us about your home," he said. He sounded bored.

"My home?" their guest echoed.

Balefire nodded. "Yes. They desire to understand the august surroundings of your unprecedented genesis."

Hearing this, Richard rolled his eyes. Where did this odd little man with his archaic manner of speech fall from? A two-hundred-year-old tree? Meanwhile, Sir Adrian Bramwell remained confused.

"Your castle, Featherstone, which reigns in peerless beauty above the sands of Clawfoot Beach," Balefire persisted.

"Oh, dear God," said Richard. Civette glared at him. She found herself wishing that Richard had chosen to spend the morning elsewhere.

An avid amateur historian, John cleared his throat. "Is there not already a castle named Featherstone? It figured prominently in early battles between the English and the Scots. The castle is in Northumberland, England, I believe."

"Yes, I know that one," said Balefire. "In its primitive form, it was the home of Abigail Featherstonehaugh. Abigail was given the chance to marry a handsome and wealthy lord but instead chose a commoner named Ridley. The scorned lord attacked the bridal party as they made their return to the castle. Commoner Ridley put up a good fight, but, alas, all died in the fray. It is said that Abigail's ghost appears at the castle each year on the anniversary of her tragic death."

"How sadly romantic," said Civette.

"How blatantly enterprising," corrected Balefire. "For it is a broadside ballad, an idiot's tale, fabricated to fill the coffers for the present owner of the fool, drafty place. Everyone simply adores a good massacre." Balefire grinned in a strange and pointed way. He turned to Adrian. "Now, do go on, dear boy. Grant these charming rustics the honor of learning about your hall at Featherstone." Balefire glanced at John. "It is a far superior castle."

Adrian Bramwell informed them that, where he lived, the sky above his head was a moving portrait of beauty. The earth's tapestry at his feet smelled of heaven, and his soul was in the air about him. In no other dwelling could any man feel more free, more alive. Adrian's words were poetry to most of his listeners' ears.

"Your home sounds positively exquisite," said Civette.

As was easily anticipated, Richard groaned. Civette swung about once again. "Go away," she whispered.

Leona noticed that Sir Adrian neither ate nor drank anything offered. In fact, he was regarding the tea tray with a good measure of apprehension. "Do you not care for tea?" she asked.

Balefire replied. "In England, tea is typically associated with a calamity. If one is ill, angry, or depressed, one has tea. Indeed, if every last penny is lost at gambling, or if one's house burns to the ground, a neighbor invariably offers tea. Sir Adrian prefers to avoid calamities. He never has tea."

"Something stronger, perhaps?" said John.

Adrian picked up a saucer and drew it to his lips. Balefire smoothly seized the plate from his grasp.

"We had such a hearty breakfast," Balefire explained.

A sudden rapping sounded within the wall. It paused momentarily before rattling once again with a low and grievous echo. From his place at the window seat, Richard leaned toward the pane. A glassy rain was striking the parched lawns with a steady, leaden beat. He peered down the length of the house. "The gutter is loose and clunking. The wind must be picking up," he said.

The ladies cared little. They remained fixated on their handsome guest.

"Considering the marvels of your home, it's a wonder you care to travel," said Leona.

"Sir Adrian cannot resist when the unknown beckons him," said Balefire. To this, his puppet nodded.

Putting down her teacup, Iris noticed something quite unexpected. "The stone on your walking stick, Sir Bramwell. If I'm not mistaken, it glows," she said.

A hush descended as everyone focused on the sparkling jewel. Balefire casually placed Adrian's left hand securely over the piece. "The jewel is from a Druid scepter, thousands of years old. It was carved from an ancient blood-red skull used by Celtic priests to foretell the future."

Richard Marlow had endured all he could. "Sir Bramwell, if that is your true name, is it a European fashion to promote pagan worship in ladies' parlors?"

"Sir Adrian is the height of fashion," Balefire replied with ease.

"This is beyond belief," Richard muttered, just as Mrs. Beals, the housekeeper, appeared at the doorway. Regardless of her abilities, she was a gruff woman with little mind for manners.

"Mr. Cairy, Mrs. Middleton, might I have a word? It is urgent," she said.

Leona was not pleased with the intrusion. Nevertheless, she rose and, along with John, went out to the hall. Mrs. Beals wasted no time. "We've got a Halloween Ball here in little less than ten hours, and one of our parlor maids has locked herself in her room," she said.

"What's wrong with the girl?" John asked.

"Marie is frightened out of her wits," said Mrs. Beals. "It was the sight of your guest that alarmed her."

"Captain Balefire is rather unsettling," admitted Leona.

Mrs. Beals shook her head. "No, missus. It was the other one. The so-called Englishman, Sir Bramwell."

John and Leona were surprised and had no reply for this. Mrs. Beals spoke on. "Marie rambled gibberish about him being pure evil. I truly didn't understand her. For certain, she's a troubled girl to begin with. But there's something about Marie's fears that seem real this time."

Leona didn't care. "Mrs. Beals, tell the girl to go to

her room and rest for an hour. And then it's back to work with her. I have a very important party here this evening."

Mrs. Beals didn't care for what the self-assumed mistress of the house said, and decided to reward her in kind. "Mr. Cairy, it may not mean a thing, but I noticed your guest as he stood in the hall. His manservant was preparing him for his introduction to you. No, I didn't see anything that reeked of evil. But I can almost swear that the Englishman is wearing a stickpin you once owned, sir—a pin you gave as a gift to someone special. Stranger still, he seemed to be hiding it."

Having accomplished the effect she was aiming for, Mrs. Beals did not wait for a reply. As she departed, the ring of keys at her side played rhythmically in the cold, damp air. John stared as the gray of the housekeeper's dress and the white of her apron blurred into the vision of a sky churning with clouds. A rush of air the color of coral, and rich with the scent of lilacs swirled round his head. Its breeze rebounded in song: *The moments of delight, how sweet, but ah, how swift they flew…*

Leona knew—knew as women with the gift of intuition do—that John was thinking of Dalby Cottage and the woman who once lived there. As for John, years of training had allowed him to sense and interpret Leona's poisonous stare.

"The maid is delirious, that is all," John vaguely mumbled.

"The maid is stupid," Leona replied. "What about your pin?"

"A coincidence. This world is riddled with them."

"Riddled with what, dear brother? Coincidences, or copies of your treasured pin?"

John was about to speak when Captain Balefire appeared in the hall. His pincer-like fingers were clasped, and his face wore an exaggerated air of concern.

"If I dare ask, what plagues the household?" he asked. "Were the scones tainted? Should we all lie down now and give up our many ghosts?"

"One of our maids is unwell," said Leona.

"The cause?" questioned Balefire.

Leona shrugged. "No idea, Captain. She appears to be imagining things."

"Ah, then permit me to tell you what I, scant moments ago in that parlor, imagined." Balefire spun about like a confident dance master. "Within a flash, the Moirai flew into my mind. You may know them better as the Fates, those alabaster-robed oracles of destiny: Clotho, who spins, Lachesis, who measures, and Atropos, who severs that final cord. Not even they can alter the course their twisting fibers foretell. And it dawned on me..." Balefire paused with a dramatic gesture.

"What, sir?" prompted John.

"Your niece Civette and my delightful charge. Fate brought Adrian to this idyllic village, this place where his father found his heart's desire. And now, so does the son. It's ever so touching, don't you see? Adrian is meant to fulfill the past's destiny. It cannot be denied, for it was written 'cross the moon and painted upon the stars. It is twice blest, as William Shakespeare so cleverly penned. Scarce moments in life these days are."

"Penned and blessed though it may seem, Captain, my niece will soon be engaged—" John said before Leona stepped in.

"Perhaps I should go and make certain the maid is

resting. John, do return to our guests. Our absence is disconcerting," she said. For all her erratic and self-centered moods, Leona was the one member of the family who recognized that this lord of a heavenly realm, this complete and utterly magical young man, could secure a future for Civette that went beyond anything her family dared to hope for her.

The two left. Balefire remained in the hall, mimicking Leona's unbearable voice to perfection. "*No idea, Captain*." He laughed. "Harrowing roots of hell, but when did the word *idea* end with the letter *r*? Oh, the grating dialect of these New Englanders. It destroys any brain matter left between the ears."

Balefire glanced around the hall. Being a spirit of the airy sort, material trappings baffled him. Through his compound eyes, he studied a gaudy vase painted with butterflies. Balefire harbored no sympathy for the creatures. While beautiful, Balefire considered them weak and useless.

"Imagine if we stuck pretty humans with pins and displayed them in large glass cases," he murmured. "There'd be little point to being attractive, now would there?"

A fury of rain sounded beyond the front door. Balefire smiled and saluted Nature's ready reply. When the deluge subsided, muffled conversation was heard coming from the ballroom. There, Balefire discovered Phoebe and a bright-eyed housemaid standing before a velvet curtain. The pair were giggling. Balefire called out, startling them.

"Oh, I won't report you," Balefire assured them. "After all, I am a servant, just as yourselves." Balefire indicated the heavy, tasseled drapes. "What have we here?" he asked.

Delighted to speak because she rarely got the chance to, Phoebe explained the supposed magic behind the Glass of Truth.

"You don't say," said Balefire. "Good heavens, girls, what if it displayed the true monster that I am?"

Giggling once again, the maids left the room. Balefire pulled the drape aside and faced the glass.

Displayed within was the visage of his true self. The argent qualities of his face were swirled and indistinct yet, in places, sharp. His image coiled about the glass, tense and charged, and never settling. The air between Balefire and his reflection was electrified with streaks of crimson and gray.

"What a delightful whirlwind you are," he told himself.

Balefire's reflection answered him with a laugh that rustled like anxious leaves before a storm.

"Back to the fray," Balefire said. With another graceful pirouette, he returned to the parlor.

There, he discovered Mr. Cairy, Civette, and his attentive puppet gathered before the family portraits. John Cairy was relating the histories behind each one. The boldest depicted Emmeline Cairy. A blacksmith's daughter, she nonetheless had caught the eye of British colonist Reginald Cairy. Lured by the riches to be had in New England, they settled first in Boston, and then upon this notched hill high above the New Hampshire village of Fairwell. Cairy Hollow had been built for Emmeline as an anniversary gift.

"Such a ravishing creature," said Adrian. His growing imagination was captivated by the triumphant Emmeline in her blood-red gown. At her feet worshiped a fragile, white papillon with a matching red bow.

"The dog's name is Ismay," said Balefire.

John Cairy was astounded by Balefire's knowledge. To this, Balefire merely shrugged. "History and I are old comrades," he said.

Leona returned. Balefire addressed her with an overblown look of concern.

"Mrs. Middleton, with all these enchanting portraits, why isn't your likeness displayed here?" he asked.

Still smarting over the stickpin, Leona did not hesitate to reply. "My brother's portrait is in his study, which is just as well. As a work, it's primitive and rough. I never had a portrait done. Only an artist the likes of Romney could convey my spirit, my looks, and he's long gone. Besides, with photography taking over, oil paintings have become passé. Wouldn't you agree?"

Throughout this, John hung his head in despair. A life without Leona flashed through the remaining webs of hope in his mind. *What I would give to go back and repair my past… Oh, what I would give!* John assured himself in such a way he was convinced the others could hear.

Civette knew that something had happened to upset her mother. Leona became unsettled so easily. With a trembling smile, Civette raised her hand and spoke. As Richard noticed, she focused solely on Adrian Bramwell.

"I adore these portraits. When I was a little girl, I used to sing to them. When thunder and lightning storms made me nervous, I would hide here in their company. Somehow, I sensed they were protecting me. Call me foolish, if you will, but I always believed that these lovely people in their walls of gold were willing to converse, if one would simply let them. Especially

Emmeline. Oh, what I would give to look like her."

"Miss Civette, you are, in your own right, without equal," said Adrian.

Driven by his praise, Civette began telling Adrian how wonderful it would be to have a portrait of herself done. Civette imagined herself in a gown that matched the green in her eyes. She'd wear rubies in her hair and spirals of diamonds about her throat and arms. How lovely her likeness would be, capturing the essence of her youth for years to come in its gilded frame.

Richard was meanwhile speaking with Iris by the windows. With his acute hearing, Balefire listened.

"Fine, fine," the impatient Iris was saying. "You're going to propose to Civette during your silly Romeo and Juliet scene at tonight's Ball. Everyone knows. If you want the truth, Richard, even Civette knows."

"Then why is Civette playing up to that counterfeit bluenose without a brain?" Richard replied.

"Why are you being unkind? And jealous, I might add," said Iris.

"I am neither. But I'll admit I'm curious about one particular item. It appears my future fiancée wishes this poor excuse for a man to flirt with her in ignorance of her relationship to me."

"Then we will fix this supposed matter of ignorance. Civette—"

"Iris, stop. I did not mean—"

Along with Sir Adrian, Civette turned to face Iris. Iris did delay a moment to consider how striking Adrian and Civette were together. Even in the dullness of a rainy day, the two seemed to glow. Squaring her shoulders, Iris went on to comment that perhaps Civette could have her portrait done as a gift for Richard. After all, Richard was her intended, was he not? Iris's question held the distinct chill of a newly dug grave. No one spoke. A moment lingered with such emotion it nearly had a sheen to it.

"How nice," said Adrian. He noticed that Civette was frowning. *"Or am I wrong?"*

No one answered. Iris faced Richard. "Are you satisfied now?" she asked.

Richard regarded Civette with such sadness in his eyes. In turn, she offered not a word, not even a swift glance of redress. How changed Civette was—altered for the worse in the blink of an eye. Richard stated that he was more than satisfied and stormed away. If this was the precursor to married life, Richard was already congratulating himself on escaping it.

Richard went outside. Iris began to follow, but held herself back. There was nothing Iris could say or do. Her presence would only annoy him. Cursing the change love had made in Richard, Iris watched him protectively from the window.

Richard stood on the terrace. It didn't matter that a steady rain fell. It was refreshing to his fretful brow. Standing above the glistening boxwood, he could only guess where his little house lay across the misty river. Everything was blanketed in a silver haze. Richard had no idea he lived in such a wild and desolate region. Perhaps it was time he changed his course. But, then again…

Richard pondered his present existence. It did not take him long. It was his future that intrigued him more. All this was Cairy and Middleton land and, if he reined in Civette properly, someday it would fall into his hands. The mountains surrounding it and the valley below were waiting to be his legacy. The mansion between would be his everlasting monument. All Richard had to do was to be patient—patient, and flatter the whimsical Civette a good deal. What cost was there in that? For all her flightiness, Civette Middleton was easy on the eye. Richard instantly regretted his hasty words. Within him, a tiny hope prevailed that Civette might feel remorse for her petty behavior and follow him outside.

Richard would be disappointed.

Chapter Eight: Quills

Adrian was alarmed by Civette's sudden distractions. Was she no longer moved by his presence? Adrian assumed, like any other new and exquisite creation, that his beauty was more than enough to please her. Never-before-felt pangs of failure gnawed at him.

Civette is simply in that nervous realm between quarreling and crying, a voice whispered inside his head. *Go to her and prove to her that you care.* Adrian recognized that voice. It was Balefire's. Erasing the confusion from his gaze, Adrian obeyed. He went to Civette and gently lifted her chin.

"What can I do to make you laugh again, as you did over tea?" he said. It gratified him that his suggestion caused her to blush.

"Civette," she heard a voice say. She turned to see her uncle standing close. Civette had nearly forgotten that anyone else was in the room.

"Civette, your mother and I wish to speak with Sir Bramwell in private," he said.

Her uncle appeared drained, perhaps even ill. "As you wish, Uncle John. Perhaps while you do so, you could invite Sir Bramwell and the captain to our Halloween Ball this evening." Civette addressed Balefire. "I would be honored if you both could attend. It's a costume party, but you needn't worry about that."

"Oh, I'm sure we can dig up something," replied

Balefire.

"Richard and Civette will be reenacting the balcony scene from *Romeo and Juliet* as a special treat for us all," said Iris.

"Then we'll dig up something special." Balefire nodded at the young ladies. It was, as Iris perceived it, a rather cryptic gesture. Balefire spoke on. "While we step away, perhaps we could prepare an introduction to your theatrical endeavor. You know, something meant to rouse your family, your friends, and any wayward and impulsive intruders." Offering Civette the crook of his right arm, he held out his left to Iris. "Allow me, Miss Middleton, to be your scribe. Miss Owen, I trust, can easily correct any errors in spelling. Now, shall we retire to a quiet corner and sharpen our quills?"

"Until we meet again," Civette said to Adrian. The tone in her voice was made all the more passionate by the sight of a rain-sodden Richard glowering at them through the window.

Adrian watched Civette leave. Every step she took tugged at the strings of his newly beating heart. "She is gone—quite gone," he despaired.

John would have none of it. "Pardon my forthright nature, young man, but you and the captain arrived upon my doorstep with no true cause. What exactly is it you want here?" he asked.

Adrian's reply was swift, for he knew not how to lie. "Your niece, Civette," he said.

"Is my daughter what brought you here?" Leona asked.

"First, the harrowed skies brooded over the cornfields. The ancient dust was dry at my feet, and the awakened wind meddlesome. My shadow is out there somewhere in silent wait for the true light. The flowers urged me to follow where the black wings flew. They led me to your door."

John had no idea what to think. "Who are you, really?" he asked.

"I am Sir Adrian Bramwell, son of the Marchioness of Guileford, nephew of the Baron of Wittenberg, and cousin to the Count of Charmbord."

"Is that all you will say?" John exclaimed. "Well, go then. Go. You are not welcome here, and you are never to speak to my niece again."

Adrian, never having faced conflict, was about to do as he was told until Balefire's voice whispered in his head. *Stand your ground,* he heard.

"Civette is yours? No, Civette is mine," Adrian found himself saying. "It was ordained that we should belong to each other."

"My daughter is an impulsive girl," Leona admitted. "Civette's experiences in life, her realities, are not equal to those of, say Miss Owen's. Civette believes in magical worlds and forever happiness. Regardless, sir, think of the concerns that should be more than apparent—and we not knowing who you really are."

Adrian assured her with a smile. "I am Sir Adrian Bramwell, son of the Marchioness of Guileford, nephew of the Baron of Wittenberg, and cousin to the Count of Charmbord."

John moved closer to Adrian's face. "You are the Devil's work, for all I know. You will leave at once."

Don't back down, Adrian heard in his mind. He agreed.

"Miss Civette belongs to me. Her eyes are mine, and her smiles are mine. Her heart will soon be my sole treasure. The forces of Nature assured me of such, right down to the spirits in torment beneath my feet. Zeus proclaimed it in the lightning, and Ra across the sun. I will not fail. Whatever you believe you can do to oppose me, you will not succeed. My plan cannot be undone. My mentor told me so, and he should know. Captain Balefire is pure genius."

"He is a conniver," said John. "And you, whoever you are, you are not titled. My guess is that you're nothing more than a scheming imposter."

"I am Sir Adrian Bramwell, son of the Marchioness of Guileford, nephew of the Baron of Wittenberg, and cousin—" Although his speech was bold, Adrian visibly weakened. He dropped his walking stick and clutched his chest. John was rendered immobile. He did nothing to assist. It was Leona who rushed about, calling to the servants, and helping Adrian to a chair.

"How extraordinary," Leona whispered. In his pain, Adrian was doubtless more beautiful.

Captain Balefire and the ladies returned to the doorway. Richard also appeared, standing behind Civette. Despite Richard's obvious despair, she would not acknowledge him. Civette rushed into the room and knelt at Adrian's side. "What has happened?" she pleaded.

"Where is his walking stick?" Balefire asked. "Ah, there it is. Miss Civette, do bring it to him."

"I will get it," said Iris.

"No," Balefire nearly barked at her. He softened his tone. "Allow Miss Middleton, please."

Civette did as she was asked. "Adrian, Adrian," she murmured, until she observed an intense light rekindling in his eyes. Despite the seriousness of the situation, it fascinated her.

Balefire moved Adrian's left hand over the glowing stone of the walking stick. "Civette Middleton has saved your life," he said.

With deliberate authority in his stare and in his speech, the revived scarecrow addressed John Cairy. "Her heart is mine," he said.

Without warning, Richard removed Civette from her place at Adrian's side. "Sir, I demand that you meet me outside."

"A duel," exclaimed Balefire. "Why, there hasn't been one of those since the *Civil* War, which is pure irony when you think about it."

"Richard, how dare you?" said Civette.

Richard laughed. "First, you support this intruder's gauche and ignorant behavior at every turn. And now you intend to speak for him as well?"

Civette did not answer. No one spoke. Amidst the uneasy silence, a distant bell began to ring. It was not the heralding of a friendly caller at the front door. The chime was vague and perplexing. The hammering sound returned as well. Low and portentous at first, it crept along the outside of the house. Its tenor alternated between curious and demanding. It was almost as if the pummeling sound was conversing with itself. The ladies huddled close together, their gazes charting the invisible movements of the noise. Still, the ethereal bell tolled. Captain Balefire went to the window and was pleased by what he did—or did not—see. He would not say.

Throughout the commotion, Adrian Bramwell remained calm. Having been brought to life in Nature's fury, these unearthly disturbances meant nothing to him. Nor did they affect Richard as he awaited Adrian's reply.

A rush of sweet floral scent engulfed the air. Leona moved about, searching for the source. A powerful gust whipped about the corners of the house. With this, the scent of lilac broadened, as if to tease its audience, before sweeping away.

"Well, sir, will you accompany me?" Richard asked.

Decided, Adrian faced Richard. "I shall remain here," he declared. "As for you, you may tumble straight to hell."

The noises, as well as the forces of Nature themselves, abruptly ceased. Everyone in the room paused at the sheer majesty of it.

Richard was prepared to strike Adrian when John ordered him to go to the study. Richard needed time to cool his thoughts, for bitter men were seldom wise. Bidding a hasty farewell, Iris wanted nothing more than to leave. She did so without her scarf and hat. Captain Balefire escorted Adrian to the library. It was best, Balefire claimed, to remove his young charge from such arrogance and audacity. Without a word, Civette left for her bedroom. There was a forsaken look in her eyes.

"You won't be troubled for long," Leona murmured.

Outside, the storm resumed. The wind and the rain bore such a bleak and taunting sound. With this, a pervading scent of lilac returned. From behind the drapes of the window, a smoky image began skimming toward Leona. The topmost of the specter swayed from side to side. The snake-like form had a woman's face with odd-colored eyes, and teeth that sparkled sharp and white.

"It's you," Leona said, and that was all.

Chapter Nine: Time

Inside the library, the workings of a fancy mantel clock had caught Adrian's eye. He watched as its pendulum pieces whirled in cadence with the weather beyond.

"The beat of this clock sounds like a heavy, human heart," he said. "I wonder if it's keeping this house alive."

Perched on the crest of an imperial sofa, Balefire scoffed. "I gave up my love affair with Time," he said. "These days, we only live to provoke each other. Now, on to our lesson, Master Pumpkin Jack. Repeat the phrase I just gave you."

Still fixated by the bright gears of the clock, Adrian recited, "Our parting brings such sweet sorrow. Believe me, ladies, with the true sincerity of my heart."

"Normally, I'd fear that many would realize these words smack of Shakespeare," Balefire said. "But this is northern New England. Culture here only grows on rocks. Now, *répétez, s'il vous plaît.*"

Adrian did as he was told, although his tone was weighted with ennui.

"Project more romanticism, and your audience will surely flutter." Balefire vaulted off the sofa and demonstrated his meaning. " 'The true sincerity of my heart,' " he exclaimed while implementing a most cavalier bow.

Balefire's puppet was not impressed by his bombastic theatricals. However, Adrian repeated his phrase with remarkable improvement. Balefire was pleased. "I blush, I weep, I swoon." Balefire twirled into an affected faint upon the couch. "Go on with the next."

"As that prince of poets, the immortal Virgil, once remarked, *Adeo in teneris consuescere multum est*," Adrian rendered with a modest smile.

Balefire applauded. "Brilliant. Brilliant, indeed. Confidence is dull, and arrogance blinding. But brush either with humility, and how the ladies will long to linger in your light."

"What does all this nonsense even mean?" Adrian asked.

"It translates to 'so much depends on habit in one's tender years,'" answered Balefire. "It's appropriate for you, my day-old prince of sticks. Alas, it is far, far too late for me."

"As if you care," Adrian mumbled.

"How true. I don't," Balefire replied.

Adrian sighed. "Why must I say such meaningless and outmoded words? Richard Marlow doesn't speak this way."

"Richard Marlow is a peasant. You are succeeding with Miss Middleton because, in her unburdened mind, you are worldly and attractive. Women adore lovely things. However, the moment lovely things are broken, they cease to be. Rely on that fact. I've witnessed women nursing unfathomable dreams and desires. Men, too, for that matter, but women have the excuse of being prettier at it. These glistening hopes are nothing more than cleverly shrouded quicksand. That which reigns in the sun is eventually pulled down by its own luster."

"I should shine forever," said Adrian.

"You shine now, and that's what matters. But, do you sense that because you sparkle like a diamond that you are resilient enough to survive a whimsical woman's change of heart? With abject apologies, my gullible pawn, you are not. You are, after all, utter mush inside. So, no more of this sighing before the watchful eye of Time. As the saying goes, she tarries for no one. Not even for a moping scarecrow. Therefore, bask in your beauty, my boy. It is a brief but glorious season."

Adrian was tired of being lectured to. "Miss Civette—may I see her now?"

"No. You must first learn to dance," said Balefire. "Stumble around on those broomstick legs, and you will surely lose her." Ignoring his creation's peevish behavior, Balefire went to the window. Throwing wide the sash, he clapped his hands. "Ladies of the mystical realm," he called into the dappled downpour. "*Entrez-vous?*"

Fearless shadows took hold. With a rush of air, the drapes rose as velvet canopies above the heads of the gleaming Raven Ladies. Swooping into the room, they settled with ease upon the colorful Persian carpet. The partially transitioned birds stood before Balefire while brushing pellets of rain from their oil-blue feathers. With their down-coated arms, curled feet, and their faces a grotesque blend of half female, half scavenger bird, they were a sobering sight.

"We were out there by the entrance gate, singing about this very house," said Mirth.

"Did you not hear us?" asked Sorrow.

"A sublime pleasure I obviously—" Balefire began, before the duo broke into song.

"There were two ravens sat in a tree,
Down a down, hey down, hey down,
They were as black as black could be,
With a down,
The one of them said to his mate,
Where shall we our breakfast take?
With a down, derry, derry, derry, down!"

"Shh," said Balefire. "I must warn you. There's a human in this house who has the gift of sight. While I could not be perceived as I really am, our lopsided scarecrow was seen clear through."

"Who is he?" questioned Mirth.

Balefire explained that it was not a "he" but a girl. "A little maid who was brave enough to speak of the evil that she saw. No adult listened. They didn't even try."

"How inept humans are," said Mirth.

"We must get rid of the maid somehow," said Balefire.

"Shall we drag her out to the kitchen yard and mutilate her?" offered Sorrow.

"And spoil the night's festivities over the demise of a little Miss Nobody?" said Balefire.

"On the contrary. It will only make a dull party more memorable," said Mirth.

"Humans always allege such sympathy, yet after two sips of champagne—poof—it's gone," said Sorrow.

Mirth nudged Sorrow. "The sympathy or the champagne?" she asked, causing them both to cackle.

Balefire clasped his hands. "My charming ladies, we have a more immediate need at hand. Master Pumpkin Jack requires instruction in the art of dancing or else he shall blunder badly at this evening's reception."

"Imagine lining up to dance with a rotted field

squash on a stick," said Mirth.

"Stranger things have been celebrated," said Sorrow. "For example, I never understood why any intelligent being would praise getting older. What's the sense in raising a glass to weak knees, fewer teeth, and a memory like a baker's sieve?"

"I respect bakers," Balefire said with a grin. "It took only one to trap four-and-twenty of you into a pie."

"And we still snipped off the maid's nose," reminded Mirth. "Ah, that's what we can do to our perceptive little miss."

"This cavernous dump could use some excitement," said Balefire. "Even the once-restless spirits within it are bored. Don't you feel it? Taste that air. This tired old house is begging to die."

"Houses often imitate the monsters who inhabit them, dead and alive," said Sorrow.

"Back to the dancing, Sorrow. You're being tedious," said Mirth. "Which woodland revel shall we choose?"

"Alas, the dance must be of this mortal world," said Balefire.

There was a distinct pause.

"Satan's fury," said Sorrow.

"Whatever for?" added Mirth.

"My sentiments exactly," said Balefire.

"I will merely copy what I see around me," Adrian insisted. "May I go to Civette now?"

Balefire looked into his creation's eyes. "Are you honestly eager to see her, or are you a finer actor than I carved you out to be? I despise admitting this, but you confound me."

The scarecrow remained silent. To Balefire's

annoyance, he even seemed somewhat amused.

"Be careful, boy. A masterpiece such as you should never invite tragedy. Keep your goals simple. Be admired, but avoid those avenues that, without fail, lead to pain."

"It is not pain I welcome. It is love," his puppet vowed.

Balefire paused in thought, which is something he rarely did. Balefire was a mad mix of metal and mischief. He judged without a heart. A heart, Balefire believed, was a vessel of poison that diffused truth. Gentle feelings were foreign to him. He had been created by and existed within a netherworld exempt of frivolous attachments. Did it bother Balefire that he felt nothing of sentimental value? Not in the least. Throughout the ages, Balefire had observed humans chase emotions that were as strong and yet as fleeting as ocean tides. Chasing waves was folly when one possessed such little time, and pure tedium when one faced all eternity.

Balefire spoke at last. "Pain and love are the same snarling beast, my friend," he said. Still, Adrian made no reply. "Remember as well that your end goal has nothing to do with love, unless you have a passion for betrayal."

"I will do as you ask, as long as you permit me to exist as I am now," said Adrian.

Balefire digested the enormity of that request. "All right, my clueless contraption," he said. "Why don't you go out to the garden and make your existing self look vulnerable in the rain. Such an image is guaranteed to strike romance in the heart of any young woman, merciless creatures that they are."

Balefire turned to Sorrow and Mirth with a request. Might they fly back to the cottage and retrieve a costume

Bess Dalby made for John Cairy to wear to a long ago Halloween Ball? It was a copy of Reginald Cairy's court attire as seen in his portrait. Leona suspected Bess would present herself as Emmeline, and she convinced her brother not to give in to the scandal this would create. Thus, there in Bess's closet the neglected court apparel hung. But now, it would do perfectly for their puppet.

"Besides, it will bring back such lovely memories for John, and especially for his sister. Don't you agree?" Balefire concluded.

"We do," Sorrow and Mirth replied in unison.

" 'Where shall we three meet again in thunder, lightning, or in rain?' " Balefire jested.

" 'When the hurlyburly's done,' " quoted Mirth.

" 'When the battle's lost and won,' " quoted Sorrow.

"Oh, I do believe it will be well before that final hour," Balefire replied.

Saluting with their burnished wings, the two stepped outside the window and bolted up like inky rockets into the agitated sky.

Adrian gladly left the room. Left to his own devices, Balefire stretched himself out upon the red silk divan. "You sigh, you weep, and you vow to write her name across the stars. Yes, for you unsuspecting fools, these are the heavenly days."

Adrian Bramwell paid no heed to Balefire's dire predictions, nor would he have cared to. In the entrance hall, he heard the echo of an odd little song. The trail of the tune led him to the ballroom. There, he encountered the same young maid who had awkwardly delivered the tea. The girl had no idea he was standing there. Cleaning out a fireplace, she was singing in rhythm with her work.

"Where is Phoebe? Where is Phoebe?

Here I am. Here I am.
How are you today, miss?
Very well, I thank you.
Run away. Run away."

Adrian chuckled, and Phoebe looked up. Blushing beneath her newly made layer of soot, Phoebe scrambled to her feet. "Pardon, sir. I didn't see you there," she said.

He wished the girl a good morning and turned to leave. As he did, Phoebe was startled by something she saw reflected between the velvet drapes of the Glass of Truth. Phoebe watched as Mr. Cairy's guest left the room. He couldn't have had anything to do with the unsettling image she witnessed. He was far too handsome.

It must have been a storm cloud skirting by the windows.

With a nervous shiver, Phoebe resumed her task.

Run away, run away, she heard herself singing in her mind.

Chapter Ten: Diamonds

Making his way across the sculptured lawns, Adrian passed a bank of teasels. A whisk of air caused the dried cones to swirl and nod. The wind through their hollows seemed to chant, "*Here today and gone tomorrow*." Their whispered messages offered the spelled scarecrow no sense of alarm. His mind and his thoughts were occupied with wonder.

Adrian veered down the hedge-trimmed path and on to the main drive. Looking back, he noticed John and Leona in conversation by a window. Adrian guessed they were talking about him. It was Adrian's first genuine feeling of self-importance and, although fleeting, he marveled at it. Within moments, he was lulled by the concept of thinking about nothing at all. He focused on the gentle persistence of the rain. There was a mesmerizing hum to it, a certain natural beauty that far surpassed what he assumed to be his own.

"Hello, there," Adrian heard through the music in his mind.

Civette had followed him. Her flared cape coat and her oddly angled hat did nothing to detract from her loveliness.

"I'm guessing you wanted time to be alone and think," she said. "My family has a way of promoting that desire in people. But, if you happen to be in the mood for company, we could walk together."

"You came looking for me in the rain?" he asked.

"I love the rain," she lied.

Images of the female ancestral portraits rippled through Adrian's mind. "I was under the impression that fashionable ladies avoided the elements whenever possible," he said.

"Iris won't go out in questionable weather. Doing so destroys her hair and her clothing and, well, her concentrated effort to look effortless," said Civette. She was pleased that he laughed. "Would you like me to tour you about the place, Sir Bramwell?"

"Call me Adrian," he said.

Civette hid her grin of triumph. She had hoped he'd say that. *Adrian.* She loved the sound of his name. It flowed like the breeze of a welcomed wind. *Adrian and Civette.* Their names blended beautifully together. To cover her playful imaginings, Civette looked up at the house. Adrian did the same. How majestic Cairy Hollow was, looming radiant in a halo of silver clouds.

"In the old days, when the nights were warm, they held splendid parties on that roof," Civette told him.

Adrian offered his arm to her. He was pleased to hold her close. She smelled of crushed gardenias. Civette's scent was made all the lovelier by the rain-kissed air. Side by side, they meandered down the winding drive.

"Who created you?" Adrian asked Civette.

Civette laughed. "By that do you mean, 'Who is my father?' If so, he was Dr. Edgar Middleton. He left when I was quite small. He moved out west and married another woman. Hearsay has it, he abandoned that one for yet another."

"Are you angry in your heart?" Adrian asked.

"Not in the least," Civette replied. "After all, my mother and I get to live here." Civette decided she had shared enough. She looked upward and pointed. "To me, it appears as though the sky and the oceans have switched places," she said. "Those clouds are now anxious ships heading for ports unknown."

"I have never seen the ocean," Adrian replied.

Civette looked at him with a brush of suspicion. "You told us you have traveled the world. How could you have done so and never seen an ocean?"

"What I meant is that I've never viewed the ocean in the poetic way you do."

Civette's face softened. She nodded and uttered, "Oh," rather thoughtfully.

Adrian gently pulled her closer to his side. "Right now, those clouds are dreams just begging to be chased," he told her.

"How enchanting," she replied.

"Shall we run after them and try?"

"I would, but my walking shoes are so awkward."

"Then take them off."

She laughed. "What?"

"Let me help." He knelt at her feet. With a blush, Civette held out her legs, one at a time. Adrian slid off her shoes. He was amazed by the prettiness of her feet. Her ankles were such delicate things.

It was then that Adrian's head filled with an unexpected memory. A young woman was kneeling at his feet. The dawn light made her hair shine strawberry gold. Taking up an old silk jacket, she stood before him. Her eyes were unusual. One eye was fawn brown, and the other the slate gray of an October sky. Holding the jacket against his chest, the young woman began to sing.

It was a strange old tune. "*When Damon languished at my feet, and I believed him true.*" She possessed a captivating voice. The air around them was warmed by a colorful burst of sunrise. In his vision, Adrian tried to shift his gaze but could not. He could not sense the means with which to do so.

"What's wrong?" he heard Civette ask.

Adrian was too new for memories. He wondered if it was Balefire filling his mind with mischief. "I thought I heard something," he murmured.

"What is that pin you're wearing?" Civette asked.

"What pin?" he asked. He was still distracted by his imaginings.

"The one inside your vest," Civette said. "If I'm not mistaken, it's a serpent on a golden coil. Where did you get it?"

"It—it was a gift," he replied. Indeed, the disguised scarecrow had no idea where the pin actually came from. He stood. "Now, run with me," he said.

They ran across the lawn, puddles shattering like silver glass beneath their feet. Pausing at a wall of dwarf apple trees, Civette ran her fingers along their boughs. They christened her with autumn rain. Droplets trickled through the silk of her scarf, down her neck, and beneath her dress. She shivered with fascination.

When she opened her eyes, Adrian was standing before her with a gaze that promised the sweetest ruin. But it was too soon. Experience had taught Civette that the best ruination was that which was made to wait.

"Let's run some more," she said.

They headed toward the gardens. Civette's laughter rode the storm-saturated air. Fog crested toward them, reminding Civette of the impatient breath of a wildfire.

The rain fell harder now. The last stronghold of flowers swayed beneath its patter.

Adrian and Civette adjusted their running into a stroll. Adrian was pleased that Civette took his arm again and leaned into his side. He could feel her warmth through her coat. Adrian decided to dismiss the woman in his memory. Forgetting was best.

"Listen to the rain," he said. "What does it say to you?"

Civette listened. "What's here is mine," she said, surprised by her own answer.

"I see—and hear—diamonds. Glorious diamonds that were meant to shine forever."

"How positive you are," Civette replied.

"In such a world as this, there's no reason to feel otherwise," he told her.

Civette spoke of the gardens at Cairy Hollow. How beautiful they were in the blush of spring, thriving well into fall through their various revivals. In those seasons of light, they adorned Cairy Hollow like a bouquet in the tender hands of a bride. Civette's uncle did not especially admire the flowers. He dismissed them as short-lived and expensive. But Civette's nanny Raylene, who had also cared for John, believed these garden beds to be havens of magic. Raylene swore to Civette that bands of pixies made their homes in the prettiest petals.

"Do you suppose they're still there?" Adrian asked.

Civette laughed as Adrian bowed to a bank of purple asters. He stood. His face was quite serious.

"The Lord Master of the Pixies claims he will answer one question for me, and one question alone." Adrian leaned down once again and asked the flowers where the true love of his life might be. He tilted his head even closer. Civette couldn't be certain, but it appeared that the flowers were lifting their faces to his smile.

"They're undecided," said Adrian. "King Aster will convene with his Knights of the Round Petals, and get back to me before midnight."

Civette laughed again. It felt so good to do so. "Regardless, I believed Nanny Raylene for the longest time. How silly is that?"

"It's not at all silly. Gentle moments never are," he said.

His response pleased her. But then she noticed the frown on Adrian's face. "Whatever is wrong?" she asked.

"I feel sad for these flowers," he said. "They don't get to grow unchecked like wild blooms do. These are forced to be discriminative. They are neat and orderly. Beyond these walls, the flowers are free to ramble where, and with whom, they wish. Here, their beauty is expected. In Nature's world, their artistry is startling."

"That is true," said Civette. "But in this garden, they want for nothing. From the last clinging frost to the first hint of a snowfall, our groundskeeper Samuel is out here, fussing and worrying over them all. It's his life's work, his passion."

Civette went on to tell Adrian that, when she was young, she used to sit in the flower beds not caring if Samuel scolded her, or if her pretty clothes got spoiled. Civette admired the flowers for their vibrant colors and the perfume that surged through their veins. Nothing in a bottle could ever compare. It never mattered to Civette that flowers fade and die. Moments like these taught her that beauty was best in fleeting things, burned into one's memory before time and selfish expectations rendered them dull and commonplace.

"I believe that beautiful things never grow old," he told her.

She looked up at Adrian and wished the very same for him. How miraculous it would be to remain as handsome as he was at this moment forever. How marvelous to gaze upon one man's face and never tire of it—to constantly bask in the light of his smile and the promises in his eyes.

They arrived at the heart of the gardens. The winding paths of the labyrinth convened at a statue of a praying angel. How commanding she was, yet compassionate, too. Civette placed her hand upon the guardian's shoulder. The coolness of the stone radiated through her fingertips. Civette felt as electric as the storm clouds in the sky. Everything around her seemed to spark with that same intensity. It was as if, beneath her touch, the angel drew breath. Shadows of falling leaves swirled like phantom dancers across her alabaster wings. The autumn flowers were brighter, surely, and the air sang to her in whispers.

Civette felt as though she were seeing the canvas of Cairy Hollow for the very first time. It was a creation unto itself. Perhaps it was Adrian's presence that made everything so beautiful. Caressed by rain, Adrian Bramwell himself was a vision of heaven on earth.

Blushing, Civette spoke. "It's amazing how the everyday world has changed since your arrival. I don't know how to explain, Adrian. But it seems that common elements suddenly live and breathe."

Her faltering words rang with truth. Now older than the girl she had been when sitting in the flowerbeds, Civette favored the lure of nightfall against candlelit ballrooms. The mechanics of day had ceased to make an impression on her until the spell of this moment. The moment embraced her. Civette could taste the wind. The playful grass tantalized her feet. The rain on her skin prompted such long-suppressed yearnings.

Civette trembled. "I hardly know you. But I will miss you when you're gone," she confessed.

Adrian was thrilled by her admission. Nevertheless, he decided to toy with her.

"Let it be known, Civette Middleton, that you will never forget me. Wherever you go, whatever splendors you behold, you will always be reminded of me. Images of my face will be in the music you hear. Passages in books will ring with the tenor of my voice. And the next time you glance into a mirror, it will be the memory of me that looks back at you."

She slapped his arm. "How dramatic you are," she said.

With a ringing, light laughter, Civette ran back toward the drive. Adrian followed her. She seemed like a golden light emerging from a dream. Adrian wondered if perhaps it were he who wasn't real.

When Civette paused to get her shoes, she seemed anxious.

"What is it?" he asked her.

Civette bit her lip. "I don't think we should go back up together. Richard's either in the study or out here somewhere, and he's in such a foul mood. Let's avoid the risk, shall we?"

The risk, she had said. Adrian congratulated himself. He was gaining ground. From the rim of the woods, the forest spoke to him. It was impatient for its reward. Adrian ignored the messages. Instead, he smiled at

Civette and delighted in watching her as she left.

Chapter Eleven: Shattered

Richard met Civette at the door.

Richard had, on the surface, dismissed his unbearable moods. He and Civette were now alone at the farthest end of the mansion's greenhouse. Against the woolen skies, it was a dismal place overrun with rusted shelves, dead plants, and foul-smelling dirt.

Surveying the gray morning through a filmy, cracked windowpane, Civette sighed. "Why do people choose the saddest of places to have important talks in?" she said.

"And why are you so wet?" he asked.

"I was looking for one of the dogs. Cicero, it was. He's always wandering off," she said.

Civette had lied to Richard before. But it had always been about trivial matters, and she felt justified in doing so. Civette made a hasty attempt to match her expression and posture to her verbal nonchalance.

"Seriously, my pet, since when have you cared about any of the dogs?"

Civette did not like Richard's insinuation, nor the way he addressed her. She refused to answer. Richard felt his world crumbling.

"Why are you flirting with that more than obvious fraud?" he asked.

Civette found herself lying again. "I'm merely being kind. The man seems—oh, I don't know—lost."

"That swindler is far from lost, and you're too much of a mindless tease to see it."

The only reply Richard received was an irritable and much deserved silence.

"Civette," he said, "you've got to understand. I was worried, hurt, and confused. You haven't been yourself since the moment that monsterish man entered this house."

"He isn't a monster," she said.

Richard took Civette by her arms and gently turned her to face him. "I don't want to talk about that so-called Sir Bramwell. The man is an oafish bore. With any luck, in twelve hours, he'll be gone and out of our lives. No, I want to talk about us."

The thought of Adrian leaving distressed her. Her mind far away, Civette looked up and pretended to listen.

"I'm hoping when we are so old that our vision is fading, and our hair turns thin and gray, that our minds will be made young by remembering this day. It is my wish that we should laugh until our few remaining teeth hurt, knowing that we survived all adversities and proclaimed our love to the world on a storm-drenched Halloween, no less. But something warns me that—for some strange and unknown reason—you suddenly want to smash everything to bits."

Civette flinched. Was she that obvious? She didn't intend to be. Civette wasn't in love with Adrian Bramwell. But she certainly was fascinated. An unexpected infatuation couldn't be as treacherous as Richard was making it out to be. Doubtless, Richard had seen other pretty ladies and entertained certain thoughts. What was the difference, really? With a start, Civette realized that Richard was still speaking.

"Please say that we may grow old together. I don't want to be lonely and brave. I don't want to admit that I gave my heart to the only woman I ever cared for, and lost. I refuse to think of you living in far-off places—exotic places with vine-covered balconies where, when you lift your ravishing face, any memory of me would be so easily blotted out by the sun. I want to feel the same sun. I want us to share the wind, the cold, and the rain. I want to spend my middle years disagreeing with you. And when the frail hours come, and that final moment strikes, I want to die with you in my arms. Nothing would make me happier."

Civette kept her gaze to the ground. While he was always a steadfast friend, Richard Marlow was not everything she'd hoped for in an everlasting love. But were the hopes she dreamed just that—fanciful, bright delusions so easily burst when one opened one's eyes to the real world?

"Promise me less cold," she said, quietly. Then Civette recalled the outright fib she'd told Adrian. Civette chuckled with embarrassment. "I don't much care for rain, either."

"Whatever comes, I will shelter you," he told her.

Civette lifted her face to Richard's. While he wasn't beautiful, he was kind. Perhaps that was enough. She granted him a kiss.

****

Leona remained in the formal parlor. She was alone, and she needed to think. She closed her eyes. There were avenues to her past Leona did her best to avoid. Now, on this bleak October morning, she'd crossed the threshold to her darker memories. Strangely, she found comfort there.

The disappointments in Leona's youth seemed trivial compared to the tedium and bitterness of her present life. She began to play that dangerous game of "what if." Had she been more honest about her feelings all those years ago, might she have been happier now? Since such memories were always wrapped with pretty ribbons of hope, Leona couldn't help but agree.

In a whirl of bright images, Leona recalled times long gone. Those years of taking lovely things for granted—those days of living like every hour would last forever. As it did in her mind, it all went by so fast.

The rhythm of the rain lured Leona away from her imaginings. It was pointless to dream. The heart she had obeyed as a young woman remained headstrong and vain. Worse still, moments of envy had led Leona to reprehensible actions and, in the end, rewarded nothing. Despite all the beauties of her brighter might-have-beens, there was no going back. But if she could have one wish granted, just one everlasting wish—oh, how life would change.

A scratching sound, much like sharpened nails on ice, disrupted her solitude. With a start, Leona realized a young woman was at the other side of the window. "Help me, please. Let me in," the girl begged. Her voice was muffled, and her frantic breath misted the glass.

Leona dashed through the French doors and went to the poor creature. She was perhaps twenty years old, thin as a rail, and saturated by the rain.

"Heavens, what happened to you?" Leona asked.

"I nearly crawled through the storm to find you here," the girl confessed.

"What is your name?" Leona asked.

"Mrs. Middleton, it's me, Sarah—Sarah Burton, the

chimney sweeper's daughter. I work as a maid for you when you have large parties. Don't you remember my face?"

Despite her dread of any disease that might accompany impoverishment, Leona nodded and held out her hand. Leona felt the girl's bones beneath her ash-colored flesh. She could smell dampened soot about the girl's clothes. With soothing encouragement, Leona led Sarah to the kitchen. The cook's eyes went wide at the sight of the girl. Without hesitation, Mrs. Wheeler went to her own bedroom off the kitchen and returned with a blanket she draped around Sarah. Leona sat with Sarah while Mrs. Wheeler went to the stove to fill a bowl with hot broth.

"Sarah's here to assist with the party this evening," Leona explained.

"There will be no working until you are warm and dry again," Mrs. Wheeler insisted.

Summoned back to work, the maid Marie entered the kitchen. The small wisp of a girl was carrying a stack of silver platters Mrs. Wheeler had selected for the party. After a bobbing curtsy to Mrs. Middleton, Marie took one look at the bedraggled Sarah. A sympathetic shiver crawled up her spine. Placing herself at a side table, Marie began polishing the scrolled trays. Her posture hunched over her steaming bowl, Sarah gave Marie a weak smile. Marie returned it.

"Eat that up. It will do you good," Mrs. Wheeler told Sarah.

Sarah stared at her soup. "I just want to hold it for a moment," she said.

Mrs. Wheeler shouted over her shoulder to Evan to bring in more firewood. With a gentle pat on Sarah's bowed and bony shoulders, the cook left to continue preparations for the party.

"If you're too chilled to help with the reception this evening, we understand," Leona told Sarah. "You may go home."

"We need the money," Sarah replied. "My father's not doing well. He hasn't worked in a while, and we don't have enough to eat."

"Well, if not tonight, there will be other parties," said Leona. Nurtured by wealth and numbed by indifference, Leona had no concept of real-life struggles. "You must feel better, Sarah. That is important. When I saw you outside the parlor window, you looked like a fright."

"Oh, that's because I saw the beautiful young woman at the tree."

Marie looked up sharply. Her gloved hands went cold.

"What woman and what tree?" Leona asked.

"I don't know who she was. But the tree is the large oak that stands at the entrance gate."

Leona was taken aback. Thankfully, the cook was devoted to her task and had not heard a word over the sounds of pots clanging about, and firewood tumbling to the floor.

"No one else was near when I met you outside," Leona told the girl.

"She disappeared when you arrived. She seemed frightened of you."

Leona regained her composure. "If she was a trespasser, she ought to be," she replied.

"Oh, I've seen her before. It was at your last Halloween Ball. It was warmer then, as I remember. One of your guests—a real fussy old hen—said she'd left her wrap at a table on the patio. She ordered me to go and get it. When I went outside, I saw the ghostly young woman beneath the oak tree. She was pale, like moonlight through mist, and she was staring at me."

"Sarah, I can only imagine that you saw another guest. We have so many at our parties."

"I thought the same at first. But she was so lovely in that light. She didn't seem real. I went over to see if I could help her. She held out her hand, and touched me on the arm. Her fingertips felt like ice. They glowed in a strange way. I can't describe it. Subdued, yet vibrant. I wanted to run, but she smiled, and her smile was gentle. I said hello, or something like that. She told me she'd see me again. Then, she vanished. I remember the odd and heavy silence after she left. Not a moment later, it began to rain. Despite the warm night, the rain was cold and mournful. The sound of it took over everything, just like it has today."

Leona stood. "You're suffering ill effects from the weather, Sarah. Rest here, and have your soup. We'll chat about your woman of moon shadow and mist later, shall we?"

Tick, tick, tick, the kitchen clock pulsed in time with Marie's agitated heart. She didn't breathe a word, but Marie had seen the moon-shadow lady too.

Chapter Twelve: Lured

Civette had not joined the others at luncheon, and she turned away the tray Phoebe attempted to deliver. Locking her bedroom door, Civette had, for the past two hours, been contemplating what to wear for the Halloween Ball.

Her intended costume was laid out on her bed. It had been decided months before that she and Richard would make their entrance as Romeo and Juliet. Their elaborate costumes had been fashioned by the head designer at the Shubert Theater in Boston. The material that made up Civette's gown was gorgeous. However, the style was not. It hung on her like a weighted drape. At least the headpiece was pretty. It was a ribboned band laden with pearls.

For Civette, the thought of reenacting Romeo and Juliet's balcony scene for their many guests had brought on pure excitement. But now, and despite her meaningful talk with Richard, Civette was conflicted. All it took for her to feel this way was to think of Adrian Bramwell again. Adrian's attentions felt new and intoxicating. Still, a nagging fear possessed her. Beneath his exceptional looks, was Adrian merely a thoughtless Casanova toying with the emotions of desperate women? This perception offended her. Civette refused to be desperate, even for a man as unrivaled as Adrian.

Wearing nothing but her step-in chemise, Civette

stood sulking before her pier glass. Sequined evening dresses were strewn about everywhere. Her dresser was covered with strands of pearls, dangling earrings, and feathered headpieces. Despite the myriad of choices available to her, it seemed not a scrap of Civette's costly wardrobe would do.

Her weary glance fell upon a cameo Richard had given her a few evenings before. Civette hopped over a mound of beaded shawls and held the pin in her hand. Civette could see that it was not well crafted. Richard claimed it was an engagement gift from his father, and that his mother wore it faithfully until the day she died. Regardless of such sentiment, Civette knew she would rarely wear it. It was old-fashioned and not pretty enough.

Civette turned the pin over, and as she did, the relief broke away and tumbled to the floor. Civette knelt and retrieved the broken piece. It would not adhere properly. She would have to attend to it later. Civette carelessly placed the cameo bits on her bureau and picked up her intended costume from her bed.

Hugging her Juliet gown to her chest, Civette went to the window. By the scant light of the storm, she studied the creation of spun silver beneath a garden of flowers. The silk stems and blossoms were delicately stitched in nature's vivid colors, and the train was a trailing tapestry of vines. It was a glorious costume for what was supposed to be an eventful day. Sighing, Civette told herself she simply had to do as expected and become Richard's Juliet.

Still, she hesitated.

Leaning her head against the misted window, Civette tried to make sense of her rambling thoughts.

When it came to Richard, she wanted to convince her heart that the misgivings in her mind were untrue. After all, she was fairly certain Richard was going to propose that night. But did Richard really love her? He appeared to. He had always appeared to, even when he was a boy and believed Civette would be impressed by the frog he'd captured for her. Richard often misunderstood the things Civette truly cared about.

Civette had accepted the idea of Richard as the man who would care for her until her final days. She now gave renewed thought to this life-changing plan. Richard's looks were moderate. He didn't eat or drink to excess. Richard never left her side to gamble at cards or to brag and boast all evening with other men. In short, Richard Marlow was disciplined and sensible. Civette now worried that "disciplined and sensible" made up the dull-plated armor of a wearisome life. Civette did not wish for a tedious existence. She could easily see that her mother was ensnared in one. No, Civette wanted laughter and light and love. Only yesterday, Civette was satisfied. But now, she was experiencing such feverish and fierce temptations.

And what of Cairy Hollow? Although she wished she could, Civette did not revere this estate the way her uncle did. Lineage and antiques and valuables locked away in a vault were all just posturing veneer. While she was rarely concerned, Civette guessed that the Cairy money was slipping away. Whatever dreams, whatever grandeur Cairy Hollow ever managed was in the memories of past owners and, like those predecessors, now long dead.

Laying her Juliet gown upon her bed, Civette frowned. "Long dead," she murmured.

A sudden idea occurred to her. Donning a gossamer dressing gown, Civette left her bedroom and tiptoed to the end of the west hall.

Emmeline Cairy's bedroom suite was the grandest of them all. Because Cairy Hollow had been built for her, Emmeline was the only bride to occupy it. Civette's mother had plans to redesign the suite to her own taste for use as her private rooms. However, to that, everyone in the house said no. This chamber was to remain as Emmeline left it. The heavy, golden-latched doors were permanently locked.

Even so, Civette knew where the key was hidden. One evening, by accident, Civette had noticed her uncle entering the room. He did not stay long. On the occasions the maid Alice was ordered to clean it, Mrs. Beals supervised like a sentry at the doorway. Civette carefully moved a small table away from the wall. A scrolled key lay balanced on a trim edge behind. Civette took the key and, with nervous fingers, placed it in the keyhole. The lock turned with a muffled snap.

The air inside was stale and mildewed from idleness and rain. Civette crept toward the tall, shuttered windows. The rug beneath her bare feet felt alive, breathing cold and damp. Civette tied back the musty drapes. A somber and colorless daylight flooded the room. It brushed over a floral arrangement, which in semi-darkness seemed stately but, by the stormy afternoon's true beams, showed withered and brown. The steady whirl of the mantel clock provided the only sense of life in that room.

A rush of wind rattled the windowpanes. Civette looked toward the glass. As a fleeting shadow passed, Civette assumed it was a bird. Ravens, in particular, were always perching themselves beneath the bedroom eaves. Civette often heard them late at night. While her mother most certainly did not, Civette found their chatter intriguing. The ravens favored the crevices near Emmeline's room. From there, they could keep a keen watch over the forest.

Civette roamed about the suite, peering under dust covers. She felt such awe, surrounded by Emmeline's possessions. With her bold portrait downstairs, Civette thought of Emmeline often. It must have been difficult for a poor, uneducated girl to be thrust into an upper class world of privilege, political talk, and parties. But Emmeline adapted and was loved.

You have to fight for what you want, a voice murmured inside Civette's head. Startled, she looked about. It seemed as if Emmeline's room was slowly restoring itself in the day's ghoulish light. Around the northernmost edge of the house, a shrill gust cried, and Civette believed she heard, *Why would you remain in a place that holds no promises? Escape. Be free. Follow what your heart longs for*. The words tumbled about in her head and then became one with the timbre of the rain.

Civette felt a rush of loneliness. Her uncle was becoming increasingly sad and distant. Her mother was, at best, indifferent to everything and everyone around her. Gruff old Mrs. Beals was more of a mother to Civette than Leona ever was. Civette sat on the floor. The timeworn carpet beneath her smelled of tea leaves. Civette sighed and hugged her knees like a frightened child. How dispiriting it was to know the envy the villagers felt for the Cairy family was aimless. No one here was truly happy.

Silence fell. Any progression the room had made

toward revival returned to darkness. One of the weaker petals from the dried floral bouquet drifted down before Civette's eyes. She watched, mesmerized, while it settled among the long-dead moths. As for her whispered advice, Civette convinced herself she had willed it all on her own.

Wiping tears of frustration from her eyes, Civette remembered her purpose for being there and went to the dressing room, where she surveyed Emmeline's gowns. Civette imagined Emmeline Cairy at the entrance of the ballroom, her porcelain complexion sublime against her red silk gown. For certain, all the wealthy women with their inbred and anemic looks simply had to resent her. And their men, without admitting it to anyone but themselves, secretly loved her.

Civette continued to browse through Emmeline's carefully wrapped wardrobe. As she moved along, garments rustled. Silk petticoats rippled with a sweeping sound in the storm-cast light. A bronze feather bowed from the shelf above, and a pair of blue taffeta dancing slippers shifted. A decorated fan furled opened and closed. Civette witnessed none of these things. What she did see were two ravens perched on the sill of the dressing room window. Someone had left it open. Water stains had crept down the raised velvet wall covering. Strangely, the water stains seemed to spell out the word *ours.*

"Shoo," Civette said, waving her fingers. "Fly away."

The ravens did as they were commanded. However, they headed first for the bedroom. Civette followed, only to discover Emmeline's portrait gown laid out upon the silk coverlet of the bed. The dress had not been there before. Meanwhile, overhead, the ravens pivoted and, with a shrill call, they sailed out the dressing room window and into the stormy sky.

Civette studied Emmeline's gown. True, it was of an antiquated style. But with its lush, blood-red tones, it would make a marvelous and most fitting costume. Civette even had a red silk ribbon that matched the one Emmeline wore in her hair. Civette smiled and was quite pleased again. Holding the gown close, she danced in circles about the dressing room. Before she knew it, she was singing an old tune she'd often heard her uncle play.

"The conquest gain'd, he left his prize,
He left her to complain;
To talk of Joy with weeping eyes,
And measure time by pain.
But Heaven will take the mourner's part,
In pity or despair;
And the last sigh that rends the heart
Shall waft the spirit there."

Whatever concerns, whatever worries Civette embraced were now vanquished. That is to say, these notions were no longer in her head. What Civette failed to notice was a curious image in the base of a brass urn. Civette was too busy dreaming and dancing to realize she was being watched.

Chapter Thirteen: Windows

Adrian was offered a chance to rest. But being newly alive, Adrian did not care to rest. As Balefire assured him, that was what death's dominion was for.

Adrian studied the guest room he'd been given. Heavily draped and furnished, it didn't impress him. Nothing of warmth existed within its walls. Even the gold-framed paintings were void of expression. It was a room where happiness seemingly never happened, a facade locked in eternal twilight. It depressed him.

He left and stood in the hallway. Muffled voices were heard, voices that seemed nearly as lifeless as the chamber he'd just escaped. The whispers beckoned him to the far end of the corridor. There, behind a partially opened door, shone a tunnel of light. He gravitated toward it.

Within that glow was a staircase far less grand than any other in the house. The wood was dry, the treads blanched and hollowed in the centers. Adrian leaned over the railing and listened. The voices were louder now, more distinct. He could hear repetitive movement. Adrian followed the sounds until he ended up in a stark hallway that led to the kitchen. The walls were crackled and scuffed in places. The late October day wafted through the thin plaster. How raw it was, how cold. The dampness crawled straight through to Adrian's spine. He felt oddly brittle.

Adrian nearly didn't see the young woman standing at the window. Dressed in drab service attire, her complexion was as fair as the mist that swirled beyond the glass. Beneath a pair of wing-arched brows, she had eyes the color of downpour gray. Tall and slender, the girl seemed breakable. Her arresting face was troubled. He could see her expression in the glass.

"Please tell me what's wrong," he said.

He startled her. The girl blushed and curtseyed. "The oncoming storm, sir," she replied.

He asked her name. She replied that it was Sarah. She looked at him. The features of her face warmed. "You're every bit as handsome as they said," she confessed.

He smiled. "Perhaps it's because, for now, you see me through other people's eyes," he said.

"How is your visit so far?" she asked.

"Of all the intriguing people I met here, I like Miss Civette Middleton best."

The young maid did not seem pleased with his answer. Frowning, she looked out the window. "I meant the house, sir," she said.

"It's lovely," he said. However, he was still thinking of Civette.

"To me, Cairy Hollow is a beacon of light at the edge of the forest," she said.

"How interesting," he replied. "I prefer the shadows that lurk within."

Adrian had frightened her somehow, and he didn't know why. He was sorry about this. Mrs. Beals appeared at the end of the hall. The girl visibly sensed the housekeeper standing there. "Sarah," the woman said. Her tone was severe.

"You should go back," Sarah said to Adrian. "This is no place for you, sir. Besides, the proper folks will be wondering where you are."

With a weak smile and a nod, Sarah walked away. She left Adrian with a cheerless image of domestic servants envying other people's lives through polished windows. There existed no hopes, no praise, and certainly no promises. Such a girl would remain in service in a house like this all of her capable days. And when she no longer proved useful, she would be relegated to a small space to die in—a space, most likely, without windows.

Adrian dismissed his melancholy thoughts and looked down the hall. The girl with the gifted gray eyes was gone. With her departure, dark storm clouds swept over the servants' hall roof and down toward the valley below.

Adrian remained until the skies no longer beguiled him. He noticed a spiral staircase at the end of the servants' hall. Adrian recalled Civette speaking about parties being held on the roof of Cairy Hollow. He followed that message there.

****

Civette stood before the balcony window in Emmeline's room. A fog blanketed the panes. "I will test you, just as I did the Glass of Truth," she informed the mist.

Civette wrote *Richard* across its cloud. A sudden pelt of rain obliterated the word. Civette stood back. Like a flower unfolding, the mist reappeared. Civette carefully scrolled out the name *Adrian.* As she moved her fingertip along the glass, angry storm clouds rolled toward the forest. It was as if she herself had propelled

102

them there.

"Oh, Adrian Bramwell, could you possibly and honestly love me?" she whispered.

Adrian's name remained clear and strong in its ethereal mist.

A blur of ebony wings fluttered past. Civette watched as two ravens soared in an upward circle and back to the roof. Civette experienced the oddest sensation that, as they had with Emmeline's dress, the Delphian birds were leading her to a choice she could make.

If her inner sense echoed with caution, Civette did not hear it. Taking up Emmeline's blood-red gown, Civette left the room. As she turned the key in the golden lock, Civette could have sworn she heard a woman's voice say, "*Bonne chance*."

Civette crept back to her own room and placed Emmeline's gown on her bed. Then back out and down the wide staircase Civette went, one hand gliding along the polished banister, the other resting over her pounding heart. With a nervous glance left and right, Civette went past the servants' hall and up the spiral staircase to the roof.

As she guessed, Adrian was there. Perhaps, in the grasp of that magical day, they were meant to be there, together, the two of them and the clouds.

Neither spoke. A driving wind emerged, void of rain. Civette turned to face it. She breathed in its power. It made her feel alive. Closing her eyes, Civette slowly raised her arms. She envisioned the house dwindling away but for a pedestal beneath her feet. The wind swept about her, cresting the tendrils of her hair and the kimono-like sleeves of her dressing gown into its clutches as wings. Lady Nature had woven an iridescent and unbreakable spell. In the embrace of her storm, Civette was made to look and to feel dangerously beautiful.

This sensation struck a startling chord of memory within her. As if it knew, the seductive wind lessened its caress. Civette relaxed her stance, opened her eyes, and remained fixated on the horizon as she spoke.

"Some months ago, I had an unusual dream—a dream I often remember in my waking hours. I was seated upon the lower garden wall and feeling tremendously upset, although I'm not certain why. Then, in the blink of an eye, I was pulled up into the night on a great rush of air. I was adorned in a shimmering gown of gold, and the wind brushed my hair with teardrops of pearl. Even though I was alone in a vast universe, all alone in that deep blush of night, my worries drifted away. I was not the least bit afraid to be cast out among the clouds. From here on earth, clouds often seem ominous. But when you're up there, you understand their innocence. They're like children set loose in a field to play. They shouldn't be blamed for bringing an occasional shadow into our lives. How would we realize our happiness without a little remembrance of gloom?

"I began dancing with the clouds, chasing them all about, and leaping from star to star. I stayed so long the heavens grew cold. It was almost as if I could feel the jealous moon breathing frost upon my face. But the loam of the stars was warm beneath my feet, warm like silver fire, and it drew up into my limbs and colored my skin with stardust. I was ever so lovely. Not only did I know it, I could feel it. The people left on this dull earth looked up into the heavens, and I proudly thought, it's me they're gazing at. But the star I stood upon cried out, 'You silly fool. You're only beautiful because of me.' And then I woke up."

From that misty rooftop, Civette surveyed all that was Cairy Hollow. She fought back tears. This estate and the life Civette had learned to lead there were much like that mocking dream. Perhaps she would have been happier as a village doctor's daughter. Expectations in her present realm were nothing more than hollow burdens.

"That star took its radiance from you," she heard Adrian say.

She marveled at how this man she'd only known for hours possessed the ability to make her worries and her heartaches drift to joy. Above all, she loved the fact that he listened.

"Who are you, really?" she asked as if this were all a dream.

"I am the one destined for you," he assured her.

His words, indeed, his very presence here, against Nature's brooding but magnificent sky, seemed torn from the page of a romantic novel. He lured her in such a way Civette could feel the depths of her being drift willingly to his. She spoke with the voice of her body.

"When you smile at me, I exist," she said.

"This is the world and the heavens themselves when you are near me," he replied.

Civette lifted her face up to his, and in her eyes, there was a wonderment he knew was his to discover. The reawakened wind moved around them. Yet all was soundless—soundless as the moments that hold a sky captive before a storm. Civette took Adrian's heavenly face into her hands and kissed him.

He did not kiss her back.

Civette, being wise, broke away. Behaving as if nothing had happened, she took Adrian's hand and led him to a bench that overlooked the sweeping gardens. They watched and listened as the treetops ceased to sway and the autumn winds returned to the west. It was as if Nature realized her powers of persuasion had failed and was now summoning them back to her core.

Still holding his hand, Civette spoke. "I have a question for you, Adrian. Do you believe in magic spells?"

"With all my heart," he said.

Civette was delighted. "I believe the same. Not to hurt anyone, of course, but instead to sense all the dark mystery and shimmering excitement—the way you feel when you blow out a candle and watch the whispers of smoke fade away in the glimmer of the moon," she said.

"Smoke fading away in the glimmer of the moon. How irresistible that sounds," he said. He was enthralled by the image her words formed in his mind.

"What kind of magic do you believe in?" she asked.

"I believe in the spell that brought me here," he vowed.

Civette shivered at the promise of his words. "One of the surest ways to prophesize is to count the crows. As simple as that sounds, crows are often harbingers of events destined to come true. Have you ever heard how the rhyme goes? It begins, 'One for sorrow.' "

"Ah, yes—two for Mirth. And what an amusing mischief-maker she is, trust me." Adrian grinned.

She delighted in what she assumed to be a jest, and laughed. "Three for a wedding, and four for a birth," she said.

He took both her hands within his own. "Five for laughing, six for crying, seven for sickness, eight for dying. Nine for silver, and ten for gold."

"So, you do know the crows' prophecies. Richard refuses to believe any of this. He's too pigheaded and lazy to try. But how can anyone with an ounce of wonder not sense that all the marvelous splendors in this world are right there before us? We only have to open our eyes and our minds."

"How true," he said.

"I never want the wonder I feel to perish and die. What's the point of living without mystery? I believe we are born with magic. Anyone who laughed with an invisible friend, whispered a spell, or wished upon a chosen star held that special power. But as we grow older, our parents lecture the magic away, and only because it was lectured away from them. Indeed, my own uncle told me—"

With a start, Civette realized something. "That's it," she exclaimed. "Follow me, Adrian, for I do own a real piece of magic. It's called the Glass of Truth, and it's in the ballroom, behind a velvet drape. If you look deep within its reflection, you will see yourself as you honestly exist. Come with me—I will show you."

Together they moved down the stairs and into the main house. Civette was prancing, just as she was when she had led Richard Marlow to that very mirror only hours before.

Civette saw no harm in this, no foreshadowed warning. Her current state of happiness clearly destroyed any sense of reason.

"Prepare to see how beautiful you are," she told him.

Chapter Fourteen: Reflections

They stood before the mirror. Just as Civette placed her fingertips on the velvet drape, a gleam of the mirror revealed itself with a rapid flash, and Captain Balefire stepped through the glass.

"Your walking stick," he announced while holding out the ruby-topped cane.

Civette could barely speak. "Captain Balefire, you startled me."

"I am excessively sorry, Miss Middleton," he said. Balefire bowed. His calculated movement disguised the smug grin on his face. "I was merely admiring a portrait of your great uncle—whatever his name was—on the wall."

"But how did you get behind the mirror?" she asked.

"My dear young woman, I am usually behind everything," he replied. This time, Balefire let his insolence glare through. "I believe you were showing Sir Bramwell—"

Civette was panic-stricken. "Nothing. Nothing at all," she said.

"No, do tell. I am all ears," Balefire insisted, and he rolled his hook-shaped hand over his abdomen.

"Enough," said Adrian. He recognized the absurd joke the grasshopper demon was playing. "Leave us, boot boy, and do not return until you can present yourself as a decent being would."

Balefire was not pleased with his puppet's tone, much less his own greatly diminished title. "Your humble servant," Balefire muttered. Turning on his heel, Balefire paraded across the hall. His metallic-hued face was burning red, and his barbed ears were pinned back like those of a scolded dog. Balefire paused, taking a dramatic stance at the doorway. His display of adversity didn't matter in the least. Adrian Bramwell would neither apologize nor call him back. Realizing but not accepting defeat, Balefire walked away. His cobbled shoes echoed pointedly across the foyer floor.

Adrian held Civette by her shoulders. "There, there, now. The evil is gone. From this moment on, you will be with me always. I will live for you, and fight for you, and forever call you my own."

Trembling, Civette did not speak.

"You are hesitating," he said. "Perhaps you are afraid to confess that all you feel for me is pity. I can accept that. Your pity is still a gift. I could be a soul if only you would love me. Be mine, Civette. Let me be yours."

"Adrian, I am honored, yet astonished, by your confession. Surely you have met so many beautiful women in this big, wide world."

"No, never."

Civette could not comprehend this. "No other women before today?"

He swore that before this hour he knew nothing. Before this moment in her presence, he did not care. Today he'd been born in her eyes. He assured her in such compelling tones that Civette was tempted to believe it was all true. A glow of passion warmed her face. With that look, Adrian realized for the first time in his terribly new life what it meant to be alive.

Whether Civette chose to believe or not, these warrants were true, for they were ordained by Balefire and the spirits of Nature to be. But there was another substance at work inside Adrian's patchwork brain and his parched wicker chest—an awakening that challenged all the harm his demons willed there. It was a burgeoning flame, a far-reaching force of goodness, and it spoke to him. What this positive power was, he did not know. However, to its urgent whispers, he listened.

"I love you," he said.

Richard stood at the doorway. Neither Adrian nor Civette saw him.

"This is all so sudden," said Civette. "How can I be certain that I love you in return?"

Civette's voice was caressing and true. It was nothing like the carefree tone she employed when addressing Richard. Nothing near it at all.

"I love you without knowing how," Adrian replied. "I love you without knowing the full power of what love is."

Richard had heard enough. "This isn't love. It's pure envy and greed," he said. His words carried such emotion they shuddered across the room.

"This is a private conversation, Richard. Why are you here?" Civette asked.

Richard stepped toward her. Standing beneath the leaden beams from the skylight, he appeared so very beaten and worn.

"Hear me out. Please," he said. "I know I'm not some romantic world traveler ready to whisk you away to adventures that couldn't possibly exist. But listen carefully, Civette. This intruder, this so-called noble and worldly man, is a swindler. Beneath that well-rehearsed smile, he is a monster out for cash and the comfort of this home. There is nothing else he wants from you."

Richard had attacked the stronghold of Civette's romantic fantasies, and it incensed her. "I want you to leave immediately," she said.

Adrian stopped her from saying more. "A moment, Civette. One insult may be remedied by another. Sir," he began with an overdone bow. "Permit me to also label you a monster, and to offer you swords."

Richard's eyes went wide. "Swords? Do you honestly want to pretend that this is the seventeen-hundreds, and we are now forced to duel over this woman's attentions? Good Lord, where did you come from? Was it a hole in the sky, or a fiction writer's time machine?"

Adrian's incomparable face colored as a memory formed in his mind. He recalled once again the young woman with strawberry blonde hair and unusual eyes. He heard her tender yet spirited voice spinning yarns about long-ago men dueling for love and honor. Apparently, these tales were merely bits of fanciful rubbish, and little else. Adrian felt such shame for clinging to them.

Richard spoke on. "Therefore, in response to your offer, I fear I must decline. But don't let that prevent you from finding some other idiot who wants to run you through. I will toast the news when I hear it. Swords! Good Lord, you really are a mildewed jumble of old world rot and make-believe."

"Richard," Civette implored, "please go."

"One last thing, Civette, and I will leave your life for good, if that is what you truly wish. Do you remember this morning and the Glass of Truth? I scoffed at its so-called magical powers, yes. Yet you believed. You said the glass reflected people as they truly were. You claimed, and I quote you, that 'not a misstep in motive or character could be shielded from its sight.' Is that correct?"

"Yes," Civette admitted.

"If you honestly believe that, then let your mirror be the judge. Test that imposter in the glass," Richard demanded.

A vision of Balefire stepping through that glass possessed her. "No," Civette cried. "Now, let us be."

"Ah, then this revered mirror has lost its ability to reflect hidden truths? How sad that such a mighty oracle should serve its gullible audience only once."

"You are detestable," said Civette.

Richard exhaled his last breath of hope. "If you see me as detestable, then I am. To this, you may add that I am skeptical and overprotective because I care about those I love. I am human. As for you, Sir-Whoever-You-Really-Are, you have nothing but my contempt. You are not true. You are not real in any sense of the word. You should pray to God, sir—pray to God to make you behave like a man."

Turning on his heel as a proud man should, Richard left. He realized, as he departed that grand home, that pride was all that remained of his life's golden plans, and he'd paid a dear and fatal price for it.

Civette heard the front door close. The sound of it sent a jolt through her. Waves of pain coiled tightly around her heart. Somehow, Civette trusted that Richard would never really desert her. She went to the door. Adrian followed her, and Civette wished he hadn't.

When Civette was deeply conflicted, she preferred that no one noticed. Through the distorted glass, Civette watched Richard disappear down the walkway. *He is leaving, he is leaving,* her heart cried out in caution. But being a stubborn girl, Civette did nothing.

Adrian begged Civette to explain her distraction. She replied that her ill mood was due to Richard. This she said with a jerk of her chin, as though Richard were nothing more than a discarded toy, a torn dress, or a cat that had grown from a kitten and was no longer adored. Had Adrian Bramwell thrived any longer than nine hours upon this earth, he might have realized that Miss Civette Middleton possessed qualities that were crueler and far more heartless than he was ever intended to be.

"How may I take away your pain?" he asked.

Civette recalled the cameo Richard had given her. Civette knew what she was about to do was spiteful. Regardless, she did it. "The pin you wear hidden within your vest," she said. "May I have it?"

Adrian unfastened the serpent clasp and readily handed it to her. "With all my heart and all my hope," he replied.

"If I decide to end my relationship with Richard, I will wear this tonight," she said. Civette was already certain she would wear it, if nothing more than to annoy Richard. Her heart had already dredged its way from wounded to revengeful. "One other thing," she added. "You should dismiss that manservant of yours, that Captain Balefire."

The suggestion stunned Adrian. "But he is my mentor, my creator—in that I mean he has instructed me as to what I should do and say in this vast and challenging world."

"My uncle told me that he learned all too late in life that a true man doesn't rely on what others think or say. He bravely thinks and speaks for himself. Let that be of advice to you."

Civette left the room. The glittering snake was clenched tightly in her grasp.

****

Adrian looked around. It was his first encounter with a stillness that seemed to speak. He wasn't certain what to do. Was this the sort of silence that was meant to be broken? Without warning, from nowhere and yet everywhere, he heard the quietude. It rang with depth and resonance. In this suspended moment of reckoning, Adrian began to ponder his existence. He lifted his faultless face to the heavens.

"God, are you here? I can't be sure. I was told to speak to you—to pray to you—and I must."

"Do you really think God is listening?" Balefire asked from the balcony above.

"Perhaps not, but you were," said Adrian. "And from now on, you will cease. I have no further need for your services."

"Are those your wishes, my fanciful slop pile, or Civette's?"

"What could it possibly matter? Civette and I, we are one and the same."

Balefire groaned. "Any man who embraces that theory is doomed."

"I intend to take her to church," Adrian vowed.

"You may take her to Hell. 'Tis all the same," said Balefire.

Adrian replied nothing. His eyes fired with newfound conviction.

Balefire merely chuckled at the sight. "All right, then, I acquiesce. You are on your own, and may you hold every moment dear. Now, go on with your all-important plea session. Please do. Just keep in mind that you are stuffed with hay, and hay is merely sod scattered upon this earth for cattle to graze upon, and endless armies to trample their muddied boots over. The master of Heaven may not have much time for a contrivance such as you. He has real souls to watch over."

The charmed scarecrow looked to the heavens once more. "Dear God, I beg of you, please make me into a man."

Balefire laughed. "Pardon my further intrusion, but if that's your true desire, you'll have no luck whatsoever up there. If you want solid results, my boy, lower your head as well as your sights, and start bargaining with the other one."

Chapter Fifteen: The Serpent

Alone in her room, Civette studied her new treasure. She was enthralled by the way Adrian's pin glistened as she turned it gently in her hands. What a unique piece it was—a coiled snake adorned with shimmering diamonds, sharp emeralds for eyes, and a ruby apple in its mouth. It reminded Civette of the tree in the Garden of Eden and the serpent who convinced lonely Eve to open her mind there. To Civette's way of thinking, the serpent was the most interesting character in the narrative. Without him, Adam's and Eve's days would have idled in ignorance of all that life had to offer.

Civette glanced toward the broken bits of the cameo Richard had given her. Without a second thought, without a moment's hesitation, Civette lifted the window and tossed Richard's mother's treasure outside. Civette couldn't even be bothered to wonder where it landed.

Beyond the gray gardens, brilliant strokes of lightning cast their splintered webs across the sky. Thunder rolled, and the storm returned. Civette heard a pelting sound. Searching about, she located the source. The mantel flue had been left ajar, and chilled droplets of rain were hammering the hearth.

Civette moved toward the fireplace. A draft in the chimney whirled and escaped with an agitated howl. Civette reached under the brickwork and attempted to close the damper. It was stuck in place. Grumbling,

Civette heard a knock at her door.

"Come in," Civette called out. The door opened, and Sarah appeared.

"I was walking past when I heard you struggling with the damper," Sarah explained.

"Goodness, was I that frustrated?" asked Civette.

"Ah, these old fireplaces are nothing but stubborn, miss. Let me have a try at it."

As Sarah curved herself under the mantel, Civette noticed how thin the poor girl was. Civette thought of all the food at Cairy Hollow that got shoveled into dust bins. What a terrible waste. Meanwhile, Sarah was waving her arm about in the hearth.

"My apologies, miss. I'm more accustomed to seeing these from the other end."

Civette was mystified. "Whatever do you mean?" she asked.

Sarah laughed. "That does sound mysterious. You'd think I was a black-eyed raven. No, my father is a chimney sweeper. I often help him."

"What a hazardous occupation for a young woman," said Civette.

"We make our money where we can," said Sarah.

Moments later, Sarah got a solid grasp on the lodged damper. With some effort, it rolled into place with a rusted groan. Just as the latch was near to closing, an irregular-shaped piece of pottery fell to the grate. Even though the fireplace was unlit, the bottle radiated fire red. Small trails of smoke rose from the rain puddle it rested in. Using a pair of tongs, Sarah carefully lifted the vessel from the cradle of the hearth.

"What in heaven's name is that?" Civette asked.

Sarah held the glazing out toward her. "Heaven had

nothing to do with it, miss. It's a Scottish whiskey bottle called the Greybeard."

"I swear to you, Sarah, I do not go sneaking swigs of whiskey in the middle of the night."

"Oh, this has not held that kind of spirit for quite some time. This is a witch bottle."

Intrigued, Civette moved closer.

"It's a counter-magical device against spells," Sarah explained.

"Why was it in my fireplace?" Civette asked.

"To protect you," said Sarah. "To be of use, it has to be hidden near the person it's meant to defend. I imagine your overcautious mother placed it here."

"Trust me, my mother does not believe in anything magical. What's in this bottle?"

"It very likely holds cuttings from your hair and fingernails. Sometimes, they're even sprinkled with urine."

Civette made a squeamish face. Sarah went on. "The person wishing to protect you would have put nails or pins in here. Next, they'd add some sort of liquid, like wine. The sharp things are meant to stab the evil that's after you. The fluid drowns it. A witch bottle like this can also be tossed into a clean fire to destroy the person who wished you ill."

"But who would plot against me in such a way? How silly is that?" Civette paused in thought, and grinned. "I propose we burn this bottle for fun. I'd love to see who in this household suddenly bursts into flames."

Civette reached out her hand. Sarah pulled the bottle away.

"It doesn't belong in this house, let alone your room.

It will do more harm than good. Dark spells draw dark souls. Regardless of its thoughtful purpose, I'm going to get rid of this witch bottle. Meanwhile, miss, you should attend to a prettier brand of magic, and prepare for your party."

"That's true, Sarah. I have so much to do to get ready."

Sarah disguised her envy by glancing around. She noticed Emmeline's gown on the bed. "Is that your costume?" she asked. "How lovely. But the hair ribbon is badly wrinkled. Shall I take it downstairs and iron it?"

Placing the silk ribbon in her apron pocket, Sarah excused herself and left. Transporting the Greybeard bottle with the fireplace tongs, Sarah crept down the servants' staircase and out into the downpour. The determined young maid didn't stop until she reached the farthest edge of the lawn. There, she flung the spelled decanter and the tongs far into a leaf-coated ravine. The tongs hit a rock. Sarah could hear the echoing clatter. As for the bottle, it careened down the hill, displacing soggy autumn leaves as it rolled. Just as Sarah turned away, a distant and indistinct tune could be heard. Wiping her wet, lank hair from her eyes, Sarah looked about. The faint song seemed to carry on the wind. Sarah believed she heard:

Have echoed to his ardent tale,
And vows of endless love.

The wind and its music whipped away. Only the patter of rainfall remained. Shaking her head, Sarah ran back across the lawn to the kitchen door.

"What were you doing just now?" a voice at the threshold questioned.

Startled, Sarah looked up. It was Mrs. Beals, the

housekeeper. "Nothing, ma'am," Sarah stammered.

"I saw you carrying something with a pair of tongs, Sarah. What was it?" Mrs. Beals asked. Her manner and her tone were none too friendly.

Sarah summoned up a fib as swiftly as she could. "It was a vase from the upper hall, Mrs. Beals. Miss Civette broke it, and she didn't want anyone to know."

"Fair enough, then," said Mrs. Beals. "Now, back to work with you. We have several guests arriving soon, and there's still plenty to do. For one, fresh wood needs to be set in the ballroom fireplaces. So, dry yourself off quickly, and get to work."

Sarah nodded and scurried past Mrs. Beals. The housekeeper's eyes trailed across the rainswept lawn. The expression on her face was a mystery.

****

After bathing and donning a thick, warm robe, Civette left her room and leaned over the railing of the grand staircase. She was enlivened by the activity downstairs in preparation for the Halloween Ball. In Civette's heady distractions, she'd forgotten all about the theatrical scene she and Richard were supposed to present. What was once considered the highlight of the evening she had now let slip carelessly from her mind.

In the ballroom below, the household and hired crews were indeed hard at work. The floors and mirrors were being polished to a solid gleam, and the tables set with starched linens. Candles adorned the rooms for, on All Hallow's Eve, no other light would do. Kitchen maid Phoebe was helping, for her initial meal preparation was done. The others were speaking of the sumptuous food served at the many parties given at Cairy Hollow. Phoebe only cared about the scraps that came back, for those were hers to dine on. She was daydreaming about a tasty hack of beef when she heard someone speaking to her.

It was the temporary hire—the girl with the sad, gray eyes and dull, lank hair. The poor thing was drenched in rain. Phoebe couldn't remember her name. But then again, as a scullery maid, Phoebe was never properly introduced to anyone. The nameless girl was crouched on the floor, setting logs in the end fireplace of the west wall. She was shivering with dampness.

"If your name is Phoebe, the cook is asking for you," she said.

"You can hear her?" Phoebe questioned. "The kitchen isn't near, and we were all talking loudly."

The girl waved her hand. "Aw, that's nothing. If I tilt my head the right way, I could hear a worm crawling beneath this ballroom floor."

"How funny you are. My name is Phoebe. What's yours?"

"Sarah."

Phoebe grinned. "Then you're in luck. Sarah's a perfect name for someone in service."

"I won't be in service long," replied the young woman. She then ducked back under the mantel to finish her task.

Phoebe shook her head at Sarah's unrealistic hopes and ambled out of the ballroom. Nearing the library, she could hear that captain with the odd name speaking to the Cairys' guest of honor. Nearly everyone in the kitchen agreed that Adrian Bramwell was such a lovely creature. Marie was the only one who thought differently. Marie declared that Satan was a lovely thing before he tumbled from Heaven's favor. Regardless of where this cultivated stranger fell from, Phoebe wanted another look at him. Phoebe had a secret hankering for lovely things. Phoebe's wish, however, went ungranted. Balefire noticed the bold little maid approaching, and discourteously slammed the door. Her shoulders sagging with disappointment, Phoebe moved on.

****

Inside the library, Balefire faced his creation. "Well, well, my pumpkin polished with brimstone. What have you accomplished with your thirty-one minutes of freedom?"

Adrian attempted to disguise lies in poetry. It was no use. Instead, he lowered his handsome head. "Civette wants time to think. What is there to think about when I am offering her everything you convinced me is important in a human's life? In the beginning, I felt invincible. Now, I am lost."

"Feeling lost is a commonplace human condition, brought on by nothing more than the individual who embraces it," Balefire said. Adrian replied nothing. "Come now. Tell old Captain B what is really wrong."

"Civette is unhappy with me. How is that possible? When we met in the garden, I found myself intoxicated by the beauty of living. My feelings for Civette grew deeper in meaning. Yet when I became the one to suffer love, she changed. She grew less compelled by what I said."

"Women, like Nature, have minds of their own. The sooner you learn to live with the storm, the better," said Balefire. "As for not being compelled by what you say, that is because you say too much."

Adrian became indignant. "But you know I have quoted everything you ordered me to."

"And added unwise witticisms of your own. Only

peasants compare feelings of love to sunshine, wind, and rain. Think about it. Apart from a first kiss beneath the clouds, who wants to be blinded, blown away, or doused by foul weather? No one. The art of deception is simple. Say little. Promise everything through your eyes. Spoken words lead to expectations. Expectations lead to accusations. However, a stolen glance is rarely punished. Now, speaking of punishment, you would do best to turn the tables on Miss Middleton. Stop fawning over that woman, and in no time at all, she will fawn over you. It will work. She'll chase you like idiots chase the wind. Trust me."

"Why should I believe you? I have memorized all your speeches, and mimicked all of your gestures. I have listened and obeyed. Yet Civette drifts further from my heart. This is your fault, all these long-dead behaviors you planted in my head."

A sinister glow overtook the harsh shadows on Balefire's face. "Then why don't I cut it off? Yes, why don't I slash your pumpkin head from your rolling-pin shoulders and mince it for a pie? Don't be tedious. Everything in your rapidly rotting skull I instilled there to make you a victor. Without me, where would you be?"

"I would still have a heart. And with this pure heart of mine, I will always despise you."

"You are without comparison," Balefire replied with a bow.

"You mock me."

"Mock you? I wish I never created you. Indeed, I'd rather my spell had brought on someone more fun, more imaginative, such as Iago. He is the very essence of evil. Lacking moral manners of any kind, Iago deludes others so superbly that not a soul suspects him. Better still, he does this for no plan of vengeance, no personal gain. His advice, like mine, was free and honest. Yes, I would have taken Iago any day. It's always romantic mush and pangs of regret with you. You don't have a villainous spindle anywhere in that bric-a-brac frame of yours. Where's your true spark of passionate torment? Where's your gnawing hunger for corruption? Perhaps you don't remember, but that's how this sad little love story is supposed to end. But no, you'd rather skip about the garden whispering to flowers and gushing about the clouds. What a bore you are. The plain truth is, I have grown tired of you."

"And I still despise you," vowed Adrian.

"Noted," said Balefire. "Being despised is music to my ears. Now go and change for your grand entrance, Jacky boy. Your audience is about to gather. And remember to bathe first. You may not realize it, but you're beginning to smell of a barnyard."

With a glare, Adrian left the room.

Balefire sighed. "Your hatred delivers only momentary pain. Gone and easily forgotten," he murmured. "But my indifference is an artful and everlasting poison. Drink deep, my former friend."

Balefire's annoyance had restored the outer rim of his true self. Glancing in the mirror above the mantel, he chuckled. With reluctance, Balefire smoothed himself into his human form.

"The world should be so lucky," he informed his transitioning reflection.

Not content with just one humor spoiled, Balefire set out in search of another.

****

With the iron-smoothed red ribbon in her hands,

Sarah made her way down the hall. Nearing Miss Civette's chambers, Sarah noticed a cylinder of amber light spilling through the keyhole of a guest room. There was a sound of rippling water, as well. Confused, Sarah looked about. She was certain the Cairys no longer had overnight guests like they used to in the old days. Sarah tilted her head to listen. Someone was singing. She couldn't comprehend the words. They sounded ancient, and were sung in Gregorian harmony, yet eerily rendered by one voice.

When the turuf is thy tour
And thy put is thy bour
Thy wel and thy white throtë
Shulen wormes to notë
What helpet thee thennë
All the worilde wennë?

The strange yet hypnotic song ceased. After a moment's hesitation, Sarah leaned down and peered through the keyhole.

Adrian Bramwell was lounging in a bright copper tub set by the fireplace. With a tiny gasp, Sarah stood. Good manners decreed she should avert her eyes and walk away. Sarah, however, had a sudden urge not to be good. She gazed through the keyhole again.

Adrian had one finely muscled leg draped over the edge of the tub. Steam rolled in curls from his strong arms and his chest. The mirage framed him in an opal mist, a mist through which his moistened hair shined heavenly blue. The copper tub mirrored the dancing flames from the fireplace. Adrian Bramwell looked every bit a god.

Sarah was not certain how long she waited and watched. Every moment, every movement was pure fascination. Sarah lingered until he stood. Crystal droplets of water cascaded down his back, which was arched and golden and smooth in all the right places. He angled his sculpted body toward the door. Sarah did not turn away.

Chapter Sixteen: Clouds

John sat in his study, toying with a glass of brandy. Catching a glimpse of his formally attired self in the glass above the mantel, John considered himself to be nothing more than a civilized reflection of grief.

Nanny Raylene appeared at the doorway. The elderly woman had the sad misfortune to resemble a shriveled apple. But that was only her exterior. Raylene was dear and kind and true. She hobbled into the room.

"You look tired," she declared. Her tone was the same she'd used when John was but a young boy in her charge. "I believe those bizarre guests of yours have worn you to a crisp. Who are they, anyway?"

"A contrived work of art, and his beastly mentor."

"Might they be frauds?" Raylene asked. "Sorry to be blunt, but that's what some of the folks downstairs think."

"The young man reeks of careless privilege. From what we were told, his father visited Fairwell years ago. Supposedly, he was in love with Elizabeth Dalby."

Raylene placed John's glass closer toward him. "Now there's a name I haven't heard you utter in years. Not out loud, anyway. When you two were young, you used to be, well, something special."

"We were both young, Raylene. However, Bess was solely the 'something special.' "

"You're selling yourself short, John. You always

did. Oh, I remember how lovely Bess was. Her looks didn't belong in this age. And she was courageous, living in those woods all alone. Beautiful and brave, that's what Bess Dalby was."

John nodded ever so slightly. Pretty memories of Bess played through his mind. He recalled her laughing and smiling. She told such stories. He remembered being enraptured by it all. Bess had a way of making the imaginary world come alive. How interesting, John thought, that the less fortunate in life were often happier. Despite the dreams greed planted, money never could produce the true joys in this world. Bess was his one true joy. The thought of her still had the power to wrap warmth around what remained of his weary heart.

"Why don't you excuse yourself from this silly masquerade and rest?" said Raylene. "Your sister and niece will be there. Besides, after all these years, the Cairy Halloween Ball is an event that practically runs itself."

"My niece needs me tonight," said John. "This supposedly secret proposal plan has everyone and everything in such turmoil. I'm guessing Civette knows about Richard's intentions. With all the overdone hints and slipped-up comments, how could she not? To make matters worse, I can see it plain as day that she's having second thoughts. She's going to turn him down. If only I could convince Civette that marrying Richard is the right thing to do. Civette would be much happier across the river in Richard's small but neat townhouse, surrounded by young and lively people."

"Just as you might have been content in that rustic little cottage nestled in the heart of the woods," Raylene remarked.

John spun his glass. "But Leona simply had to remind me of my duty and reroute my course. At least I've got my memories. They're still here, buried deep within my heart."

"Memories are fine in your heart. But sometimes, they can't breathe. To fix this, you must let happiness back into your lungs," said Raylene.

"My lungs?" John questioned. He was intrigued.

Nanny Raylene smiled. "Yes, your lungs. Now, just as in your youngest days, John Cairy, listen and do as I say. First, draw in a huge breath. With that breath, laugh or sing with what you're remembering. That laughter, that song, will surge through you, restoring the glory of your memories back into your entire being."

Samuel, the head groundskeeper, appeared at the study door. It was time to prepare the walkways for the party, and Mr. Cairy's approval was needed. John recalled years past when this task, heralding the start of the annual Cairy Halloween Ball, had the ability to enliven him. He remembered the thrill he used to feel when the first guests arrived in their magical costumes. One year, Bess made her appearance in a gown that billowed like a summer cloud. What a vision she was with her hair held back in place as if by the wind.

John did as Raylene suggested. He drew in a deep breath. As Bess walked toward him in his mind's eye, he began to sing.

"*Beautiful dreamer, wake unto me,*
Starlight and dewdrops are waiting for thee,
Sounds of the rude world heard in the day
Lull'd by the moonlight have all passed away."

Nanny Raylene applauded him. The head groundskeeper simply smiled with amazement and confusion. He hadn't seen Mr. Cairy this lighthearted in months, perhaps even years. "Shall we begin, sir?"

John followed Samuel out into the hall. The tall clock in the foyer struck the hour of seven. Attired in rented livery, Samuel's son Evan was standing at the entrance to the ballroom, waiting to announce the arrival of the first guests.

"Go relax in the servants' hall, Evan," said John as he walked past. "We won't see a living soul for another hour."

Samuel went outside and summoned the hired crew. Positioning himself at the front door, John looked upward. However, he did not see the true sky. In his mind's eye, cheerful clouds blanketed the horizon.

As it did mere hours before, a rush of coral air scented with lilacs engulfed him. Its breeze carried a continuance of the very same song. *The sunny hill, the flow'ry vale, the garden and the grove.* John paled as the lyrical voice in his head drew a deep breath and altered itself, uttering *the grave.*

Balefire arrived to find John Cairy motionless, as if in a trance. "What do you see so intently up there, sir? A woodland witch on her broomstick, sweeping cobwebs from the sky?" he asked.

A cold dread overtook John, leading him to suspect that Balefire, somehow, had everything to do with the disturbing messages he'd just experienced. He knew there was something ominous about this strange little man. John did his best to respond with calmness.

"I see something even more portentous. I see storm clouds gathering overhead more treacherous than the ones before them."

"'Tis Nature's way," said Balefire. "No matter what

time you set for your party, she will attend—and ruin it—whenever she damn well pleases."

John replied nothing. Balefire was not in the mood for silence. "You're not wearing a costume," he said.

"My one privilege as the host," said John.

"Noted," said Balefire. "As for me, this look is a masquerade to my true self."

"Noted," John answered in a like tone.

A figure approached on the mist-laden walkway. It was Iris Owen, lumbering along in a dress fashioned in a hue reminiscent of badly poached salmon. The varying degrees of the evening rendered her sluggish and inelegant. Her hair, which had been meticulously curled in the modish "careless" style, was carelessly at fray, and her too-small shoes were already pinching her feet. John felt for the girl. He knew Richard's intention to propose to Civette was a great disappointment to Iris. Furthermore, John knew firsthand that the pangs of a lost true love would live in Iris's heart forever.

He opened the door for her. "Miss Owen," he said. He then softened his voice. "Iris, I am pleased that you did come. In many ways, you're like a second niece to me."

A smile broke through Iris's miseries. "Thank you, Mr. Cairy. You're too kind. But then again, you always were. Speaking of first nieces, has Civette come down yet?"

"Civette has been upstairs this entire afternoon getting ready," he told her.

Iris knew all about spending great lengths of time getting ready. The only difference with Civette was that it accomplished something. Holding the skirts of her gown away as though they were drenched with rain, Iris went up the stairs. "Damn it all," Iris declared as she stubbed an already painful toe on a riser.

Beyond the arched doorway, workmen could be seen preparing the terraces and the paths. Fog curled in spirals from the manicured lawns toward the tumbling clouds. All seemed ghostly gray. One lanky man was methodically unfurling a long entrance rug. The burgundy hues of the carpet suffused the growing brume. Balefire watched, his eyebrows wrenched high on his misshapen head.

"It's like your life unraveling into haze right before your eyes, and you can't stop it. There's no way to reel back the years with all their hopes and dreams and those deeply cherished ought-to-have-beens," he said.

"That is true, if one sees it only your way," John replied. "For, on the other hand, one can always roll up the good memories and keep them safely tucked away from prying eyes."

"Well said, Mr. Cairy. You have outwitted me."

"Perhaps this time, Captain Balefire. As for the next, who knows? With any luck, you'll gain your ground. And when you do, I shall glance back at you and wave."

"Touché," said Balefire. He was impressed.

The men continued to watch out the front door. Five crows with silver-tipped wings soared through the gloom. Settling themselves upon the lawn, they went about destroying the gardeners' diligent handiwork.

"The Devil take them," John muttered.

"Those crows?" Balefire laughed. "The Devil has no need for blackened souls. He houses far too many as it is. No, I trust the prince of darkness is on the lookout for the righteous variety. An honorable soul would be quite the addition to his trophy case." Balefire placed his hands behind his back and rocked on his cobbled heels. "If only he knew where to find one."

Leona appeared in her customary ballgown of gold. Balefire glanced knowingly from Leona to John. "He's still looking," Balefire murmured in a sing-song voice.

Barely disguising a well-deserved smirk, John excused himself to speak with the workmen. He stepped outside, his elegant formalwear fading into the fog. Iris, having paused at the top turn of the stairs, felt a slight vibration at her feet. It had a tremor to it, like a heralding of lightning about to strike. Iris was engulfed with the sensation that she could actually feel Captain Balefire thinking.

"A question, if I may, Mrs. M," Balefire began. "Have you been wondering all this time if Bess Dalby is watching you?"

Leona was stunned into silence.

"I can feel her presence here. Can't you? Bess Dalby was so admired, so loved."

"Bess Dalby was a lunatic and a money-grubbing whore."

With a savage fluttering, the five silver-tipped ravens flew toward the open front door. Waving at them with her arms, Leona cried out for the head gardener Samuel, or indeed anyone, to come at once and shoot them all. With mocking cries, the band of ravens wheeled back over the lawn and sailed away.

"'Tis a pity there's no rifle propped up here in the foyer," Balefire observed. "You could have easily taken them down yourself. Pardon my apt observations, madam, but you do seem the type not to allow anything—or anyone—to stand in your way."

Leona's back stiffened. "Those lawless birds need

to realize they should never pass the boundaries nature has set for them," she said.

Balefire laughed. "Nature has no boundaries. Nature takes what she wants, and she takes it without warning. Perhaps, Mrs. Middleton, she'll come like a thief in the night, wrap her agile limbs 'round your ankles, and drag you squirming and screaming to the roots of Hell."

Leona had endured enough. Straightening her hair and the folds of her golden gown, she excused herself. "I must see to the preparations for this party," she declared. And with that, Leona departed for the servants' hall.

Balefire saluted Leona with a song half poetically true and half spun from his own wicked imaginings. Iris stepped back into the shadows, and listened as he sang.

"Come into the garden, Leona,
For that black raven, night, has flown,
Come into the garden, Leona,
I am here at the gate all alone;
And the woodbine spices are wafted abroad,
And the musk of the rose is blown."

Mrs. Beals appeared in the foyer. She blanched at the sight of Captain Balefire.

"You don't like me, do you?" he said.

Without a whisper of reply, Mrs. Beals moved on. Balefire was highly amused. His derisive laughter trailed away with him into the ballroom.

Chapter Seventeen: Break

Iris didn't know what to make of anything she'd witnessed or overheard. What she did sense, however, was that the creature known as Balefire was beyond the limits of normalcy. Shaking her head, Iris hobbled into Civette's bedchamber. "Shoes, shoes, my kingdom for a comfortable pair of shoes," she exclaimed with a groan.

"You can borrow a pair of mine," Civette quietly replied. Attired still in her oversized robe, Civette was seated at her dressing table and crying.

"What's wrong?" Iris asked. She'd never seen Civette cry before. Not even as a child. The Civette Iris glorified always refused to give way to tears.

Civette went straight to Iris's arms. "I'm so confused," she said.

"Dear God, Civ. What about?"

"Adrian Bramwell. He has such a hold on me."

Iris's head clouded with so many realizations and sudden hopes that she hardly knew what to say. She held her friend tighter.

"I am haunted by this," Civette went on. "The feelings I have are unexpected, yes, but too overwhelming to be anything but true. I honestly don't know what to do."

Iris paused, bracing herself for a fight. "What you're really saying is that you don't know what to do about Richard," she said.

To Iris's surprise, Civette nodded. Iris led Civette to a sofa and coaxed her to sit. Iris spoke to Civette with thoughtful kindness.

"Think things through, my dearest friend. Are you sure you want to upset the apple cart over someone you've only known since breakfast? Seriously, Civ, Adrian Bramwell is nothing short of spectacular. That's undeniable. But what do you know about him, I mean *really* know about him? He could be a complete and utter fraud. And Richard is, well, steady and reliable. He's trustworthy. Maybe those aren't the most romantic attributes in the world. But when you're old and fragile, those will be the qualities that see you through."

Civette did not answer. Iris glanced over toward Civette's bed and noticed Emmeline Cairy's portrait dress laid out across the virgin white coverlet.

"Is that what you're wearing?" Iris asked.

Civette nodded. "I'm going after what I deserve," she announced.

There was much that Iris could tell her—so much that a lonely woman in pain could share about her own mistakes in love. But Iris hesitated. Civette was stubborn and strong-willed. She would never listen, never understand. Sheltered in a life of luxury, Civette had no need, no reason, to question her future. Civette expected what she wanted now.

Iris forced Civette to look at her. "Perhaps you should stay with your Juliet gown for now, and avoid unnecessary gossip and embarrassment. After all, everyone for thirty miles around will be here. Play it safe, Civ. You can discuss your feelings with Richard later, when everyone's gone."

"Oh, why is there always such a need for

appearances?" Civette bemoaned.

"Because once you're someone ornamental, you're not allowed to break," her true friend replied.

"You sound like my mother," said Civette.

"Someone has to," Iris replied.

A trembling smile crept across Civette's face as she thought of a possible plan.

Chapter Eighteen: Invitation

Balefire was pacing in the ballroom mentally choreographing his vision for the evening when he heard the rustling of silken skirts from the hall. He ducked behind a curtained door just as Civette entered.

Observing Civette in Emmeline's gown, Balefire chuckled. "Oh, the intrigue," he murmured. With his forehead pinned against the filmy drape of the door, Balefire watched on.

Civette moved with single-minded steps toward the Glass of Truth. Standing tall, she swept back a tasseled drape. Her image glared back at her, smug, selfish, and arrogant. A chill encompassed Civette. Was she truly as vain as her reflection showed her to be? For the first time in Civette's life, such a possibility unsettled her. Civette raised her chin, smiled, and toyed with her fan. This did nothing to lessen her reflection's imperious stare. As was her way with all of life's challenges, big or small, Civette allowed herself to become distracted by something else. There was a curl in her hairstyle that had fallen out of form. Picking up a mirrored tray from a side table, Civette viewed her reflection from behind.

Marie and Phoebe entered the room. Marie was carrying a delicate tray of glasses, while Phoebe was struggling with an overloaded sling of firewood. One glance at Civette, and Marie was shocked.

"Miss Civette," she cried. "Begging pardon, but you

shouldn't do that."

Civette was preoccupied with pushing her unruly strand of hair back into place. "Do what?" she asked.

"By holding two mirrors opposite each other, you have invited in the Devil."

"If you want my steadfast opinion, Marie, the Devil has resided here for a very long time."

"Do you feel it, too?" the little maid asked.

Without answering, Civette dropped the velvet curtain, walked out of the ballroom, and never looked back. Marie placed her tray of glasses on the sideboard and scurried away. As for Phoebe, she allowed her load of firewood to tumble loudly onto the marble hearth. Placing her hands on her hips, Phoebe enjoyed a good laugh and called out to what she believed to be an empty room.

"If you want my humble maid's opinion, I think the Devil would add a whole lot of fun to this duller-than-dishwater place," Phoebe exclaimed. "And if you disagree with me, old house, that's too bad," she added for good measure.

Phoebe waited a moment for an answer that never came. Satisfied, Phoebe wiped her nose on her sleeve and trudged out to the hall. Moments later, Balefire stepped out from behind the door.

"What a spunky little hellion that one is," he said. Phoebe had indeed impressed him.

Moving to the dance floor, Balefire smiled at being center stage and lit to perfection by bold candlelight. Rapidly waltzing about the gleaming parquet floor, he sang:

"She left the web, she left the loom
She made three paces through the room

She saw the water-lily bloom
She saw the helmet and the plume
She look'd down to Camelot
Out flew the web and floated wide
The mirror crack'd from side to side
The curse has come upon me cried
The Lady of Shalott."

With Balefire's final and resounding note, the windows of the ballroom magically lifted. Balefire calmly watched as a legion of forest vegetation slithered and crawled over the sills. Japanese maple leaves dredged their vibrant red colors across the polished floor, while fan-shaped maidenhairs curled themselves around vases and bowls. Dogwoods swirled and callicarpas danced. A band of lemon queens flew in on a cloud. Garnet daylilies arrived by the dozens, riding the backs of fall-blooming anemones. Bee balm, goldenrod, and clover took up the colorful parade, with a lengthy tangle of grape arbor as its end guard. Within moments, these plundering blooms had ensnared and suffocated the hothouse flowers, conquering their places of honor about the room.

"Welcome, my friends," Balefire announced with pride. "Welcome to the last and indeed most memorable Cairy Hollow Halloween Ball for mere mortals."

Following a swift bow, Balefire danced his way over to a large porcelain floor vase that dominated a shaded alcove. With each step taken, he diminished in size. A single bound, and he settled inside. Balefire's haunting laugh echoed all the way to the bottom of the vessel.

From two of the raised windows, the Raven Ladies swooped in and settled in the center of the brightly lit ballroom. Their heads stiffly darting, they looked left and right and all around.

"Balefire," Sorrow whispered with a ruffled shiver.

"I am here."

Balefire's hollow and reverberating reply caused the Raven Ladies alarm. They spun about on their awkward feet.

"Where?" Mirth asked, all the while looking up.

"I'm not dangling from a chandelier, you fool." Balefire surfaced from the depths of the painted vase. "You really are a couple of rumple-heads."

"I have no comb," Mirth replied in her own defense.

"What are you doing in that ugly jug? Looking for money?" Sorrow asked.

"It's not a jug, Sorrow. It's a pretended Ming—pretended like everything else in this anemic mansion. The Cairys have no money. All they've got left is a sliver of pride. It isn't even enough to revive a starving mouse."

Balefire vaulted over the rim of the vase and, regaining his illusionary size, he landed gracefully upon the floor. Prancing toward the Glass of Truth, Balefire chanted, 'Mirror, mirror, here I stand. Who's the fairest in the land?' " He peered within and was enchanted by the creature he beheld. "'Tis a wise wind that can move mountains," he said.

"You are wise because you are old," said Mirth.

"Old age may bring wisdom, ladies. But in youth, one is better off exercising his wiles." Balefire grinned. "Speaking of which, it's nearly time to eradicate the bitter Richard Marlow."

"How are you going to do that?" Sorrow asked. "You lack a pistol, you own no knife, and pardon my saying so, but you are also an absolute despair at swordsmanship."

Balefire was not offended. "With my impetuous and flighty nature, I don't have time for the serious study of anything. No, ladies, we shall take Marlow down with his own misery."

"That sounds predictable," declared Mirth. "I believe I shall nap. Wake me when it's reckoning time."

"Oh, you will know when it arrives," said Balefire. "No one for miles around shall miss it."

****

John returned to his study. Leona appeared not long thereafter. In her hands were two gleaming glasses of champagne.

"Here, John," she said while holding the one on her left toward him. "Let us drink to our present successes."

"Your hand is trembling," John observed. "Why?"

"So many marvelous things have happened this day. Yet I still have the boldness to wish for a few more triumphs."

John took the ornate glass. He watched the bubbles play against their fluted prison. *What price freedom*? he asked himself. Sighing, John put down his glass. She certainly didn't mean to, but Leona shuffled with disappointment. "What marvelous occurrences are you referring to?" he asked. "I seem to have missed them all."

"My daughter and our miracle guest of fortune," Leona replied. "While it may seem sudden, they are drawn to each other, like a lightning bolt to the sea. I believe they will marry."

"Are you referring to that more-than-obvious schemer and Civette, or to nature's anger and the waves?"

"John, do be serious. I believe Adrian and Civette will announce their love and marry. Civette will move to

England, of course. And when she does, Cairy Hollow will remain with us, just as it always should be."

"If they leave, perhaps you should as well," John informed his sister.

Leona couldn't fathom the words she heard spoken. "What are you saying?" she asked.

"The only triumph I perceive in all of this would be you leaving. Nearly every day for the last twenty years, I have dreamt of your departure. Oh, the indescribable visions I had! Hope is a powerful tonic, Leona. The mere taste of it can fuel one's mind for days. You may ask yourself how one seemingly weak and indecisive man could bear such patience and loathing. It was my love for this house—my unnatural passion for this mound of bricks and mortar—that forced me to hold my evil prayers and endure your nagging presence. Cairy Hollow is a thing of beauty in my eyes, and she belongs to me."

"Just before mother died, she vowed that, as her eldest child, Cairy Hollow should rightfully go to me."

John laughed softly. "While we are on the subject of fantastic lies, Leona, why don't you tell me what really happened to Bess Dalby."

Leona sat and held her head in her hands. John placed his untouched glass of Abelé on the table next to her.

"Cheers," he said.

Leona never looked up. John left the room.

Chapter Nineteen: To the Ball

As the tall clock struck eight, Evan announced the arrival of the first guests.

"Miss Priscilla Reed, Miss Hannah Reed, Miss Elizabeth Reed, and Steven Reed, their nephew," he proclaimed.

"Grand-nephew," corrected the eldest. Evan tried not to react to the sight of Miss Priscilla's chins flapping as she spoke.

The Reed sisters had costumed themselves as the Fates at every Cairy Halloween Ball since the first ever hosted by John's grandfather. Now, the elderly trio seemed more like victims of Fate than their proprietors. John went forward to greet them. His voice boomed across the empty hall.

"How wonderful to see you ladies," he lied.

"The privilege is ours," said middle sister Hannah, whose vanishing eyebrows made her appear permanently surprised.

"How marvelous it is to see this old house shining," said Elizabeth who, despite being the youngest, was still quite old. She was a delicate creature with a little mouse voice. People often uttered, "Pardon, what?" whenever Elizabeth ventured to speak.

"Amen to survival," said Priscilla, wagging chins and all. "Now, where might we find your niece Civette? She should be here at the door to greet us, as is her duty.

Besides, the birdies are chattering that she and Richard Marlow—"

"It's early yet," John interrupted. "However, ladies, we do have a special guest in our household. His name is Sir Adrian Bramwell, and he will appear shortly. Meanwhile, permit me to introduce his mentor, Captain Balefire. Captain Balefire, the incomparable Reed sisters and their grand-nephew Steven."

Balefire grinned in that singular way of his. "I spoke of the Fates earlier and, voilà, here they are." Balefire bowed and kissed their bejeweled and wrinkled hands. "Of all the interesting creatures set upon this earth, a righteous woman intrigues me the most," he said.

"Oh, sir," squeaked Elizabeth.

"How polite," said Priscilla.

"How kind," said Hannah.

"How true," concluded Balefire. He studied their obnoxious nephew. "You appear to be getting along in years," he said.

"I'm twelve," the boy flatly replied.

"A miraculous dozen. My, my. Now, what do you intend to be when you double that count?" Balefire asked.

"I wanted to be an outlaw, like Jesse James. But my moldy great-aunts won't let me." The boy paused to demonstrate his displeasure on his face. "So instead, I'm going to be just another rich and lazy politician."

"Precisely what this country needs," concluded Balefire.

Elizabeth may have added something, but no one heard her.

The Reed sisters wished to know about Sir Adrian. Where was he from?

"The British Isles," replied John.

"Oh, an island. How mysterious," said Hannah, who had no idea Great Britain itself was an island.

The hired maid Sarah approached the elderly women with champagne on a tray. Exclaiming to the positive, Balefire reached out and took two glasses for himself. Priscilla refused "the Devil's brew," shooing the bewildered Sarah away as though she were a pesky fly. Doing her best to ignore Balefire's two-fisted drinking, Priscilla wished to learn more about Adrian Bramwell and his island home.

Balefire obliged. He cleverly described the Rookeries as a realm of its own. In this magical place, the sand swirled in hues of violet and ebony, and the turquoise waves were capped diamond-white. It was a paradise, really, overflowing with fruit, the sweet spices of which sugared the air. Many breeds of vividly colored birds flocked there from tropical regions. The Rookeries, with its unique volcanic base, kept the feathered creatures content all year. These exotic birds sang night and day. Why, there was even a toucan who told tales of piracy from his perch on the mansion's veranda. A sunset at the Rookeries was a miracle of Nature. One never failed to feel humbled by the crest of the sun descending in bursts of bittersweet and pearly pink. The heavens would then play out above one's head with a symphony of shooting stars. The sisters were awed by his story. Priscilla clung to his every word through her ever-present ear trumpet.

Seeing that guests were beginning to arrive, the hired orchestra opened with a lively background number. Raising his voice over the din, Evan announced the arrival of Richard Marlow and an acquaintance of his by the name of Philip Osgood. Philip Osgood was not very tall nor very special. It was doubtful that many people would glance at him twice. Philip was costumed as Napoleon. It did not suit him.

Attired in his Romeo ensemble, Richard went immediately to John's side. Philip dutifully followed. John asked Richard how he was faring. It was an ill-timed question. John could easily surmise that answer by looking at the young man's face. Richard Marlow was miserable, and it was all the fault of John's niece.

"Tolerable, I suppose," Richard replied. "And perhaps less so, now that I'm apparently playing my Shakespearean role alone."

"Civette should be here shortly," said John. "And then the two of you should hide. You're supposed to be making your entrance on the staircase."

"What, no balcony?" Balefire jested.

"I'd rather head straight to the swallowing of poison, myself," said Richard. "Well, I imagine I'll have to go look for her."

Richard left. Sensing the awkward pause, Philip spoke. "Thank you, Mr. Cairy, for including me in this special evening," he said.

"The pleasure is all mine," said John. He then introduced Philip Osgood to the hovering Reed sisters. He knew Philip was overly polite and would entertain these overly dull women. John glanced about with a fervent hope that other partygoers would soon arrive, so that he might step away. To be trapped in conversation all evening with a trio of elderly women who smelled distinctly of camphor and crushed moths would surely be the death of him.

"Mr. James Alexander and family, Mr. William Hall

and family, Mr. Theodore Fiske and family," Evan declared.

John's hasty prayer was answered. Seeing that Philip Osgood was regaling the spinsters with a play-by-play description of harvesting apples, John excused himself and went forward to greet the gentlemen. Their daughters, mostly similar in age to Civette, curtsied to Captain Balefire. They had curious looks upon their faces. They'd never seen anyone quite like him before. Balefire returned their greeting with a grandiose bow. The girls giggled.

"Oh, sir, if you are indeed a captain, why aren't you attired like one?" asked Miss Hall.

"How observant you are, young miss," Balefire replied. "Alas, I was discharged by Senator John Sherman for not trusting him in 1890."

"How sad for you," uttered Miss Fiske. "Are you quite recovered?"

"Yes. During my convalescence, I turned Lincoln's Emancipation Proclamation into a kite," he claimed.

"A kite, sir? For what reason?" asked Miss Hall.

"To see if it could still fly. I even tore up the Declaration of Independence into eleven splendid ribbons for its tail," Balefire replied in the guise of a great confession.

The girls giggled again. This time, Balefire giggled back.

"Miss Eira Corbin," Evan announced, and many heads turned.

Eira Corbin had been a midwife longer than anyone in the village of Fairwell could remember. With her bowed back, cloudy gaze, and twitching, talon-like fingers, most people feared her. That fear suited the old woman just fine. Eira Corbin lived high above where the Connecticut River surged around a jagged point. That crag, as was often observed, resembled an outstretched wing of a raven. Strange stories had been told about the reclusive midwife. A band of children who had wandered into the woods late one evening swore they saw her evolve into an albino raven with blood-red eyes. When her transformation was complete, Midwife Corbin lifted up and away. From all around the forest, swarms of ravens cried out and followed her into the shadows of night.

How chilling it was that, on this evening, Midwife Corbin had adorned herself in a white feathered gown. The train that fell in pleats from her shoulders to the floor resembled wings. The dress was old, but remarkable for its preserved beauty. The woman who wore it was nothing short of radiant, especially when one considered her advanced years.

"How old can she be?" asked one woman.

"I don't have a clue, but she delivered my grandmother, who is now eighty-three," said the other. The two women stared at Corbin in respectful shock.

Captain Balefire moved through the animated crowd to speak with the midwife. "I am surprised to see you here," he said.

"Really?" replied the old woman. "I am surprised you are surprised. What baffles you, you whirling weathervane?"

"I believed you felt, as I do, that the present company here at Cairy Hollow is a dull and artificial society. For example, that man over there—the one who speaks volumes, yet knows nothing. I'll wager he's either the village idiot or its chief," claimed Balefire.

"So close, Captain, and yet so far. He is both," said Corbin. "Now, just imagine what these townspeople would label us if they knew."

Midwife Corbin smiled and strode away, her slight form within its wing-like dress disappearing into the fold.

Chapter Twenty: Wallflower

Despite the many guests arriving, Leona remained hidden away in the study. No lamps were lit. The fireplace provided the only glow. Leona preferred it that way. Staring at a portrait of her brother upon the wall, Leona displayed little heed to the door opening and closing. Richard appeared. Knowing that Leona adored being the center of attention, Richard was surprised to discover her here.

"Mrs. Middleton, are you all right?" he asked.

In something of a daze, Leona poured out her memories.

"Over twenty years ago, a young seamstress by the name of Bess Dalby embroidered that jacket for my brother. John admired the work, and the artist, so much that he insisted on wearing that jacket for this portrait. His likeness is not the best it could be. But that jacket is impeccably portrayed."

Leona ran her fingers over her face as if to restore the youth and exuberance that once reigned there. It was a futile gesture. Leona spoke on.

"It pains me to admit this, but Bess was an attractive creature with personality and talent. My brother John was completely taken with her. This, I knew. And he was not alone in his admiration. Olen Devereux loved her, too. Olen Devereux owned an estate on the other side of the forest. It's in ruins now, and he has moved far, far away, so I heard. For all his hard habits, Olen is likely dead. But in those days, he was a handsome man with a reputation. The air about him always smelled of expensive whiskey and fine leather. When he spoke, oh, the allurement in his voice and his eyes. I remember it well. Girls of my class were warned to stay away from Olen Devereux. Naturally, we did."

Leona had faltered in her vow. Richard noticed, but said nothing.

"Women were drawn to Olen like pretty moths to a flame. Bess was one such woman. Because of her looseness, polite women stopped patronizing Bess. It was widely known that seamstress Bess began earning the bulk of her pay through other unspeakable talents. With her unique eyes, she was an easy magnet for men. Her eyes were brighter in her earlier days, I imagine. But I remember one as dirt brown and the other dust gray. I can also easily recall the streak of silver-gray hair that trailed down behind her right ear. It proved that Bess Dalby never listened to God.

"I knew she wasn't innocent. I spied upon her. Bess was a conniving Killarney witch who communicated with trees and flowers, and conned devilish imps into performing her infinite tasks and spells. Bess Dalby called upon evil when need be, for evil knew her name."

Richard remembered Civette's words about the Glass of Truth belonging to a sorceress in the woods, and was horrified. "Are you quite sure?" he asked.

Nodding, Leona stood and went to the fireplace. "Although Bess's kinship with the dark side can't be proven, I am positive of it. My inner voice is never wrong."

"And you never made your discovery known?"

Richard asked.

Leona stirred the glowing embers. "I feared what that woman might do to me," she confessed. "Everyone believed that Bess and I were friends. I kept up that ruse for appearances, and especially for the sake of knowledge. Bess had cast her spell over my brother. I needed to remain close, to hopefully determine her next moves in advance. Bess was angered beyond reason when John came to his senses and decided against marrying her. I'm certain she blamed me."

There was a weighted pause. "What happened to Bess Dalby?" Richard finally asked.

"She died. Took her own life, so it was said. I doubt anyone truly knows."

There was something in Leona's stare, and within her rigid but vague tone, that Richard saw as not quite right. He watched as Leona knelt by the withering fire and added a log. The blanched limb caught with a convulsive hiss. The flame cast fitful shadows across the skirts of Leona's golden gown. Leona herself remained fixated on the fire. It was as if the demons of a thousand taunting dreams were dancing there.

From beyond the study door, Richard could hear Civette saying in a strong and clear voice, "O Romeo, Romeo, wherefore art thou, Romeo?" Richard was elated.

"I must go now," he said. "That is my cue."

Her focus still on the raging fire, Leona replied nothing.

Chapter Twenty-One: Worth

Overjoyed that Civette was carrying through their original plan, Richard spoke as he stepped out of the study.

"*Shall I hear more, or shall I speak at this?*" Richard recited with grand enthusiasm as he strode across the polished ballroom floor. Still smiling, Richard looked up to the top of the stairs, only to find Iris standing there, costumed as Juliet.

" *'Tis but thy name that is my enemy; Thou art thyself, though not a Montague,*" Iris replied before Richard held up his hands.

"What is this?" Richard begged to know.

"*What's Montague? it is nor hand, nor foot, nor arm, nor face, nor any other part belonging to a man. O, be some other name.*" This Iris managed to say before her voice froze in her chest and tears rose to her eyes.

Richard observed the faces of those in the crowd. Everyone was looking at him with vivid expressions of alarm or concern. "Iris, how could you do this?" Richard asked. "What kind of trick are you playing on me? Where is Civette?"

John went to Richard's side. "Come with me, Richard. We must leave."

"No," Richard exclaimed. He was experiencing the oddest sensation that he wasn't even there in that room with everyone staring at him. Time had, somehow,

154

walled up around him. He could barely find air to breathe. "Where is Civette?" Richard repeated. He sounded so lost, so afraid.

No one spoke. No one moved. With great sadness in his entire being, John led Richard away.

****

Since an invitation to the annual Cairy Halloween Ball was meant for everyone residing in Fairwell, Sorrow and Mirth—despite Mirth's urge to nap—decided that such an invitation included them.

On impulse, the two flew out the library window and up and around to Emmeline Cairy's dressing room casement. This was where Civette had discovered them earlier. The clearly distracted girl had neglected to close it. Hopping inside, Sorrow and Mirth studied Emmeline's encased wardrobe with dazzled curiosity.

"Perhaps we shouldn't disturb these lovely things," said Sorrow.

"Sister! What has caused you to become so righteous?" asked Mirth.

"I'll show you how righteous I am," answered Sorrow. "Follow me."

In their half-female, half-savage bird forms, the two marched through Emmeline's hushed bedchamber and out into the hall. The gilded doors to Emmeline's chambers were, for the first time in such an age, left wide open and undefendable. Blustering noises from the party below assaulted their ears. Mirth scoffed at what she considered the forced merriment of it all.

With a wave of her hand, Sorrow silenced Mirth. Ducking her head quite low, Sorrow halted. "This is the room," she whispered. There was an intense glimmer in her eyes.

Sorrow put her feathered ear to the keyhole and listened. Nothing. Without a moment's hesitation, and a frightening grin, Sorrow kicked open the door to Leona's bedchamber.

"Here's where we'll do the disturbing," Sorrow announced.

"Bravo," exclaimed Mirth.

The pair practically flew to Leona's dressing room. There, they rummaged through the woman's clothing like the wild creatures they were. A silver satin gown with vivid blue fringe was much admired. Sorrow and Mirth both claimed it for their own. Fighting over which victor the gown might best suit, they tugged and tore the delicate garment to shreds.

Mirth noticed a monogrammed label stitched within its folds. Fortunately, years before, Bess Dalby had taught the sister birds how to read. Mirth held out the label for Sorrow to see. "How blatant is that?" she murmured. "It says *Worth*."

Because the Raven Ladies preferred so many of the same gowns, a compromise was met. Sorrow and Mirth would share bits and pieces from every favored dress. Old-fashioned bustles were created from various disassembled ruffles and bows. A voluminous pink skirt etched with golden ferns got rent in two for matching shawls. Jeweled bodices became elaborate turbaned headpieces. Fringes, beads, and feathers adorned the hems of their hodgepodge but fascinating skirts. In short, the sisters destroyed thirteen of Leona's treasured creations in their quest. They also made short order of Leona's finest dancing slippers, as well as her perfume and jewelry.

"How splendiferous we are," announced Mirth.

"I say we parade right down the main staircase and give everyone the surprise of their lives," suggested Sorrow.

"No, sister, no. We must be announced at the entrance to the ballroom, just as all the other distinguished guests are."

"Then what should our names be?" said Sorrow. "We can't use our own."

"I'd vote for Jovie and Tristana Wingstrom," said Mirth.

"And I'd second that," said Sorrow.

One last glance of approval in Leona's looking-glass and off the two went.

****

The night sky had wrapped itself in storm clouds. Most of the intended guests had arrived for the Ball. A select few would appear, as society dictated, fashionably late. There was a good deal of laughter and the clinking of glasses over greetings and happy conversations. Despite Richard's initial dread, his odd scene with Iris was dismissed and forgotten. It was as if Richard's heart-wrenching moment had never occurred and, worse still, had never mattered.

Civette emerged from a side door. She was wearing Emmeline's dress and didn't care who noticed. Walking past Richard and her uncle without so much as a glance, Civette placed herself near Evan. It was obvious she intended to be first at Adrian's side when he appeared. Civette was focused on the outer hall. She did not sense Richard's approach. In truth, Civette barely heard his voice.

"And why is the lady of the hour not showing herself off as the highlight of it all?" Richard asked.

Civette's response was to turn her head in resentment.

"What is this childishness I see? Have you no warm and loving greeting for your intended?"

"None given, none returned," said Civette.

"Why is it that I must always go first?"

Civette sighed. "Don't be ridiculous, Richard."

"It appears I was born for it," Richard replied. He placed his hand lightly on her arm. "Civette, please. Go put on your Juliet costume. We'll make our entrance on the staircase. Everyone will think the prior debacle was a Halloween prank, a jest for fun. Our guests will smile and raise their glasses, and this whole miserable charade will dissolve into a faint and distasteful memory."

Civette neither moved nor answered.

"If you, somehow, come to your senses, I'll be waiting," Richard concluded, and he walked away.

John was now at Civette's side. His face was chalky white and pinched.

"Why are you wearing that?" he asked.

"I changed my mind about performing *Romeo and Juliet* with Richard. It all seemed so pointless," she said.

"And was it pointless as well to make a mockery out of Richard and Iris? Are they both so easily broken and thrown away?"

"Oh, Uncle, really. Look around you. No one cares."

"I care. Now, about that dress. It was Emmeline Cairy's, and should be preserved as such. It isn't yours to toy with. You have disappointed me beyond measure. I demand that you go and change at once."

Civette had grown weary of ill moods and condemnation. Spotting her friends, Margaret Hall and Gertie Fiske, Civette conceived her escape. "At last," she cried, waving to the girls. "Come over here. I have so much to tell you."

"This wretched plan you have dreamt up, niece, mark my words, it will end in ruin," John whispered. He, too, walked away.

Civette dismissed her uncle's dire warnings. She was convinced that by evening's end Uncle John would recognize what her goals truly were and be happy for her. Civette watched as her two friends approached. Margaret Hall had created a rather clever bee costume. Her skirts were done in alluring swirls of gold and black. Gertie had attired herself as a lighthearted bat with a golden nose. Squealing admiration for Civette's bold dress, the girls hugged one another while trying not to entwine their wings and headpieces.

"Where is Iris?" Gertie asked.

"And what was that strange scene with Richard all about?" asked Margaret. "After all, isn't he *your* special beau?"

Civette pretended to laugh. "It was a practical joke, that's all."

"Well, I, for one, didn't get it," said Gertie.

It was then that Cora Alexander appeared at the threshold. She was a slight girl with bold, laughing eyes and a cloud of lovely dark hair. Truth be known, Miss Alexander was considered the prettiest girl in all of Fairwell. Cora had attired herself as a bride. Naturally, her choice of costume inspired an outburst of gossip among those in the know. Undoubtedly, this was Cora's intention all along.

Gertie motioned with her sprawling bat wings for Cora to join them. Cora tossed back her highly embroidered train and, with sashaying steps, paraded across the crowded room. Many of the party guests watched Cora with looks of delight. She grinned. Cora was fully aware that she was captivating. Reaching Margaret, Gertie, and Civette, Cora allowed herself to be embraced and admired for the briefest time before waving them off and adjusting her veil.

"What's this I hear about a handsome visitor to Cairy Hollow named Sir Bramwell?" Cora asked Civette. Much to Civette's displeasure, Cora did so without first complimenting Civette on her dress.

"We heard the same. Where is this mythical man?" asked Margaret.

"Oh where, oh where can he be?" chanted Gertie.

"He is indeed handsome, girls—just you wait and see. Sir Adrian and I, well, we're special friends now."

"Special friends, you say?" murmured Cora.

"Yes," claimed Civette. "I'm sure he'd like to get to know my acquaintances better. I'll introduce you girls. You as well, Cora. He should be here soon."

"Praise the day," murmured Cora.

"Do you think he'll dance with any of us?" asked Gertie.

Margaret clasped her hands. "Oh, I do hope I get a shot at him," she said.

"My dear Margaret, this isn't a duck hunt," Cora advised.

Sweeping up a glass of champagne from a passing maid, Cora strolled away. The pearl satin of her bridal gown showed ripples of heavenly blue in the candlelight.

"What do you think got into her?" wondered Gertie.

"The same sauciness that's always been there," replied Margaret.

The girls fell silent. Their eyes were on the prowl for

Sir Adrian Bramwell.

It was true that Adrian's appearance was greatly anticipated. All about the ballroom, at card tables, in corners, and over the punch bowls, colorful stories flared up about him. Despite his name not being known until today, it was rumored that he was a Russian Count, a French Baron, and a Prince of Egypt. Claims were made that, when he was only seventeen, he saved lives when a merchant vessel ran aground off Cornwall, England. He was the special guest of Swedish Princess Margaretha at the Royal Opera House on the evening before her wedding. It was noted that Margaretha paid more attention to Adrian than to her betrothed, Prince Axel of Denmark. While visiting America, Adrian was offered a background role in a Rudolph Valentino picture. Adrian lost that opportunity, however. Valentino was worried that moviegoers would be more enthralled with the extraordinarily handsome extra seated behind him. Adrian Bramwell then embarked on a steady round of world traveling. His life became, if possible, even more exotic. Heads of state held dinners in his honor. The Zulu Nation considered him an ancestral spirit. Women of nobility adored him to distraction. A duke's daughter nearly strangled herself with the tie of Adrian's smoking jacket when he politely declined to marry her. With his Romanesque beauty, Adrian Bramwell was the offspring of a god; with the tenor of his voice, the prodigy of angels. He was, in summary, supreme.

All these speculations delighted Captain Balefire. Indeed, he had invented every last one. To further test his powers of persuasion, Balefire sent round a whisper that Richard Marlow's modest wealth had collapsed, and that his family was near to ruin. Balefire laughed over his delicate flute of champagne. After only minutes, the word *penniless* was being hissed as if uttered by a pit full of snakes.

Philip Osgood made his way to where Richard stood with a group of gentlemen. "Were you aware that you're being labeled as nearly bankrupt and destitute?" Philip cautioned his friend.

"Really? For what cause is this?" Richard asked.

"I'm not certain," said Philip. "More disturbing still, some people here are saying that you're not proposing to Miss Middleton because you no longer have the means to pull her family out of debt."

Richard was stunned. However, he had little time or ability to react. All attention turned as Evan called out, "Sir Adrian Bramwell, son of the Marchioness of Guileford, nephew of the Baron of Wittenberg, and cousin to the Count of Charmbord!"

Sir Adrian Bramwell made his appearance. Richard found himself even more bewildered than before. Adrian was wearing the same court regalia as seen in Reginald Cairy's portrait. Richard was loath to admit it, but Adrian seemed born for the look. The man was, as that sneering Balefire declared, the height of fashion.

A bold energy ignited the room. Many of the guests surged forward with the hopes of meeting the long-awaited Sir Bramwell. Whatever observations had circulated now renewed with fresh momentum. This mystery guest was more noble than any courtier from any region, more fit to be king, and far more godlike than Adonis could ever claim to be. The rapture spun about Sir Adrian Bramwell was undeniable, and undeniably out of control.

"Witnessing his bearing, I sense he has royal blood

in his veins," said one man nearby Richard.

"My wife believes him to be a Dutchman, although her odd reasoning escapes me," said a second.

"I can see that my wife finds him heavenly regardless of where he's from," observed a third.

"I think he's a fake," said Richard.

"All I see is a man who could turn heads faster than a guillotine," said Philip.

"A guillotine is more than that absolute horror deserves," said Richard.

They watched as Civette broke through the throng of admirers, approaching Adrian in her shimmering dress of red. Her movements were graceful. They always were. Civette Middleton had the ability to flow to music that played in her head.

Nothing good was going to come of Richard's present state. He excused himself and went toward the door. Richard made the unfortunate mistake of turning. In doing so, he witnessed Civette embracing the man who had stolen everything dear to him. Richard left, but not before cursing Civette, the house, and everyone in it. He didn't care about the consequences of his dark wish. In Richard's mind, when the heart of love was sentenced to die, everything surrounding it should also be condemned to suffer.

As for Civette, she saw Richard go and, this time, she didn't care. She was completely taken by how breathtaking Adrian was in Reginald Cairy's court regalia. She was so consumed, she failed to wonder how he came by such attire. Instead, Civette shivered with the suspicion, perhaps even the knowledge, that she'd been guided by some unseen force to costume herself as Reginald's beloved wife. Standing before Adrian, she felt electrified. The glow of the chandeliers caressed her lovely blonde hair.

"Sir Reginald," she said playfully. Civette was delighted by the murmurs heard about the room. She was waiting for Adrian to recognize, as many others did, the portrait recreations she and Adrian had made. Civette expected Adrian would commend her for being clever.

"Do you approve of my gown?" she prompted.

Adrian was about to tell Civette how beautiful she looked, when Balefire's voice hummed in his head. *You would do best now to turn the tables on Miss Middleton,* it said. Adrian decided to give his mentor's myriad of advice one last try.

"You're not wearing my pin," was his calculated response.

Civette was stunned by the coolness in his tone. "I-I have to think of Richard," she stammered. "I must break the news of my decision to him carefully. I planned to wear your pin later, when the dancing begins."

"Then I shall wait for the dancing," Adrian said. His voice had not warmed in the least. Adrian looked past her, sweeping the room with his magnificent gaze. He paused at the sight of Cora Alexander. Cora noticed and flirtatiously ducked her head.

"What an enchanting creature," said Adrian. "Who is she?"

Civette regretted that she had to answer. "Her name is Cora Alexander."

Adrian rendered such a heavenly smile. "I believe I shall go and present myself."

There was nothing further Civette could say or do. She had no choice but to let him go. Her breath halted in her chest, Civette watched as, with an elegant bow,

Adrian Bramwell introduced himself to Cora.

"How creative and lovely you look," Adrian told her.

Cora was shocked. She knew by their stares that some of the guests were upbraiding her for wearing a wedding gown to a party where the young lady of the household was supposed to be proposed to. But what did Cora care? Civette was not Cora's special friend, and Richard had courted Cora just before he turned his material attentions toward Civette. Besides, the wedding gown was just a costume. If anyone wanted to make more of it, then that was their own dramatic need to be difficult.

Cora raised her eyes to meet Adrian's. How handsome he was. If it were possible, Adrian Bramwell was more attractive than he was reported to be. "Do you really like my costume?" she murmured.

A most special phrase came to Adrian's mind. "My dear Miss Alexander, you are without comparison," he vowed.

Cora stepped toward him. His court attire was glistening. He smelled of fresh cut hay and autumn spice. She had a sudden desire to be outside with him, strolling hand in hand beneath a hunter's moon. It was a strange impulse for a social girl like Cora. Still, the image burned like a bright and seductive fire in her head.

"No one has ever spoken to me as kindly as you have. No one ever," Cora lied. And how wonderful he was to lie to. His presence was intoxicating.

"Forget what others have failed to do," Adrian said. "Nature creates us all with beauty in mind. Honor her by telling yourself that you are without comparison and, before you know it, confidence radiates from within.

Now, repeat those words. Lady Nature and I are waiting."

"I—" Cora hesitated on purpose. "I am without comparison," she declared with a pretty little peal of laughter.

"You should witness what that laughter accomplished. It brought an added gleam of loveliness to your face. Miss Alexander, you are indeed the envy of angels."

"How you flatter me, even when—" Cora beckoned Adrian closer. "Is it true that you are attracted to my dearest friend, Civette?" she whispered.

"Yes. But Civette is unsure of her feelings for me."

The confirmation of this sent a chill down Cora's spine. But, for all the things Cora was feeling, pity for Richard Marlow was not one of them. Cora looked up at Adrian and smiled. "Perhaps Civette is only pretending to be unsure," she said.

"I do not understand," he said.

"Some women like to tease the man they intend to accept," Cora explained. "It gives us ladies an advantage for a short while."

They both laughed, each with their own thoughts powering it. The golden reflection of the chandeliers in Adrian's eyes was mesmerizing.

"I know how to help you—that is—if you'll let me," Cora said. She was amazed at how calm and genuine she sounded.

"Any method at all, Miss Alexander. Please explain."

"It's simple. Make her jealous."

"I've never made anyone a gift of jealousy. How is it done?"

Cora paused. How startling and yet how true his words were. Impressed, Cora spoke on. "Whenever Civette ignores you, give all your attention to me. If any true feelings for you exist, she will make sure you know it."

"Ah," said Adrian. "It's similar to turning tables, then."

"You could say that," Cora agreed. "So, are you game, sir?"

"A challenge most gratefully accepted, Miss Alexander. How wise you are."

"And without comparison," she added with a deliberate blush.

"While we're at our ruse, let's call each other by our first names, shall we?" he said. "It will seem more convincing."

"As you wish, Adrian. Let the games begin," said Cora.

Together, Adrian and Cora disappeared into the midst of the waiting crowd. Captain Balefire appeared from behind a nearby gold silk serving screen. His already fierce features were troubled.

"Let the games begin, indeed," he said.

"Miss Jovie Wingstrom and Miss Tristana Wingstrom," Evan announced.

Balefire watched as Sorrow and Mirth made their entrance. The two were vexed that not a single partygoer turned and looked at them. Sorrow and Mirth expected to be acknowledged and applauded for the cleverness behind their costumes. However, everyone was preoccupied with their pretty puppet instead. Balefire waved at the despondent Raven Ladies to join him by the ponderous food table.

"So, you invited yourselves," he said.

"You can thank me for that," said Sorrow.

"I'm not certain of my gratitude as yet," said Mirth. "I still believe I shall nap."

With that, Mirth crawled under the skirted table. Balefire glanced at Sorrow. "Humor me, Sorrow, if you can. How many murdered ballgowns went into the making of yours?"

A sneeze erupted from beneath the table. Balefire lifted the cloth and peered below. "Mirth, really, what are you doing under there?" he asked.

Mirth yawned. "Trying to rest, but it's so noisy in here."

"Naturally, it's noisy. It is a hall full of greedy people clamoring in high-pitched voices for free food and drink. It makes the antennae on my head spin."

"Send me down something tasty, will you?" Mirth asked. Balefire tossed a canapé under the table. "Mother of buzzards, what foul concoction is this?" Mirth asked.

Balefire laughed. Through the window beyond, a force of low-lying clouds took hold, making the sky and the land all one tapestry of mist. A shadow passed the beveled panes of glass. Looming tall, it moved in sadness.

Chapter Twenty-Two: Winter Stars

Richard was that shadow.

With the ballroom candlelight as his guide, Richard made his way over the tiered lawns and through the rainswept gardens. He paused by a crepe myrtle tree. A sudden breeze caused its branches to nod and creak in its wake. Richard started down the hedge-trimmed path, and on toward the misted drive. Murmurs from the house party floated about his ears. Their echoes seemed false and contrived. *A fairytale land for fools,* Richard told himself. The farther away he moved, the more ghostlike the voices became. Within moments, all Richard could sense was the vastness of the universe. Despite his grief and confusion, Richard was comforted.

He reached the imposing oak at the entrance gate. The tree was mournful gray beneath a ladder of veiled moonlight, and the ground about her roots smelled of long-dead lilacs. Richard touched the bark of the tree as gently as if the old guardian were human.

"Oh, the sights you've seen," he murmured.

"Filled with changes both happy and sad," he heard a tentative voice say.

Iris appeared against the gloom of the deep valley. She had changed out of that accursed Juliet gown, back into her own sensible clothes. Moon-shimmer disguised the dullness of her gray evening dress and her tepid blonde hair. She walked toward him as if in a dream.

"Iris, I-" Richard began.

"We're not going to discuss our playacting skills, or lack thereof, " Iris told him. "That was all a foolish and headstrong mistake, and I couldn't be more sorry for my part in it."

Richard could have easily expounded on his anger and his disbelief. Richard could have berated Iris for being careless, and not a true friend. Instead, he decided to mask the moment with lightheartedness.

"You're still wearing the costume headband," he said.

Iris was grateful Richard didn't comment that at least the pearls looked nice in her hair. She removed the ribboned wreath and placed it upon a branch of the tree.

"As for this oak, now that is a happier subject," she said. "I believe trees really do listen. Have you ever confessed a wish or a hope to a tree, and had it rustle its leaves in reply? With their advanced age comes wisdom. This oak has been my loyal companion for years. She has heard all my dreams. She knows all my secrets. Yet not once did this grand old lady whisper a word. There's nothing wrong with confiding in trees."

Richard uttered a tired laugh. "And Civette would say the exact opposite, just to be, well, Civette."

It did not please Iris to hear her rival's name mentioned so soon. *Civette, always Civette*. To cover her thoughts, Iris ran her fingertips slowly along the great oak's lowest limb. "I've often sensed that this oak is troubled. I believe I know why. The house is too far away to offer shade from the sun or shelter from the rain."

They both looked up the drive. Candles flickered through the panes of the manor house. They reminded Richard of the golden flecks in a proud cat's eyes. He held his gaze there. How commanding Cairy Hollow appeared against that endless vault of night. To Richard, the estate was a living treasure that would never die.

"Richard—" Iris began.

"Yes?" Richard said. However, his tone was vague and he did not turn his head.

Iris longed to confess that she had always loved him. Richard was Iris's hero. His words and his manner had the power to soothe her. He'd always been kind, even when other men were indifferent or cruel. Forever friends and fiends, it was as if Iris and Richard each knew what the other was thinking. Without effort, they could finish each other's sentences. The two were inseparable at holiday gatherings and social events. Richard despised interacting with others, and Iris was shy. Until Civette made herself available, Richard and Iris were a perfect match.

Iris wanted to reveal the correctable pain in her heart. But she couldn't gather the words that flowed so freely in her mind when she wasn't near him. His presence always caused her true feelings to become burrowed deep within her, tightly curled up, and so very afraid of being hurt.

"May I confess something you might find a bit unusual?" he finally said.

Relieved that he was speaking, Iris nodded.

"I was thinking you might be my guardian angel in human form. Maybe you're here at this very moment to watch over me, to save me. Whatever good, whatever bad, you are my protector. Oh, I know how odd this all sounds, Iris. I've gone and said it, and it doesn't even make sense to me."

Iris spoke softly. "And what do you need saving

from, Richard Marlow?"

A sliver of moonlight broke through the troubled clouds. Brushing over half of Iris's face, it streamed in a pool over the chiffon of her dress. In this rare and goddesslike light, Iris was quite beautiful. Her eyes shimmered like winter stars. For Richard, it was as if he were seeing Iris for the very first time.

Iris watched his expression change at the sight of her. She saw hope. "Richard, I—" she began.

Rampant thoughts and images flew through Richard's head like leaves in a cyclone. Around they spun in a frantic confusion until not a single thing about it seemed right. A wrathful cloud skirted the sky. Richard could only stare as the pretty glow upon Iris's face crept away.

"I honestly do love Civette," he blurted out. Richard placed order to the trembling tone of his voice. "She may not be perfect. God knows I'm not. And she hasn't got the loving heart that you do, Iris. Or your goodness. You and I—we're comfortable together. But there's no spark. I don't know how to say it, but there's something about Civette that makes me feel alive."

Iris immediately felt the pangs of loss for something that was never really hers in the first place. How demoralizing it was to hear that goodness and heart meant nothing, except perhaps for some trite words dashed off in a sympathy card.

"I therefore have no right to infringe upon your inner thoughts," Richard was saying. "I can only ask for your forgiveness, and the hope of your future friendship."

Iris's heart dared her to attempt one last chance. She complied.

"Have you ever met someone for the first time, yet

felt you'd known them forever? That's what happened when I was first introduced to you. I can't explain it, really. It could have been that we met on a road where we once passed as strangers, several lives ago. We might have accidentally ended up by an honored oak tree, exactly like this. There's no mistaking that intuition, that blinding realization, that our yesterdays were intertwined. I happen to trust in a notion that on that long-ago road, we turned to each other, and we knew our present time together was meant to be. Might I be so bold, Richard, as to ask if you ever felt that way too?"

Richard sensed that Iris was about to spill the secrets of her heart, and he wanted to save her from making a mess of things. Taking a deep breath, he confessed to Iris a tender wish that when they were older, they would recall this moment, raise their cocktail glasses, and laugh together.

A hollow gust blew. They both shivered. Iris's opportune moment had been embezzled by the wind. Iris smiled wistfully at Richard and replied that their future meeting had better be a promise. Richard was relieved to hear Iris say this. Romantic love between friends jeopardized something which, if not the shiniest prize on the shelf, still did not deserve to be destroyed.

As for Iris, laughter was the last thing on her mind or in the core of her wounded heart. It was over. Iris had gambled at a worthwhile chance, and lost. Worse still, that loss was not in gradual pieces, but all at once, like a solitary lamp extinguishing in the darkest hour of night. One might have thought she'd weep tears. She did not. The cut of her pain was far too deep. Iris lowered her head, her entire being drooping back into the look, the loneliness, and the life that had never failed to suffocate her.

Without a further word, they hugged each other, as friends with a shared but innocent secret would do, and made their way up the candle-cast steps toward the main house.

Chapter Twenty-Three: Black Is the Color

"My darling girl!" Civette heard over the lively hum in the room. "How happy I am to see you!"

A young gentleman acquaintance of Civette's was weaving his way toward her. His name was Freddy Fairfax. Blond and indolent, Freddy represented the new breed of New York sophistication. He went to an office by day, dawdling with papers he barely read and making long, drawn-out decisions for people he hardly knew. Luncheons were lingering affairs at the likes of the Ritz, where the waiters were attired better than most of the patrons, and a dish of roasted canvasback duck cost the astronomical sum of three dollars. By no later than five, Freddy would be lounging with his fellow faux office dwellers at his club. And thus, his days would unfold, one after the other after the other. What many envied Freddy saw as a life of drudgery. Sensitive to city heat, as well as to the incessant needling from his third stepmother, Freddy Fairfax escaped in prolonged weekends to New Hampshire. Here, where tall trees replaced endless rows of townhouses, Freddy savored the delicious freedom to be more himself.

Civette extended a gloved hand. Freddy kissed it and looked at her face.

"Come now, precious thing, why so glum? It's old Freddy Fairfax, here before you and groveling at your feet."

Despite her anguish over Adrian and Cora, Civette managed to smile. "You're the furthest from a groveler there is, Freddy Fairfax. You were the only man to have ever courted me and neglected to propose."

"Oh, Civette—I don't know how to tell you. I assumed you'd guessed. The reason I never proposed is because I respect you too much to ever pretend to love you. And why should you care? Tittle-tattle has it you've roped in an accountant. While not a prince, perhaps, he'll be more steady than this here Freddy."

Civette laughed, and Freddy was delighted to see her do so. He glanced around the room. "I see the old place is decked out in style," he said. "Except, perhaps, for your mother's taste in floral arrangements. Tonight's choices are, well, *très* gloomy and cheap."

Civette finally noticed the strange vegetation that had taken over the hothouse vases. She shrugged. "They must have wilted," she said.

Freddy waved his hand. "That's always the way with expensive florists. Give them an address like yours, and they'll rake you over the coals for last week's dregs. Anyway, I have someone I must introduce to you. He's quite the charmer, Roger is. The reason I mention him is that Roger and I have been to a séance, and we're simply dying to tell you all about it."

"A séance? Where?" Civette questioned.

"A large estate outside of Boston. Very hush-hush, although I swear there were a hundred talkative people there. It was conducted by a certain Madame Dhruva. The claim is that she's a Bengali princess. If you want my humble wager, I'd say she worked on her backside in a New York brothel. But all the same, it was astounding. Roger got us in due to his being neighbors with her manager. I know how you can't get enough of all that harum-scarum stuff, my dear, and that's why you and Roger simply must meet. So, come along, Civette, come along!"

Freddy led Civette through the crowd and introduced her to Roger. In many ways, Roger Manville was like Freddy, being careless, elegant, and highly entertaining. Roger had made the acquaintance of Captain Balefire and was instantly captivated by him. Roger possessed a mania for anything or anyone with a dramatic flair. It wasn't long before the group was chatting with ease about the occult.

"Yes, Miss Middleton," Roger was saying. "Ever since Mary Todd Lincoln lifted the thin veil in search of her dead son, séances have become all the rage."

"Oh, it goes back much further than that," said Balefire.

"Do you have an interest in communicating with the dead, Captain?" asked Roger.

"Not only an inherent interest, but the skill," he claimed.

Swiftly dismissing the fact that she couldn't tolerate Captain Balefire, Civette leaned in. "Could you conduct a séance in this house right now?" she asked him.

"How brilliant and daring of you," Freddy declared.

"Why, yes," the captain answered to both.

"Do we have enough time?" Civette asked.

Roger Manville held up his glass. "Indeed, Captain Balefire. Before the ever-important dancing begins, do you believe you could conjure up more spirits to twirl before our eyes than bubbles in this Veuve Clicquot?"

Civette turned to Roger with laughing eyes. "Then we're already defeated, good sir. You're drinking

Abelé."

"Be it stark vinegar or a Chateau Margaux, I could summon a legion of demons sprung from the depths of your darkest dreams," Balefire replied, and everyone reacted accordingly.

"Once Sir Adrian returns, I would love for you to prove your claims," Civette said. She glanced about the great hall. "Sir Adrian respects magic. He told me."

"Quite so," agreed Balefire. "Let's have him sent for."

Civette nodded and signaled for Sarah.

"Sir who?" questioned Roger. He was intrigued.

"His name is Sir Adrian Bramwell," said Civette. "He's ever so worldly and handsome."

"Then we will wait for him," Freddy declared. "And what about your intended?" he asked Civette. "Should we include him?"

"Richard?" Civette scoffed. "Absolutely not. Richard Marlow doesn't believe in anything magical, especially me."

"The ardor cools," murmured Freddy.

After instructing Sarah to bring Sir Adrian to the formal parlor, Civette led the way there. They were stopped in the hall by Leona.

"I overheard you asking for Sir Adrian to be summoned here. Do be mindful of manners, child. He must be properly introduced to our guests," she said.

"Later, Mother, when the people who truly matter are here."

"I say," claimed Freddy in mock protest. Groaning, Civette pushed Freddy into the room.

"Civette…" Leona began. However, the parlor doors were closed before her face. Leona remained, unmoving, in the hall. Those doors had been shuttered to her, but bitterness and regret, like the old comrades they were, crept along the floor and the walls toward her. Leona breathed deeply and let them in.

****

Balefire and the gentlemen went about rearranging the room for an impromptu séance. Adrian made his appearance in the company of Cora Alexander. With her arm entwined through Adrian's, Cora was behaving like Lady Triumphant. Civette refused to reveal her displeasure at this. She laughed as though Cora's fakery amused her. It was now Cora's turn to display indifference. She didn't do half as well.

"Come in, come in," Balefire declared. "By refusing to cross the threshold, you are confusing the spirits."

"Are you really conducting a séance?" Cora asked.

"No, silly girl, we're playing charades with a troupe of imaginary friends," Freddy replied.

Cora looked up at Adrian. "I'm—I'm not sure I care to remain. My mother is strictly against spiritualism."

"What little your mother has to look forward to," said Balefire. "All right, young lady, if your sensitivities prefer, we will begin with the juvenile version of a séance. A demonstration of clever parlor tricks, if you will. I know all the gimmicks, all the sleights of hand. I've lived through, and practiced, each and every one."

"If you promise it's only a trick for fun—a lark, if you will," said Cora.

"Oh, with me involved, it's rarely anything else," Balefire assured her. "So, do sit down and allow the lark to sing."

Cora settled herself with noticeable hesitation. She put on quite a show of playing helpless and scared. Over their gold-rimmed champagne glasses, and with their eyes alone, Freddy and Roger critiqued Cora's gala performance. They'd seen more capable vaudevillians in the opening acts at the Palace Theater. Adrian went to Cora's side, giving Civette momentary cause for concern. Civette then rationalized that Adrian would only want her more once he realized what a needy little manipulator Cora could be. Moving her abundant skirts aside, Civette placed herself between Roger and Freddy.

"I believe in ghosts," claimed Freddy. "When I was a child, I was elevated out of my bed and carried through the air to the garden where I was dropped in an unhappy bed of hibiscus. I believe it was the spirit of my first stepmother. She never liked me."

"Oh, Freddy, enough! Do show us, Captain, how a false séance is done, so we can move on to a real one," said Civette. She frowned at Cora, for good measure.

"First of all, the room must be very dark," Balefire instructed.

"Shy ghosts believe they look frightful in the light," Roger added, and nearly everyone laughed. Freddy and Roger extinguished the candles about the room and returned to their seats.

"Silence, everyone," Balefire instructed. "Ladies and gentlemen, remove your gloves." Balefire waited while they did so. Civette was staring at Adrian's fingers. How tapered and long and seductive they were. She recalled the sensation of his touch. Balefire noticed Civette's diversion, and smirked. He waited until everyone had secured their gloves in their laps.

"Thank you. Begin by placing your hands flat upon this table with your outer fingertips touching your neighbor's. Excellent. Feel the energy flowing between us? Now, bow your heads and concentrate on a long-lost loved one." Balefire glanced up at the portrait of Emmeline Cairy. "It can even be a once happy little dog, if that's what pulls at your heartstrings."

The company did as Balefire instructed. The ensuing silence was interrupted by a light knocking sound. Startled, Freddy screamed. It was only the temporary maid Sarah arriving with more champagne. Sarah glanced about the room with unmistakable envy. If she'd been wellborn, Sarah told herself, she would have thrived in an environment as lovely and as exciting as this. Sarah left the darkened room and paused in the hall. A shimmering movement on the grand staircase caught her eye. Sarah couldn't be certain, but she thought she saw a figure moving toward the west wing of the house. Steeling herself, Sarah ran back to the kitchen.

****

Inside the formal parlor, moments passed. Nothing happened. Cora, who had been holding her breath, gasped loudly. Muffled sounds from the party could be heard through the walls. The distraction of it caused everyone to shuffle in their seats.

"I really must leave," Cora claimed. She looked at Adrian with feigned concern. "Please, Adrian?" she begged.

"As you wish," said Balefire. "However, I do feel an actual moment from the past trying to break its way through."

Cora stood, prompting Adrian to do the same. Adrian placed his arm about Cora. "The past, even my own immediate one, holds no interest for me," he informed the others.

Adrian's words filled Civette with dread. Adrian

and Cora left the room. Civette felt an overpowering urge to follow them. As she was about to stand, a low and lamentable noise rose up from the floor. With it came the shrill effects of a cold wind. Encased in a silver sheen, the echoing whirlwind enveloped itself about those seated at the table.

Balefire rolled his hands toward the ceiling. "The moment I spoke of has arrived."

"Captain," they heard a woman's voice say over their heads, "light the fire."

Everyone pivoted toward the fireplace. The hearth was stone cold and the embers gray. However, within the wink of a knowing eye, a breeze whistled down from the tip of the chimney. Fluttering over the grate, that breeze exhaled. Phantom-like ribbons of smoke rose between the logs. The cradle of ash beneath glowed a deep devil-red. Soon after, the fireplace was ablaze. Satisfied, the current of air yawned and crept back up the bricks.

"Thank you, Captain," the alluring voice said. "This place must be warm when Olen arrives."

The hearth flames and the invisible force above it crackled in reply.

"Needle and thread, needle and thread," the woman's voice chanted as it bounced from corner to corner and wall to wall. A silvery shadow skirted the trail of her voice. The room filled with a pronounced scent of lilacs. Two ghostly, snow-white mice appeared on the floor by the fireplace. Huddled for safety and warmth, they began to chitter.

"Keep that up, and I'll have you turned into chimney sweeps and whisked out the door," the voice sweetly threatened. With tiny shrieks of terror, the phantom mice scurried away and vanished into a wall.

Silence followed. Those about the table heard the tall clock mark the moments that passed. *Tick, tick, tick,* it pulsed in rhythm with their captivated hearts. The whirlwind that had shrouded the group at the table rolled past and rattled the parlor windowpanes. Freddy squealed.

"Shh," Balefire commanded.

They watched as the leaded-glass windows overlooking the garden unlatched and drifted open. The moon's fogbound light flooded in, bathing the room and its occupants in a nebulous glow.

"There's someone in a hooded cloak outside," Roger said in a near whisper. "Do you see? He, or she, is standing by that birch tree and appears to be spying on us."

A chilled wind swept by, billowing the intruder's hood and revealing the contours of a woman's face. She raised her left hand. In her grasp was a vial. The storm's light played against the leather-bound glass. As quickly as this was revealed, the woman vanished.

Not a second later, a muffled bell rang. Freddy's eyes went wide.

"It's the front door," whispered Civette. "We are hosting a party."

With a sudden and menacing shriek, the whirlwind wrenched the murky light from the room and pulled the casements shut. At first, no one reacted. Soon thereafter, Roger, who always appreciated a good show, began applauding madly.

"How did you do that?" Freddy exclaimed over Roger's accolades.

"Smoke and mirrors, and a brief yet powerful moment to reflect on," said the grinning Balefire.

"Mr. Olen Devereux," Evan could be heard announcing in the ballroom beyond.

Without a word or a warning, Civette left the room.

"What got her corset in such a crunch?" asked Freddy.

Balefire began to laugh uncontrollably.

"Shall we follow her?" said Roger. "Perhaps this Devereux fellow is the ghost to beat all Cairy Hollow ghosts."

Balefire wiped tears of laughter from his stony eyes. "We'll never know by sitting here, will we?" he asked.

The men raised their glasses, stood, and promptly departed.

****

"Mr. Olen Devereux," Evan had announced.

Within the ballroom, the fervent din rolled to silence. Group by group, the guests turned their heads in a dreamlike flow. Olen Devereux? He'd been gone for ages. No one knew where. As Olen Devereux stepped forward in his elegant evening attire, curious whispers grew. Olen had to be in his mid-fifties, but he looked no more than thirty. How handsome and magnetic he still was. Everyone continued to stare.

"Who sent an invitation to him?" John Cairy asked under his breath.

Appearing at his side, Balefire readily admitted that he had.

"I want all these people gone," said John.

"Is that an official wish?" Balefire asked.

"Never more so," he said.

"Indulge me, Mr. Cairy. Whisper it in my ear."

Balefire leaned his angular head toward him. John was in such a foul mood that Balefire's request was the least of his annoyances. John repeated his desire to have everyone gone.

"Consider it done," Balefire said, and he walked away.

John laughed bitterly and watched as Captain Balefire rushed forward to greet the guest John could see only as a painful reminder of his past. Whatever words, whatever wishes he'd just uttered flew out of his head. All that remained for John Cairy was a feeling of disgust.

"Olen Devereux, how delightful it is to see you again," said Balefire. "Come, be reunited with your long-lost friends."

Civette was moving through the throng. Her eyes darted about anxiously in search of her mother. Civette knew. She'd heard the stories. Leona had been deeply in love with this Devereux man and probably still was. Fortunately, her mother was nowhere to be seen.

Olen Devereux and Captain Balefire headed straight toward Adrian. Civette rushed to get there first. "Sir Adrian Bramwell," she said, "may I introduce—"

"My clasp. You still do not honor me by wearing it?" Adrian asked her.

"I haven't yet talked to Richard."

Adrian looked away. "Miss Alexander shall introduce," he declared.

Cora tossed a knowing smile toward Civette. With the seal of that smile, the victor and the vanquished traded places. Civette had stolen Richard away from Cora. Now Cora was luring Adrian away from Civette. The events of the evening, as Civette had imagined them, had turned for the worse. It was Cora who stood by Adrian's side. It was Cora who held Adrian's cool hand and tilted her head toward the heavenly tone of his voice.

The look of adoration Cora gave Adrian reflected in the response on his heavenly face.

Look at me, look at me, Civette begged in her mind. But Adrian would not. Civette had gambled at a losing game. Her heart rent in two, Civette was forced to stand tall and face the shiny trappings of someone else's fascination.

With Balefire's assistance, Cora introduced Sir Adrian to Mr. Devereux. Cora then brought Adrian before the Reed sisters and their mundane nephew. "Miss Priscilla Reed, Miss Hannah Reed, Miss Elizabeth Reed, Steven Reed, allow me to present my friend, Sir Adrian Bramwell."

Adrian placed his perfectly sculpted hand over his heart. "Verily, ladies, as that prince of poets the immortal Virgil once remarked: *Adeo in teneris consuescere multum est.*"

"Good sir, you must be a university man," said Hannah.

"And so very accomplished," squeaked Elizabeth.

Priscilla grinned at Adrian and Cora. "I say you two should get married," she said. "You're far more exciting than Leona's bratty daughter and that bloodless Marlow boy."

"How wonderful then that Miss Alexander is dressed for the occasion," Adrian replied. His smile was irresistible. The often overlooked Reed sisters took such delight in it.

Cora then led Adrian to where an assemblage of mothers, her own included, stood in a corner of the grand hall. Their rhinestone-and-feather-adorned heads bobbing, they were all gossiping about the fact that Olen Devereux had gone straight to the study where Leona had been hiding since the Ball began. Despite having their backs to the room, the ladies could feel Adrian's approach. He radiated such charm. They turned and basked in the presence of this exotic man.

Cora presented Sir Bramwell to them as her dearest friend.

Now he's dearest, Civette complained in her head.

"Miss Alexander," said Midwife Corbin, who hovered nearby, "I see you are as vivacious as ever."

"Trust me, kind lady, I will inform Her Majesty of your courtesy," Adrian replied.

Midwife Corbin cackled. "That straight-laced grump? What would she care? Save your courtesies for a better figurehead, my son. Someone like John James Audubon back in the day. Now, he was a vision for my highborn tastes. And he was for the birds, as well, the Devil praise him."

Adrian laughed, which allowed everyone to pass over the midwife's strange words and do the same. Adrian's glee lit up the lovely angles of his face. The ladies were enchanted.

On what felt like a magical rush of air, the sounds of the orchestra filled the room. The grand hall came to life. Philip Osgood met up with Richard, who was standing alone by the punch bowl. Richard was the room's only element that was not animated. He was thinking intently about something and would not speak.

Philip looked from his friend's dour face to that of Adrian's far more composed one. "I fear he is perfection," Philip said with an apologetic sigh.

"Perfection is only found in highly romantic novels," replied Richard. "Even then, it's all a well-plotted ruse."

"Ruse or no ruse, this Sir Bramwell is still utter completeness," said Philip.

"But would he be revealed as such in the glass?" Richard wondered aloud.

"Whatever do you mean?" Philip asked. Richard seemed suddenly alert.

"There's a mirror behind those velvet drapes, over there," Richard said, motioning with his chin. "It's claimed to be a Glass of Truth. The mirror supposedly displays people as they honestly are."

"Does it now?" Philip laughed.

"It is true. Well, as a fanciful story it is."

"Then leave it as such," said Philip. "It's a make-believe prop for bored people, Richard, and nothing more."

Civette appeared. Strolling with a group of enraptured young men, she was attempting to look popular. From his place with Sorrow and Mirth near the buffet, Balefire picked up a chicken leg and crammed the crest of it into his mouth. Crunching the bones, Balefire watched as Adrian excused himself to Cora and went to Civette.

"Have you changed your mind about my clasp?" he asked.

"I will go talk to Richard now. You'll see," Civette pleaded in return.

Adrian replied with a curt bow. "I have discovered that Miss Cora Alexander is a most agreeable young lady. Would you not agree?" He did not wait for Civette's answer. His manner implied he had no interest in hearing it. With elegant strides, Adrian returned to Cora's side.

Cora was elated. For her, the evening was so

splendid that it pressed upon her heart. Some women, Cora told herself, would wish for such a night to last forever. But Cora knew better. The beginning and the middle of beautiful things never did last. One should always expect an end to anything worth cherishing. So instead, Cora vowed she would never forget the wonders of these special hours. There was the difference.

"My dear Miss Alexander," Adrian said while taking her hand, "will you do me the honor of delighting this assembly with a song?"

Cora curtsied in a most elegant fashion. "It would indeed be a pleasure to sing for you, Adrian, and for our guests."

The words "*our* guests" burned in Civette's head. On his part, John Cairy could only stare at Adrian. That upstart, that blatant imposter, was taking over as host of his party. However, John knew not to react. Everyone in the ballroom was calling out with encouragement. After speaking with the orchestra leader, Cora stood before the crowd, preparing herself to perform.

Sorrow groaned. "Why is it, at every gathering of humans such as this, the empty-headed flirt always sings?"

"That empty-headed flirt, as you call her, is rapidly becoming a threat to our plan," said Balefire. "I even heard her say, 'let the games begin', as she conquered the attention of our dear but distracted puppet."

Sorrow and Mirth gave serious thought to what Balefire had just said. The room fell to respectful silence and Cora sang:

Black is the color of my true love's hair
His face is like some rosy fair
The prettiest face and the neatest hands

I love the ground whereon he stands
I love my love and well he knows
I love the ground whereon he goes
If you no more on earth I see
I can't serve you as you have me
The winter's passed and the leaves are green,
The time has passed that we have seen,
But still I hope the time will come
When you and I shall be as one.
I go to the Clyde for to mourn and weep,
But satisfied I never could sleep.
I'll write to you a few short lines,
I'll suffer death ten thousand times.

Civette was outraged at Cora's choice of music. However, Civette kept her face clear of expression. All eyes were on her. She knew this. *I am the only true ornament in this room,* Civette reminded herself, *and I will not break.*

Chapter Twenty-Four: In Durance Soundly Caged

Cora's song concluded with great praise offered by everyone except Balefire, Sorrow, and Mirth. Peeling off bits and pieces of Leona's once lovely wardrobe, Sorrow and Mirth left the party. They had endured enough and were now on a mission.

As the applause died down, the sound of downpouring rain engulfed the room. The drapes rose with the wind the deluge created, agitating the hundred flaring candles. Evan moved swiftly about the hall, closing the windows against the hammering gale. Evan was a typically unruffled young man, but there was something about this storm that troubled him.

Evan was further troubled by the sight of Midwife Corbin outside. Her face raised to the tempest, and her white-feathered gown fluttering, the old woman appeared to be talking to someone. Evan knew he should go and encourage her to venture back inside. The poor thing had to be a hundred. Most likely, Midwife Corbin had gone batty. Evan was relieved when she decided to come in on her own. Evan did note, however, that the midwife had an agitated look upon her face, and was mumbling to herself.

Once the windowpanes were secured, Balefire stepped forward. "Miss Alexander, that was indeed a lovely tribute to Sir Adrian. For those of you who don't know me—and that makes you fortunate—" Balefire paused for the anticipated laughter. "My name is Captain Balefire. I have pleasure in announcing that my charge, Sir Adrian Bramwell, shall regale our present company with a poem."

There was a general murmur of surprise. The guests settled into chairs and into groups against the wall to hear him speak. Balefire looked beyond the ballroom to the foyer. The storm's light through the beveled panes painted the vestibule with a netherworld glow. Seeing this, Balefire was pleased.

Meanwhile, Adrian looked about. An uneasiness loomed beneath the beauty of his features. "A poem?" he repeated.

"Certainly, being wellborn, you were raised on the works of Milton, Jonson, Cowley, and Blake," Richard Marlow suggested. It was his fifth sampling of punch that had provided him with such bravado.

Had anyone else challenged him, Adrian would have accepted his shortcomings with grace. Richard Marlow was another story. Adrian recalled his etiquette training with Balefire.

"You forgot the greatest writer of all, William Shakespeare," Adrian replied.

The room resounded with laughter and applause.

"Of course I'll recite a poem," Adrian announced. Much to John and Richard's dismay, the guests were even more effusive. Adrian strolled about as confident and winning as a stage actor. "However, I will select something earthier than the classics for your listening pleasure. After all, my new and treasured friends, it is All Hallows' Eve."

He paused before Civette. "My clasp, Civette. Do you remain uncertain?" he whispered.

Civette nodded. "Please give me a little more time," she whispered in return.

Adrian brought a golden tapestry chair to the center of the dance floor. "My darling Cora, I shall dedicate this poem to you," he said.

Cora looked pointedly at Civette. "It is an honor, Adrian," she said.

Cora settled herself so that her satin wedding gown showed to its best advantage. All the guests were smiling at her. Their praise made Cora's face glow with loveliness.

Adrian cleared his throat and began:

Of thirty bare years have I,
Twice twenty been enraged.
And of forty been three times fifteen,
In durance soundly caged.

There came a distant cawing of crows. The guests reacted in various ways. Some were even humored. The chorus of the crows' call grew in strength as they flew overhead. Everyone followed the vibrant sound with their eyes. The clamor hit a crescendo and faded, drifting off toward the east. A humid silence followed. The ladies who had fans began pulsing them like wings before their faces. Adrian drew breath to speak and, as he did, erratic shadows flickered against the ballroom windows. A few of the onlookers turned their heads in question. One man simply muttered, "Leaves."

Adrian continued:

I know more than Apollo,
For oft, when he lies sleeping,
I see the stars at blooded wars,
In the wounded welkin weeping.

The shadows at the windows grew with intensity.

More people looked this time. The same man who believed the shadows were merely leaves now uttered, "Heavy fog." Everyone returned their attention to Adrian.

Cora, being the only one truly facing the windows, peered toward whatever was rapping at the tall panes. There, in the grim shade of night, she saw two rain-drenched creatures clinging to the glass. They were blackened corpses, tall, lank, and female in form, with large purple veins bulging at their necks and thighs. Their large hands and feet were clawlike, their faces long and tormented. As dark as their faces were, the circles about their merciless eyes were even darker. Both creatures had rings around their mouths that appeared to be dripping blood. One attempted to speak. Its jaw unhinged to its collarbone. The creatures finally spoke in a way only Cora could hear. In a hollow tone, they chanted:

She lifted up his bloody head
Down a down, hey down, hey down,
And kissed his wounds so drenched in red,
With a down,
She pulled him up upon her pell,
And carried him straight down to hell,
With a down, derry, derry, derry, down, down!

Throughout this, Adrian Bramwell was calmly reciting:

The moon embraced her shepherd,
And the Queen of Love her warrior,
When the first doth horn the star of morn,
And next the heavenly Farrier.

Cora was about to cry out when the two creatures propelled themselves backward with an unheard screech.

Large, oil-black wings sprang from their sides and they flew upward, their flight of passage hampered in part by the ponderous rain. The guests saw none of this. They were fixated upon Adrian and his curious, archaic poem. Only Gertie Fiske noticed Cora's paralyzing anxiety. Before the spellbound crowd, Adrian concluded:

With a host of furious fancies,
Whereof I am commander,
With a burning spear and a horse of air,
To the wilderness I wander.
By a knight of ghosts and shadows,
I summoned am to tourney,
Ten leagues beyond the wild world's end,
Methinks it is no journey.

The brazen chorus of crows returned, now from east to west. The guests once again followed the trail of sound. With Adrian's last utterance, the torrential rain ceased, as if on command. No one knew how to react.

To everyone's surprise, Priscilla Reed madly applauded with her thin, mottled hands. "Beautifully done, beautifully done," she warbled as loudly as she possibly could.

Balefire grinned. "Praise from a righteous woman. Ah, how the spirits shall roar at our next revel," he murmured.

The room resonated with applause and shouts of *Bravo!* The men raised their glasses, and the ladies waved their feathered masks. Basking in his adulation, Adrian looked to Civette. He could see the want in her eyes. She nodded yes. His smile sealed the deal. Extending his hand to the distracted Cora, Adrian drew her close as she stood.

"As it is with many games, the time has come to

switch players," he whispered. "I believe, Miss Alexander, that you and I are through."

Disoriented, Cora followed Adrian's gaze to where it rested on Civette's face. Despite her intense confusion, Cora realized that nothing could be more clear. Always the winner, Civette Middleton had triumphed over her yet again.

With little more than a feeble nod, Cora stumbled toward a quiet corner of the ballroom. There she stood with her back to the music, the hum, and the laughter. Nervously clutching the train of her gown, Cora's eyes were closed. Her lungs drew frantic, ragged breaths. Gertie Fiske appeared by her side. The fear on Cora's face alarmed her.

"Whatever is wrong, Cora? You appear as though you've seen a ghost."

Cora answered in a trembling voice. "I saw not only one but two." While an array of brightly adorned dancers whirled past, Cora related what she believed she had seen at the window. Gertie's expression was rendered more incredulous with every descriptive phrase.

"Cora, what you're claiming is beyond belief. It has stopped raining, at least for the moment. Shall we go outside and stay near the house for safety's sake? We could look around. Perhaps in doing so, it will put your fears to rest. There simply cannot be creatures out there as you describe. Perhaps what you really saw were partygoers playing cruel tricks on you."

Cora was hesitant to step away from her windowless refuge; however, Gertie was insistent. Gertie took Cora by the hand, and they ventured toward the side door that led to the gardens. Before they stepped outside, Gertie put her punch glass down on a table. Housemaid Marie saw this and went dutifully with her tray to pick up Gertie's crystal glass. Marie watched through the service hall window as the two young ladies moved cautiously about by the terrace wall.

There appeared to be nothing but darkness outside to trouble them. The night was coarse with clouds— scratchy billows of oyster gray and black, unsettled and beset with rain. Not even the dimmest ray of a single star could thrash its way through the present gloom. Cora and Gertie were about to return to the house when a fluttering was heard overhead. Sorrow, in her barbarian state, dropped low. Her spanned wings were barely visible against the gloom of night. With her vein-gorged talons, Sorrow grabbed Cora by the bustle of her satin wedding gown and, with a hideous shriek, Sorrow lifted the unsuspecting girl into the sky.

"Let the games begin," Sorrow declared in perfect mimicry of Cora when she had, little more than an hour before, attempted to lure her puppet away from Civette.

Cora wrenched around in panic. The depths of an endless sky offered her nothing to cling to. Without hesitation, Gertie reached up and grabbed Cora's flailing feet. Gertie leaned back as steadfast as she could, trying to hold at bay whatever monster it was that was attempting to fly off with her friend. Other fearsome creatures rode overhead. Their rhythmic wings flapped like heavy sheets in a sharp wind. The wet air rang with rolling whispers of *Sorrow, Crying, Sickness, Dying.* Sorrow was struggling against Gertie's heroic stronghold. The determined Sorrow would not relinquish her victim. With a thrust of her wings and a vicious growl, Sorrow dug her talons deep into Cora's back. Gertie could hear Cora's spine splintering.

"Don't give up, Cora," Gertie shouted. "Don't give up! I have you!"

With a battering rush of air, a large raven swept into view. It easily knocked Gertie to the puddle-drenched ground. Landing upon the wall of the terrace, the raven's claws crumbled the stonework. Her feathers were tipped with gray, and the crest of her head was arched like an ax. With a twist of her body, the phantom bird lurched to the ground and slashed her way across the flagstones toward Gertie. Hovering above the delirious girl, the bird lowered her head, showing smoldering eyes of red.

"Give up," the raven commanded. Its gravelly voice swept over Gertie with a pungent blast of sulfur.

Gertie responded with a resounding slap across the bird's face. Gertie's nails drew streaks about the raven's hellish eyes. The bird snarled and arched her back, and during those few harrowing moments, Gertie grabbed a garden spike and drove it through the demon's chest.

The bird staggered back. Her blood oozed in foul-smelling streams of black, and her cloudy breath rattled in her throat. The other clamoring devil birds immediately swooped to the ground. One landed with her razor-sharp talons at each side of the quivering Gertie.

"Do you honestly believe you can put an end to us?" it asked.

Inside the house, the laughter and the happy music played on. Not a single guest suspected the horrors that were playing out beyond the shuttered windows. Only Marie had the slightest clue, and she was too numbed by fear to move.

Trembling on the cold and wet ground, Gertie looked past the agitated wings of her attacker. There, she saw her battered friend getting tossed among the airborne creatures like a commonplace toy.

Gertie was too frightened to cry. "Goodbye," she whispered.

"Goodbye," echoed the bird. In a flash, it grasped Gertie by her throat and snapped it. The black pearls Gertie had been wearing broke away. They clattered like frozen tears atop the terrace stones. The demon bird rose into the air, the lifeless Gertrie held dangling by her heel.

Marie dropped the tray she was holding. The sound of cackling rippled the outside air. Mirth, in her horrific monster form, settled herself before the window that shielded Marie. Pushing her face to the glass, Mirth searched about through her large and luminous eyes.

"Step outside, dearie," Mirth whispered in a hoarse and terrible voice. "We merely want to snip off your nose."

Recoiling in horror, Marie pressed her body against the plaster wall. Marie watched Mirth's grotesque shadow slink across the hallway floor and disappear. Outside, the other savages arched their wings, threw back their heads and, with shrill cries, became one with the stormy sky.

Cautiously, Marie moved toward the window. The Raven Women had taken flight, their prey firmly fixed in their clutches. Over the great oak at the entrance gate they soared, making their way like threshing blotches of ink toward the shadowed treeline of Ravenswood Forest. The sky showed no pity. Callous lightning illuminated the underbellies of the clouds. Into the silent, gray light the hellions flew and were gone.

Marie ran to her attic room, binding whatever meager belongings she possessed within a cloth bag.

Donning a dark cape, Marie made her way down the service stairs. Everyone in the kitchen was too busy to notice Marie slipping away through the side door. Looking up warily, the frightened housemaid scurried beneath the cover of Cairy Hollow's trees. Marie had had enough of witchcraft and demons and death. Despite the near poverty and hunger that awaited her in the village, Marie was going home.

Chapter Twenty-Five: Freed

Observing the party through vacant eyes, Richard stood alone. Enveloped in his own misery, he didn't see Civette approach at first. Richard only became aware when he heard his name being uttered with no level of feeling at all.

"You wear your intentions well," he told her. "The manner in which you are attired, everyone will easily assume you are seeking a different man to fulfill your future, not to mention exactly which one. And for those who don't care to think—and in this I include your intended victim—you will merely look desperate."

Civette despised what he said, but she remained unmoved and said nothing.

"Witnessing what you've become to ensnare this two-bit imbecile, I sense I want nothing more to do with you," he concluded.

"Suit yourself," Civette murmured while smiling at a passing guest. It was then Richard noticed something about Civette's smiles. They were self-indulgent and never meant to please anyone but herself. Why hadn't he realized that before? Or perhaps he had. As a child, Civette only smiled when she wanted others to do her bidding. That was the sad beginning of it all. Richard now found himself begging for the end.

"Has he proven that he loves you?" he asked her.

Civette answered without looking at him. "Yes, and

in so many ways I can scarcely name them all."

How vengeful she was. How thoroughly callous Civette had become in less than a day. Richard wondered for a moment if this was all but a dream. But such wonderment came from his heart alone. His steady mind knew better. Richard braced himself. "Answer me one last question, Civette. Did you ever care for me?"

Civette's face readily supplied his answer. A bleak rawness filled his chest. Richard's trembling heart had made peace with his mind, at last. He became inexplicably calm.

"I have given this matter much thought over the course of this one devastating and demoralizing day," he began. "Not surprisingly, I have arrived at the conclusion that you are nothing but a greedy creature who thrives on being loved. We should have stayed as we were. Your trifling romantic woes amused me when we were just friends. But you dared me to love you, and that was cruel. You intended to give nothing in return."

"And what about you, Richard? Did you ever care for me? Or was Cairy Hollow your one true obsession?"

Her eyes were glaring. Richard laughed and hung his head low. "Perhaps, underneath it all, we're both monsters, you and I," he said.

Despite all the things Civette could have said or done, she realized the better person she could be, and took Richard into her arms. Iris watched this entire scene from across the ballroom. Without words to hear, without emotions to bear, Iris had no idea what Richard and Civette were talking about. However, seeing the two embrace defined everything in Iris's whirling mind.

"Why doesn't anyone think of releasing someone they truly don't love?" Iris whispered. But she knew the answer. It was vanity that made cruel people aim to destroy that which they no longer wanted but desired no one else to have.

Iris loved Richard. She loved him with a fierceness that would never die. But, for now, Richard Marlow was in for everything he deserved.

Iris left Cairy Hollow and everyone in it. Halfway down the walk, Iris paused and clutched her hands over her heart. She knew she'd always cherish the image of that ballroom alive with light. In her head, she'd often hear the lively strains of music and laughter rising on the breeze, and picture the dancers swirling past the candlelit windows. But even while presently standing there, it all seemed like a blurred hope that was better cast to darkness. There were other hopes, other dreams out there just begging to be born. Iris merely needed to welcome them in. She faced the long and winding drive. With every step taken, Iris Owen knew that she would, eventually, heal.

She passed the tiered gardens. Beyond was a grand hill that sloped to the country lane toward town. A moment from her past flared in Iris's mind. Iris was perhaps ten, and running down this very hill with the equally youthful Richard and Civette. Iris caught her foot on a rock and tumbled. Richard's only concern was that Civette did not suffer the same. How hurt and angry Iris was then. But the present day Iris couldn't help but laugh.

She reached the majestic entrance gate. Iris then recalled that Civette's dancing slippers were still on her feet. Leaning against the polished rails, Iris removed the silver slippers and, with a victory cry, she flung them far onto the rainswept hill.

"Sometimes, certain people get exactly what's coming to them," Iris proclaimed to the seething skies.

A chill wind blew past. It rustled Iris's bland hair and her bleak dress. After one last look at Cairy Hollow, one last toying with the pretty fabric of her memories, Iris Owen squared her shoulders and walked away.

****

"So, we're done, aren't we?"

This Richard whispered in Civette's ear as she held him. Her only response was to step back, nod, and leave him standing there alone.

With trembling fingers, Richard put down his glass. He'd withstood all he could manage. Civette had officially abandoned him and was making a fool of herself with a man who was nothing more than a stick figure mannequin saying and doing things without an ounce of true human care or concern.

A stick figure mannequin, Richard repeated to himself. His own words overwhelmed him with a preposterous thought. That very morning, Civette's mother had spoken of Bess Dalby boasting that she could spell life into her scarecrow. It was a boast, perhaps, but said by a supposed sorceress all the same. And there was that odd poem Adrian Bramwell recited for the guests at the Ball. It brought to mind the snippet of an odd song Richard had heard one morning when he was walking through Ravenswood Forest. It echoed through the trees toward him. When Richard followed the trail of that tune, it led him to an abandoned cottage in a dell. No one was there. A decayed scarecrow hung, weather-beaten and forlorn, in the weed-clenched field. Richard did his best to remember the song that had lured him there. Suddenly, the memory of Adrian reciting that poem overlapped the lyrics in his head.

By a knight of ghosts and shadows,
I summoned am to tourney,
Ten leagues beyond the wild world's end,
Methinks it is no journey.

The antiquated words were one in the same.

Richard went to Philip. "I need you to run an errand with me," he whispered. With a hasty bow to the company about them, the two departed. They made their way to the foyer where that despicable Captain Balefire was staring intently out the window.

"Going somewhere?" Balefire asked without turning.

"We'll be back shortly," Richard replied.

From the misted window, Balefire watched them leave. Sipping champagne from his tall, fluted glass, Balefire took it all in.

"There they go on a wild goose chase," he said, "yet all the foul creatures are here."

The moon broke through the woolen sky. A misty light flooded the windows, bathing the vestibule in an eerie blue glow. The night, it seemed, had found something to say. Across the windowpane, the word *soon* was written out by an unseen hand. Balefire saluted the missive with his raised glass.

The sounds of scuffling and heavy breathing made Balefire turn his head. That spunky kitchen maid Phoebe was lugging in wood for the foyer fireplace. Balefire experienced a sudden and unusual desire to be kind. There were coats and wraps lying about on the benches nearby. Balefire picked up a handsome chesterfield and reached within the pocket. As luck, or magic, would have it, a leather billfold was there. It was loaded with cash.

Balefire held it up.

"Here, girl," he said. "I want you to take this and run."

Phoebe replied with a sound somewhere between a laugh and a snort. "Whatever do you mean, Captain?" she asked.

"I mean for you to leave this place as soon as possible. I won't go into detail. However, disaster is about to strike, and a distant but warm core within me desires that you avoid it."

"Disaster, sir?"

Balefire nodded. "No questions, please. Just leave."

"I can't take some stranger's money. I'll get sacked," the girl replied.

Balefire waved the wallet over a flaming candle. "Then do you suggest that I burn it? Take the money, Phoebe. The present owner will never miss it where he's going."

Phoebe could see the seriousness in Balefire's glassy dark eyes. A strange wave of realization swept over her. Phoebe let her load of firewood fall. Both she and Balefire grinned. Reaching out her hand, Phoebe took the money and promptly did as she was told.

Chapter Twenty-Six: The Forest Dark and Deep…

A mile or so from Cairy Hollow, Marie paused at a curve in the road. But for the raindrops trickling in the oak leaves above, all was silent, all was still. Even the once vicious wind failed to whisper.

Holding the small bundle of her belongings tight, Marie leaned against a fence rail and focused on the village in the valley below. Nestled in Nature's bowl, the tiny lights of Fairwell were a welcome sight. Chimney smoke curled in ribbons toward the pepper-colored clouds. Struggling to be seen, the moon broke through. Her gossamer rays brushed the roads and the rooftops. Sweeping shadows overtook the moon's brief and tender light. Still, the village slept without care, while watchful lamps flickered on wide window sills. The night smelled of mist and mushrooms. Marie sighed, and with that deep sigh, normal breath returned to her lungs.

But Marie's moment of serenity was not destined to last.

The wind resumed. A tremor rumbled the ground at her feet.

As if out of nowhere, a glass-sided hearse appeared. The plumed horses were soundless on the murky, wet road. Not even their elaborate harness offered a jingle of brass, or a rhythmic brushing of leather. The four phantom-like horses moved in unison. The wind did not touch them in any way. It blew past, cold and weary.

The driver, noticing Marie at the side of the road, tipped his distinctly crooked hat to her. Perched high upon the box seat, his face, with its long, hook nose, was ghostly. His cheeks were hollow, his furrowed eyes dim, and the pallor of his skin ashen gray. Tapping his hat back in place, he returned his gaunt hand to the reins. His long cape, like his hat and his horses, matched the somber color of night.

Marie could only stare.

This is not real, none of this is real, she told herself.

As if carried on air, the funeral coach floated by. Carvings of flowers and doves were strewn about, with elaborate scrolls embellishing the trim. The curtains beyond the beveled glass were drawn and held fast by tasseled cords. A coffin was carried within. The stark white box was tipped on its side toward Marie. No fragile corpse lay anywhere nearby. Marie thought to say something to the driver but changed her mind. For some strange reason, she knew he wouldn't hear her.

Silver clouds masked the troubled face of the moon. The fringe tassels above the toppled coffin shimmered and faded into shadow. Down into the peaceful valley the hearse proceeded, a single lantern swaying hypnotically at the back. Marie watched until the light grew smaller and disappeared somewhere near the doors to Graham's Tavern. As it vanished, the sound of a single bell tolled in the raw night air.

One for impending.

Ah, yes.

It answered the question in Marie's troubled mind.

Marie turned to the landscape behind her. She had no idea she'd paused at an ancient cemetery. Crumbled headstones laid forlorn about the dewy ground. It was a lonely and forgotten place. Even the entrance gate had rusted off its hinges. Marie couldn't make out the names the stones bore in that fogbound night. However, one particular epitaph was clearly legible. It read:

Here by the forest
dark and deep
I offer you
eternal sleep.

A heavy and hollow wind rushed through the trees, rustling the last of autumn's leaves and causing the arched branches to waver and groan. Holding the hood of her cape, Marie glanced up and, as she did, a cluster of white satin material tumbled from the tree. It hit the root-tangled ground with some force. Marie looked down.

It was the body of a slender, young woman. Her face lay buried in a puddle rippling with moonlight. The white satin gown she was wearing had long tears and shreds, and the ruffled train of it was knotted tightly about her throat. The woman's thin arms were slashed and bruised, and some of her pale white fingers were missing.

Marie dropped her bundle in panic and fell to her knees.

"Miss, oh, miss, are you alive?" Marie begged. Marie's voice was tight with fear, for she knew no such thing was possible. With trembling hands, Marie reached out to turn the poor girl over. With little effort, she did so. The body seemed light as a feather. Marie peered closer and gasped.

It was Cora Alexander. Her lovely cloud of dark hair was nearly all but ripped from her head. Her face was gashed, and her once vibrant eyes brutally pecked out. Cora's head tilted slightly, releasing a trail of bloodied rain from her ravaged eye sockets. Marie fell backward onto her meager bundle. Crying hysterically, she scrambled away until she had the strength to stand. Marie then ran to the village, ran with all her might, and not once did the terror-stricken girl look back.

****

A distance up that winding country lane, Richard and Philip arrived at the threshold of Ravenswood Forest. Tall in shadows and shrouded in mist, it loomed like a fortress before them. Chokeberries bowed in gray slivers of light. The men entered the hallowed grove of trees. Here, the breath of night sank into heavy clouds at their feet, and the two spoke little because of it.

At one bend, upon a grotto of crushed stones, they discovered a nearly devoured rabbit. The matted animal's gaze registered the agony of its final moments. This visage of life's fragility caused the two men to stop and stare. Scents of spilt blood and storm clouds invaded the air. Holding handkerchiefs to their faces, Richard and Philip ventured into the pulsing heart of the woods.

What once was a road now dwindled into darkness. Nature had reclaimed it as her sanctuary—a place where the commands of night would be heard and obeyed. Treetops swayed, and the shrill wind carried the chorus of their scarlet leaves up into the never-ending sky. Tiny lights flickered about the men. It was too late in the season for fireflies. Philip reached out for an errant glow and, just as his curling fingers drew near, it vanished with an audible hum.

All around them, vines and crouching bushes whispered to one another in the shadows. Their shapes and colors were indistinguishable in the gloom. The wild growth exhaled a misted perfume. The grass at their feet swirled and flattened with each scented breath. It was clear that everything altered its form in the cradle of night. Yet the forest did not sleep. The men could sense the many eyes of Ravenswood upon them. Sentinels of secrets they were, guarding the age-old mysteries that belonged to Lady Nature alone.

Richard ducked beneath the branch of a gnarled and moss-covered oak. Above his head, an alarmed owl screeched. Its burnished stare was deep with warning. Richard stepped warily toward the creature and it screeched again. "Blasted owl," he said.

"We could circle the tree. The owl will follow us with his eyes and eventually strangle himself," said Philip.

"Philp, even in your Napoleon Bonaparte costume, I believed you to be a man of reason," said Richard.

"This from some Romeo traipsing about on Halloween in search of a scarecrow," Philip said in reply.

The men walked on. The forest floor was strewn with years of fallen foliage. The top coating held a scent of mulled cider on a brisk October day. But the slick and forgotten layers below reeked of molded graves. There, in that earthy hollow, the men arrived at a divide in the woods. Ahead lay identical trails into obscurity. Richard couldn't recall which path to take. Ribbons of moonglow filtered through the arched branches. What scant light there was played above their heads like bony fingers to a harp. Richard looked toward the sky. It was filling in fast with newly braced storm clouds. One menacing billow blew past, creating the smoky outline of a raven's wing. Richard's eyes followed the shadow as it flew toward the west.

"That's the way," he said.

The wing tip hovered until Richard and Philip reached a clearing in the forest. Once there, the crepe feather cloud charred and fell to earth in the form of ashen snow. *We are born in water and perish in ash* both men heard within their heads. Neither commented to the other, believing his thought to be his own. The two men ran through the thick, unyielding Indian grass, dodging cinder drops. A trail path in the meadow swayed before them, as though a phantom scout on a horse of air were leading the way.

Just beyond, and huddled in shadow, was Bess Dalby's cottage. The wind wrapped around the weathered walls, making a low shudder, before whisking away. The old place was quiet and forlorn. The men paused at the uneven porch steps. Leaning forward, they gasped as they caught their breath.

Why are you here? Richard thought he heard somewhere above his head. Nervously, he glanced about. Tree branches were trembling, yet there wasn't a hint of a breeze. *Why are you here?* they seemed to whisper again.

"Did you hear that?" Richard asked Philip.

Philip did not answer. He was watching the vines that coiled slowly around the porch rails. At least, he believed they were. He blinked, and they stopped. Therefore, Philip trusted in all good faith that he had imagined it.

Richard watched in disbelief as the last of autumn's leaves leaned down. As they rustled, it seemed they sang:

The moments of delight, how sweet,
but ah, how swift they flew…

Why are you here? the murmuring ground repeated. Philip heard it this time. He looked at Richard and shivered.

"Now, whose mournful cottage is this, and why are we looking for a scarecrow?" he asked.

"The owner of this lonely abode was a woman named Bess Dalby. She's gone now. Died mysteriously, so I heard. Civette's mother claimed Bess was a witch of sorts. Who really knows? Maybe these woods are full of them. I learned only today that Civette's uncle was in love with Bess Dalby. Leona, apparently, despised her. My guess is that Bess was involved with a man Civette's mother was taken with."

"Remind me to leave this licentious little village and move to an indifferent city as soon as possible," said Philip.

Richard replied nothing. Philip put his hand on Richard's shoulder. "It might be best for you to consider moving away. You know, Richard, some place where life is meant to be lived by young people, and not all these old ghosts from the past."

"I intended to marry Civette," Richard reminded him. "Civette and Cairy Hollow should have been mine. And if it weren't for this complete counterfeit of a man, this supposed Sir Adrian Bramwell, Civette and I would be engaged this very night. I know it. That phony doesn't care for Civette. He's lavishing attention on her only to annoy me. Oh, and he went after Cora Alexander only because he learned she and I once were involved. That monstrous man wants nothing more than to bedevil me."

"Oh, Richard, really. You're believing your wild thoughts and behaving badly because of this supposed rich man who showed up at the Cairys' door? He's handsome. So what? You're giving the situation too much weight. The man is a rogue, and he's pursuing

Miss Middleton not to annoy you but simply to flatter himself. When all is said and done, and Sir Whatshisname wanders away in pursuit of someone else's lady, Civette will calm down and once again be your love."

Richard hesitated before speaking. "The plain truth is, she never did love me," he said. For the first time, perhaps, Richard comprehended the words he had uttered. "We've known each other since she was five and I was a worldly seven. We've been like brother and sister, Civette and I. When we grew older, she always confided in me about her trials and tribulations with other men. I suspect even in marriage she'd continue to do the same. A marriage, I will now confess, which no longer includes visions of me. She told me so tonight, Philip. Civette and I are through."

Philip shook his head. "Nonsense. People in love are always imagining things. Now, enough about your unwelcomed rival, and on to the scarecrow. Where was this mysterious effigy when last you saw it?"

"Over in that forsaken patch of field. There it stood, all sticks and spokes and molded hay. I remember thinking that scarecrow had a distinctly evil tone to it, even if it was headless. And now, the demonic creature is nowhere to be found."

"Well, it's not like it up and strolled away on its own, Richard. Let's go have a look around, shall we?" said Philip.

The two men went to the field. The horizon's edge and the curtain of night were one and the same. They could have easily been turned upside down. Richard and Philip wandered through the wilting stalks of corn and discovered no ramshackle guardian for any part of Bess

Dalby's diminished gardens. If there were any mysteries to be had here, the night was shielding them.

The wind grew bolder as the sky deepened with thick brushes of blue. The moon broke through momentarily, but with a misty and meager light. It was almost as if the silent orb was weeping. Above their heads, ten ravens rode the crest of the wind. Their feathers were oily blue in the scant moon-spill. Richard and Philip watched as, upon the ground, the ravens' shadows reflected the startling silvery image of a demon's face.

"The Glass of Truth," Richard murmured. He then shouted to Philip above the gale. "What we've been looking for has been at Cairy Hollow all along. The mirror in the ballroom—the Glass of Truth. It holds the key to everything, Philip. We must go back."

The men turned and fled into the beckoning woods. The ravens frolicked with frantic jeers at Richard and Philip's determination. The murder of ten circled again, and with a flap of their jet-black wings, the storm clouds blew with a vengeance toward Cairy Hollow.

Chapter Twenty-Seven: Messages from the Past

Having welcomed his guests with elegant smiles and elaborate worries over the cost of this evening's spectacle, John Cairy retired to his library for a much-needed moment of solitude. A muffled knock sounded, and the door opened over the musty carpet. John turned and frowned.

"Olen Devereux, what might I do for you?" he asked.

Olen Devereux entered the room. John recalled the night, now more than two decades before, when his sister confirmed that Olen Devereux and Bess Dalby were lovers. When he'd heard the news, John Cairy had never conceived of living as long as this. His reasons and his hopes had died that very hour.

"Bess told me stories about this place," Olen remarked, as if to himself. "For obvious reasons, I was never invited. Bess said there were always parties here, and so many guests. She wondered if it unnerved you to be alone."

Bess was correct. John despaired of his life without her. The bleaker of his recollections preyed upon him in his quiet moments. Like gaunt, gray ghosts, never speaking, never warning, they were always present as a reminder of the errors that paved his existence. When he was young, John had no qualms in allowing his life to be governed and arranged. Because of his happy youth, he trusted there would still be chances. However, Time, with her ever-spinning hands, had brutally ripped them all away. Time was no healer of wounds. Time delighted in keeping one's wounds open to bleed.

"You took away the only thing that mattered to me. What more could you possibly want?" John asked.

"My sole desire is that you listen. I have no other yearnings left. Whatever I craved along the way in life means nothing to me now."

John looked at Olen, truly looked at him. Much to John's dismay, Olen Devereux was still a youthful-looking man. Not a year, not a moment, had marred his handsomeness. But there was something odd about him, too. Olen's voice seemed to be a separate entity from his lips. His gaze was distant, and the air about him deathly cold.

"I remember one particular morning, oh, years ago now, when you were supposed to visit Bess," said Olen. "I can still see her in her lovely green dress with hawthorn flowers pinned in her hair. She was wearing that clasp you gave her. The jeweled one with the serpent on a limb. Bess was pacing back and forth before the windows, watching, ever hopeful, as the mantel clock marked the time. As she paced, Bess told me stories about the two of you—enviable stories that I always held in my heart as a hope that, someday, a decent woman like Bess would feel the same for me."

John was startled by Olen's confession. What did he mean? John did his best to dismiss the wild thoughts in his head and listen.

"On that day Bess waited for you, you never came. Three days passed. I went to see Bess again. She was so thin, so pale. She was exhausted, she said. But in truth, it was much more than that. Being what and where I am now, I know. Her hopes had been such fragile things, fashioned with memories made prettier by time. Nothing lingered to offer her strength. Not a single wish survived.

"I stayed with her that entire day and into the night. Bess spoke to me in faint whispers. Beyond the window, the creatures of the forest stopped their busy chatter. They knew. They were helping Bess to be heard. She told me what she needed to say, closed her eyes, and vowed to dream no more.

"Hour by hour, I sat by Bess Dalby's side, clutching her cold and lifeless hand. And when a forceful wind swept through the house, rustling curtains, and slamming doors, it took Bess's spirit along with it. I felt it leave, just as a light from your golden pin flared and fled for the open window. I heard Bess's voice as though she'd spoken from the clouds. She said, *Look for me in the light—never in the dark. I will always be near.*

"But she meant those words for you, John Cairy, not me. Yes, I loved her. I loved her then, and I love her still. But I never stood a chance. So I took what I could of her kindness, and remained her friend. Bess had so few people in her life after Leona got through destroying her with accusations and lies. Worse still, Leona swayed Bess's mind when Bess was at her weakest. If only I hadn't waited three days to return. At least I was with our darling girl at the end. While they say it can never be so, I know Bess Dalby died for love."

Olen reached into a pocket of his dress jacket. Retrieving a folded sheet of paper, he held it out with a smooth and veinless hand. "This is for you," Olen said. "Bess told me when the time came to give it to you."

"How can I ever thank you?" John asked.

"By telling Leona that you know everything, and that she's lucky if you don't kill her. Best of all, John, you needn't explain a thing. I've just spent the last hour in the study with her. Your sister is now immersed in a hell of her own making."

Without so much as a farewell, Olen departed through the terrace doors. John watched as Olen Devereux became one with the mist. John wanted to stop him. There was so much John could have said. But he did nothing. Leona had inflicted a lifetime of pain. That was true. However, John had himself to blame as well. There was a better life John Cairy might have lived, but his many weaknesses had tied him to this one.

The moment John unfolded the paper, he knew what would be written there. It was a handwritten copy of the poem *Thanatopsis*, by William Cullen Bryant. John recited from memory along with his own handwriting:

To him who in the love of Nature holds
Communion with her visible forms, she speaks
A various language; for his gayer hours
She has a voice of gladness, and a smile
And eloquence of beauty, and she glides
Into his darker musings, with a mild
And healing sympathy, that steals away
Their sharpness, ere he is aware. When thoughts
Of the last bitter hour come like a blight
Over thy spirit, and sad images
Of the stern agony, and shroud, and pall,
And breathless darkness, and the narrow house,
Make thee to shudder, and grow sick at heart;—
Go forth, under the open sky, and list
To Nature's teachings, while from all around—
Earth and her waters, and the depths of air—

Comes a still voice—
John could read no more. Bowing his head, he wept.
****

Emerging from the study, Leona took herself to a distant corner of the ballroom where she stood not speaking, not feeling. On impulse, Leona turned her head and looked out the window. Her gaze fell upon the towering oak at the entrance gate. Leona half expected to see Bess Dalby there, fully alive and gazing with knowing eyes upon this lavish gathering of fools. But no—Bess was dead. Only the memory of her lingered there. Leona laughed bitterly. Even in death, Bess had won. Leona's brother and the only man Leona ever truly wanted were both in love with Bess. For John and Olen, Bess Dalby would never grow old. She would always remain the warmth in their hearts and the delight in their minds.

Meanwhile, Leona would grow older, day by day. She would begin to feel pain, and suffer from it. Her child would care less and less for her, moving in a world of pleasure meant solely for the young and the beautiful. This moment marked, for Leona Cairy Middleton, her stark realization of the beginning of the end.

The bright colors and noises of the ballroom restored Leona to the present. She watched as Sir Adrian Bramwell asked her daughter for a dance, and she accepted. As a couple, they were breathtaking to behold. They placed themselves beneath the fiery blue light of a chandelier, while Captain Balefire addressed the orchestra.

"Please play *Come, Dear Civette, Quit the Town*," he instructed.

The conductor politely informed Captain Balefire

that the lady in this tune was named Amanda.

"We care not for Amanda," Balefire declared. "We care not for any name but that of Civette. And now we shall dance." He turned to the waiting guests. "A dance, everyone! A jolly dance," he exclaimed. Balefire then waltzed about the room with Adrian's walking stick in his hands. Placing the walking stick by the draped Glass of Truth, Balefire turned and studied Adrian and Civette with such evil satisfaction.

The musicians cued up for the song. The conductor tapped upon his music stand with his baton, and the resonance of it tore through Leona like the jagged edge of a broken glass. The night, with all its searing suspicions and truths, was draining her. Leona watched as her daughter took command of the room. The glistening floors were Civette's stage, the walls her canvas, and the candlelight a beacon for her reflective charms. It was evident that Civette had conquered Leona's place as the ornament of the house.

The music began, and the poetry of it soared in graceful circles toward the frescoed ceiling. *Behold the wintry storms are gone, a gentle radiance glads the sky. 'Tis love and beauty all we see.* For Leona, this vision was marred with wretchedness. Leona watched the dancers glide past as if on wings. The air in the room grew heavy. Evan opened the shuttered windows, and as each pane rose, storm breezes tenderly caressed the thin drapes and the party guests' costumes. Those on the dance floor turned their heads at every corner, smiling and nodding to the others who stood admiring from the sidelines. Not once, however, did anyone's eyes meet Leona's. It was as if they all knew the secrets and the shame Leona had stored in the darkness of her soul. And now, like her brother, they all wished her gone.

From the corner of her eye, Civette saw Richard and Philip return to the entranceway of the ballroom. Richard began watching Civette with triumphant vindication. Civette no longer cared. She turned her head in slow motion toward Adrian. With billowing pulses that matched the beat of her heart, the dancers, the music, and all the onlookers suddenly vanished. There was only one man Civette intended to be with and to cherish forever. She would choose the man who understood her. She would be with the divine creature who saw her as more wondrous than that taunting star in her dream. Civette was settled. Her incessant longing for happiness finally focused on its cure. Civette was officially finished with Richard Marlow and the transparent world. Civette was through with the light. Desire possessed her. It drove through her like water in darkness.

With a wave of her hand, Civette signaled the musicians to cease. Civette waited until everyone's attention was focused on her. Removing Adrian's clasp from her long satin glove, she held it up as though it was a trophy won in a match. "I will wear it now. I will be yours," Civette pledged. Her eyes were intent upon that which she believed she wanted.

"My darling, my own," said Adrian. For the first time ever, Adrian could feel his heart fully pounding. He took Civette into his arms and kissed her deeply. Her breath became the life he realized he was always meant to cling to. Across the stunned room, Balefire folded his arms and leaned against the wall. Despite its few and unforeseen twists, his staged masterpiece was drawing to a close. He was grateful that his one major obstacle, namely Miss Cora Alexander, had been efficiently carried away.

"What the Devil hath joined together, let no honest man even try to put asunder," Balefire murmured.

Richard's voice boomed across the floor. "And I will destroy your plan, Sir Adrian Bramwell, if it's the last thing I do."

A wave of conversation swept over the crowd. "I stand corrected," Balefire said with an astonished grin.

Chapter Twenty-Eight: A Clock Stopped

A Clock stopped—
Not the Mantel's
Geneva's farthest skill
Can't put the puppet bowing
That just now dangled still—

~Emily Dickinson

"See for yourself what you really are," Richard exclaimed.

The bewildered guests looked to where Richard and Philip stood by the Glass of Truth. The two men drew back the velvet drapes. At first, no one reacted. The light of the nearest chandelier engulfed the glass. Its brilliance overpowered the room, blinding everyone in its path.

Shielding his beautiful eyes, Adrian moved toward the mirror. Civette, with her hand on Adrian's shoulder, cautiously followed. The party guests either craned their necks or inched their way forward as well. Still, the haunted mirror was aglow. How could so much light spring from one ordinary looking-glass? Adrian moved close enough to block the radiance. Leaning forward, he was horrified by what lurked within.

Adrian grabbed his gilded walking stick and raised it in defense. Whatever it was that existed in the reflection raised the rusted spoke of a weathervane. Adrian recoiled. The image did the same. Adrian dropped his walking stick. Its clatter echoed on the polished wood floor. The spoke within the glass jounced noiselessly.

"What prank is this? Who is this deformed creature?" Adrian demanded to know.

With hesitation, Civette looked around Adrian's shoulder. What she saw caused her to cry out with fear. Adrian held her back.

"Don't be afraid, Civette. This is merely an illusion brought on by that fiendish Captain Balefire."

"Oh, this is no illusion," vowed that very man. Balefire held his arms out wide. "This, my friends, is truth brought about by black magic."

As Balefire spoke, the alien plants in the ballroom began to quiver and crawl. Curious lemon queens invaded a silver punch bowl. Buzzing knots of maidenhairs attached themselves to a lady's cape. Dogwood blooms and garnet daylilies bowed with laughter, while long tendrils of Japanese maple leaves and tangles of grape arbor snapped free from their restrictive bowls and slithered their way toward the mirror.

The guests began to run. Men were shouting to the ladies to exit in any way possible. One woman climbed out a window. In her fear, she was not proud. The younger Reed women were leading their elder sister out. Priscilla Reed kept halting, cupping her ear, and demanding to know what the riot was about. Their nephew Steven lobbed a heavy vase at the Glass of Truth. The vase fractured into pieces, while the mirror and its hideous image remained intact.

The light in the ballroom was trembling. Agitated candles reflected in the windowpanes, mimicking wheels of fire in an endless sky. In an alcove beyond, bench seats and music stands overturned as the musicians deserted their posts. Scrolled sheets of music fluttered in the unsettled air. A disoriented woman ran through the kitchen. The silk panels of her harlequin costume were streaked with food from the jostled buffet. Throughout the hall, trays, dinner plates, and delicate glassware tumbled upon chairs or crashed onto the floor. A candelabra plummeted, extinguishing itself in a sculptured pool of wax. Beneath its lazy smoke, the silver piece appeared to be choking.

Convulsing with tears, Margaret Hall claimed she could not find her friends. Where were Gertie and Cora? Where could they possibly be? Philip Osgood rushed to Margaret's side and gently guided the delirious girl to the door. With a great burst of noise, the Cairys' dogs emerged from their basement lair. Around the ballroom they raced, mindless of the abandoned shoes, melted wax, shattered glass, and sticky streams of wine. Evan whistled sharply to them. With slinking movements of guilt, the dogs followed him out the front door. Their incessant barking echoed in the night.

Sarah was about to leave when she thought of Phoebe and Marie. Without hesitation, Sarah dashed up the stairs and along the dark passageway that led to the servants' quarters. A strange light moved in phantom streaks along the polished doors. Sarah could hear the chaos from the ballroom below. The frantic sounds crawled up the walls around her. A floorboard creaked, long and slow. Sarah paused.

"Hello," she called out quietly.

At once and all together, every door in the hallway opened wide and slammed shut. Sarah screamed and stood rigid. The force of the air current rustled her clothes. A scent of misted fog permeated the hall. Sarah sensed a presence.

"Hello," she said again. This time, she spoke in a whisper.

A beam the hue of sunken gold flared and died. There, at the far end of the hall, Sarah saw a pale imitation of herself. Her counterimage slowly approached, floating several inches off the ground. Even though she knew she was staring at an alien form of herself, Sarah asked the specter who she was.

The apparition ignored Sarah's question. "We're going to exist here forever," it claimed as if spoken from its mind. Sarah found herself unable to reply. Her mirror self merely smiled and repeated, "Forever."

Within a fierce gust of wind, the ghostly being flew backward through an opened door and disappeared. Sarah followed her image inside. It was a maid's room, with crackled walls and no windows. No one was there. As Sarah turned to leave, the door slammed shut and fastened itself. Sarah tugged at the handle and called out for help. No one could hear her. No one ever would. Sarah was locked in to stay.

****

Downstairs, John entered the ballroom from his library. The horrors before him fully registered on his face. John looked anxiously about the hall until he found Civette. Making his way through the capsized furniture and the frightened crowd, John called to her. Across the lawless room, Richard was doing the same. Civette could not see or hear either man. A small child was clinging to a leg of the sideboard. Richard knelt and, with soothing words, he carried the crying child out. Richard would return for Civette as soon as he found this poor girl's mother, he vowed.

Immersed in the shadows of an archway, John discovered Raylene. Her entire being was white and expressionless. John looked to Civette, who finally noticed him, and then again to Raylene. John guided the unsteady nursemaid to safety. John was certain his niece would easily escape on her own. Civette was an intelligent girl. She was nothing like her mother. As John and Raylene departed, madness still reigned.

Leona managed her way toward her daughter. Civette held out her arms to her mother for comfort. Her plea was not met.

"Give me that pin," Leona demanded. Civette could only shrink in horror. "Give it to me now, girl. It represents nothing but betrayal and pain." Leona's expression was wild. She threw her arms wide, indicating the ballroom and all that was Cairy Hollow. "It's gone now. Everything that was supposed to be mine has been miserably lost," she told Civette. Leona did not wait for Civette's reaction. She tore the jeweled serpent from Civette's bold red dress.

"Save me, Mommy, please," Civette begged.

Her own daughter's anguish didn't mean a thing. "There's nothing left to save," she said. Leona turned and stumbled away. Not once did she look back.

Restored to her half-lustrous-raven, half-grotesque-human form, Sorrow flew into the room. Eira Corbin noticed her, nodded, and calmly hobbled toward the door. "I must fly," the old woman said.

Once outside, Midwife Corbin moved against the wind. With a claw-hold on her loosened hair, she approached a gnomish grove of apple trees. With her arrival, the grove electrified. An ivory down covered the old woman's face. Her fluttering train became feathers of white, and her feeble legs grew sturdy and grasping. In the flickering light, Corbin turned her head to reveal all-knowing eyes that burned copper-bright. The raven-like being took three odd hops and was airborne. As foretold, Eira Corbin flew away.

****

Inside the ballroom, Civette cringed as she heard the man she once knew as Sir Adrian Bramwell speak. "Don't leave me, Civette. Balefire was lying to you. He was lying to all of us. That abomination is nothing more than a magic trick."

Adrian took Civette by her arm. As he did, Civette could see and feel the twisted flails and withered sticks that comprised his being. The sound Civette made was that of a scared and wounded animal.

"Civette," Adrian begged. "I am not what lies in wait beyond that mirror. I am not altogether what you believe. It is possible that beneath this there is a man who loves you with all the power of his newfound heart. It is possible!"

This the poor creature tried to say, but he could hardly be heard against Civette's screams. The once incomparable Sir Adrian Bramwell let go of her arm. Civette collapsed to the floor. Trembling and crying, Civette began to crawl away. She was mindless of her rich clothing and her clean white hands. Tears flooded the makeup from her eyes, and her golden bracelets rolled in circles from her wrists.

"How can you turn against me like this?" Adrian begged. "How can you be so cruel?"

Richard Marlow returned to the room. Civette ran

like a wild thing into his arms. Richard sheltered Civette close. Still Civette screamed and cried, her chest heaving against the soiled silk of Emmeline's dress. A delicate hem of blood-red beads broke away. The tiny pieces bounced about the floor like tiny shards of ice. Civette kept uttering, "*Monster, monster, monster,*" as Richard coaxed her toward the door.

Hearing this added frightening images and feelings to Adrian's already reeling mind. He felt his scalp being pierced by quills. Wafts of decaying hay and the hot iron aroma of charged clouds filled his lungs. He heard a hollow chorus of voices beneath his feet. An echo of thunder bore through him. His newborn heart pulsed against it. His body lurched. An unearthly sound surrounded him, forming a cyclone. It chanted in his mind:

From the hag and hungry goblin
That into rags would rend ye,
The spirit that stands by the naked man
In the Book of Moons defend ye,
That of your five sound senses
You'll never be forsaken.
Now wander from your selves with Tom
Abroad to beg your bacon.

Adrian realized that Balefire was singing the very song he heard in his head. All the guests were gone. The hum of Balefire's unearthly voice echoed about the ballroom. Once his mocking tune was done, Balefire dissolved into laughter. At least, that's what Adrian believed to have happened. The great room fell to silence. Only Sorrow remained.

A sudden vision burned through Adrian's frantic mind. He saw himself hanging lifelessly from a wooden frame. At his side was a gentle young girl, telling stories and singing songs. Together, they watched storm clouds and sunsets and shooting stars. The girl would, with time, confess all her youthful heartaches. He never said a word. But she knew he understood. One autumn day, she stood upon the stonewall and announced, "My name is Bess." The sound of her voice echoed around the somber room. *Bess, Bess, Bess.* The girl got older with each whisper of her name. She made him fine clothes, and cared for him as a constant friend. But then, one day, she was no longer there. Something horrid had happened to her—something Adrian was not able to see. But the woodland creatures knew. They came by the dozens to mourn. Days and months and years passed. Adrian had been left alone, until one troubled morning an ebony woman stepped up before his disheveled self and kissed him. Her kiss became the spark that brought him power, that brought him beauty, that brought him life.

The semblance of Adrian Bramwell looked back into the mirror and finally understood.

"Oh, heavenly God, I am that monster."

Everything within him went cold.

Chapter Twenty-Nine: Glimmer of the Moon

Moments passed. Adrian faced the unmoving Sorrow.

"Everyone has deserted me but you—and that." Adrian pointed toward the mirror where his true reflection aped every gesture he made. "Civette has left me. Her heart has turned away. All the light and the warmth within me has disappeared. That which I loved, and all who pretended to love me, are gone."

With reluctance, Adrian addressed his own image. "If you are me, if you feel the same loss, then show some pity. Speak to me. Who are you? What am I? Why are we put on this earth, only to be made to feel and to guess and to suffer?"

His reflection merely gaped at him in a mum and demented way. Its stick shoulders were sagging. Strands of rancid pumpkin dangled from its coarse and quivering mouth. The creature in the glass could barely stand.

"You will not answer. No, you merely ridicule my doubts with a vacant look of horror. You poor, delirious mute, all made up of broken chairs and flails and rotted gourds. You cannot escape your prison of moonlight and glass, no more than I could my own miserable creation."

Something of his wretchedness got through to Sorrow. Crumbling to guilty tears, she threw herself at his knees. Adrian broke away. "You created me out of straw and mud for your own selfish schemes. You are the monster."

"My dreams were for all of us, and never selfish," she vowed.

"Between the dawn and the close of one brilliant day, I walked this realm of yours. I was thrilled with wonder and calmed by knowledge. I trembled with joy and passion, and was exalted by sympathy. The gifts of power, beauty, and love were right there before me. I believed that this existence and even time itself were mine to conquer. But no. Look at me. Look at me, Sorrow, if you dare. I am nothing more than corrupted dust."

Adrian lifted his once revered face to the heavens. "You must despise me, God. You had no hand in my creation. Why would you breathe life into something as vulgar as me? No, it was a senseless demon and his followers who put me here to be despised and tortured for their own amusement, for their own narrow-minded plans. At least I can thank you, God, that I now know who I am." He indicated the horrid phantasm, trapped in glass. "Monster!"

The specter pointed back, the cracked and dried leather flails upon its hand lurching to and fro. "Hear me, scarecrow. I am thy soul," it vowed.

"It lies," Sorrow said through her tears. "It is nothing more than an apparition. You are a man."

The so-called apparition sneered at Sorrow. "And what, pray tell, is a man?" it chanted in a harsh and broken whisper. "Man is but a mirror wherein imps and angels play charades, make faces, mope and pull one another's hair, until that sly urchin Death slivers the glass, and the bare coffin boards show underneath."

Adrian seized his walking stick. The ruby sphere

was glowing bright. "If we are only illusions, I'll play your urchin Death and shatter the glass. Let's see which one of us survives."

Just as the heated stone came close to striking the mirror, Adrian's grisly reflection rippled away. Captain Balefire appeared, bathed in shadows of maligned gold and green. His voice seemed to emanate from a distant plain.

"I don't recommend it. Break this glass and beware—your youthful soul, Civette, and this irresistible world itself shall crash in a million shattered dreams to the ground."

"If I cannot be beautiful, if I cannot be loved, I don't want to live."

Adrian made ready to strike once again, when an aroma of gardenias enveloped the glass. The vision before him went static with a great wiry noise and became Civette. Her lovely face was eclipsed by shadows yet veiled in light. Adrian dropped to his knees.

"My darling, you did come back to me. Your smile is my hope. I can almost feel the touch of your hand. You no longer despise me, me your desperate admirer, humbled at your feet. Please tell me that you love me. Oh, Civette, my fiery angel above this cold, uncaring earth! Only you can change my fate. In your radiance, I am no longer a mockery, but a man."

The scent of gardenias flared and was gone. A celestial echo filled the air, and Civette drifted away as though she were sinking in a pool of lucent water. Ashen curls of smoke rolled over the glass and Balefire reappeared, roaring with laughter.

"Oh, the drama. Has nothing I taught you stuck in that festered gourd you call your brain? *Oh, Civette, my fiery angel above this cold earth.* Until you've studied the course of a woman's heart, you will be forever miserable."

"You do not understand," said Adrian. "Through Civette, I was born to live."

Balefire shook his head. "Never, never mix up mothers and hopeful wives, my friend. It's positively fatal."

"I want another chance at Civette's love," Adrian pleaded. "Allow me to try again."

"Another spin on life's cruel carousel?" Balefire replied. "Well, why not! It was highly entertaining in the first round. And every director, like myself, prays their production survives opening night. But do you honestly believe you can provide your audience with the same thrilling finale on a second run? And your actors—can you trust they're up for one more go? John Cairy seems spent. I do worry about his health. And the sound of his sister's voice is not to be endured. She behaves as though she's French and talented. Guess again, dearie. My fear is that Leona Middleton will demand even more of the stage action and forever ruin the deeper meaning of the piece.

"I sense we can all agree that Richard Marlow was a wretched bore. We really should've discovered a more praiseworthy rival for you—someone with strong looks and brave words, and not that lazy excuse, whining and moaning and taking up air. At least Miss Iris Owen recognized her shortcomings, cut her losses, and quit. Goodnight and goodbye. The maids, I will admit, did splendidly in their minor roles. Marie added depth to what should have been a dead-end part, Sarah was a superb tragedian, and that dark horse Phoebe showed some spunk. But, back to our main core, and especially to our ingénue. Will the audience find Civette as alluring and lively the next time? I have my doubts. She crawled out of this ballroom like a rabid racoon. It wasn't the prettiest performance I've ever witnessed, I can guarantee you that."

"Please," Sorrow begged. "I can't stand any more of this." She took Adrian by his hands, feeling the weathered flails, and trying her best not to flinch. "We ravens from the forest, this was our doing. My sister, with my urging, was the one to finalize the spell. Forgive me. Forgive us. I never realized what our drive for vengeance would do."

Sorrow looked deep into Adrian's eyes. The golden light she had admired at the onset of his magical creation was gone.

"My poor broken and shunned creature," she said. "There are thousands upon thousands of good-for-nothing humans in this world, all made up of inferior trash. Yet they never see themselves for who they really are."

Sorrow turned to Balefire in the mirror. "Why should Bess's scarecrow be the only one to know himself, and then be made to grieve for it?"

Balefire sighed. "Oh, do stop. You're becoming dreary."

"This was a hideous idea from the start, Captain Balefire, a sick, twisted scheme."

"You and Mirth were more than satisfied with the 'sick, twisted theme' until now, my dear. Why the sudden remorse? Revenge and Sentiment are oil and water to each other—they don't mix. You'll never see them invited to the same party, and for good reason. You must raise your glass to only one at a time."

"Have you no feelings, no heart?"

"Sorrow, Sorrow, Sorrow. You know where I came from. I am an empty creature without cares. When nothing matters, nothing can be lost. Your good opinion gone bad does not scar my well-being. My moods and my heart are nothing like yours. They pulse with great intensity to the beat of evil. I am gloriously dead inside."

Sorrow stood tall. "You're nothing but an instigator sprung from a cursed weathervane. You tricked us into this. You know you did."

Sorrow's threatening posture had no effect on Balefire. "To be sure, I dragged you two kicking and screaming all the way," he calmly replied. "You and your sister changed the course of Civette Middleton's life forever, and you never should have. All your sulking and dramatic revenge over a cottage which, in the long run, was better off getting leveled to the ground. Your anger was entirely misdirected. Whatever happens to Civette now is on your hands. I merely made your wish come true. Don't accuse me of its consequences. Those are also yours to bear."

Sorrow was reduced to silence. Balefire frowned at Adrian. "As for you, my hodgepodge of sticks, stop groveling. You shame me."

Adrian looked up. His decaying likeness peered warily from behind Balefire's back. "Is that really me, Balefire? Can I honestly be that repulsive thing?"

"When man questions fate, it's bad timing. When a monster does, it's simply bad taste. You mustn't be so skeptical. Of course you are that repulsive creature. I should know. I created you. And you ought to appreciate that honor, as short-lived as it may have seemed,"

Balefire replied.

"You should have let me be."

Balefire scoffed. "May I remind you, *Sir Bramwell*, that twenty-four hours ago you were a stenching clump of compost on a stick? I gave you potential. What other scarecrow can claim he ruled a gentleman's estate for all of one glorious day?"

"Remove that vision from my sight," Adrian pleaded.

"That vision you're despairing of is your true reflection. You could no more remove it from your sight than you could your own shadow," said Balefire.

Adrian held his head in his hands. He could feel it rotting away. He trembled. "I am nothing but a fool."

"All mortals are fools. Like you, they were rummaged out of earth's endless muck, and like you, they'll all get flung back to the dunghill. If anything in the interim was gratifying, then the messy voyage was worth it. Wouldn't you agree?" said Balefire.

Adrian Bramwell was losing strength. He could barely speak. "Civette was everything to me. To her, I was not pitiful. Because of her, I knew what it was to love and be loved."

"Not this rambling rubbish again," said Balefire. "You earthly creatures and love. You take a simple emotion that is so easily acknowledged—*Hello, how do you do? I believe I'm in love. You as well? Now, isn't that nice.* There. Wasn't that effortless? But, no, you weaklings insist on burdening desire with chaos. What starts off as madness and moonbeams always ends in misery, yet you stupidly try for it again and again and again."

Sorrow held the scarecrow close. "You have too

much heart for this cold, compassionless world. We will go home—home to the forest where all will be as it was before the heartache and the pain. I promise you. Oh, I do promise you!"

"Good luck to you all when that cottage roof finally gives up its ghost and caves in," Balefire declared.

As if Balefire had willed it, splintering glass resounded above their heads. The domed skylight fractured and gave way beneath the force of Mirth's talons as she swept into the room. Restored to her artificial beauty, Mirth landed in the center of the ballroom with effortless grace. Taking in the carnage all around her, Mirth grinned.

"Well, well, look at the fun I missed," she said. With rigid strides, she approached the grieving Adrian. "You disappoint me," she trilled at him.

Balefire snapped his fingers. "See? I told you. As with all fascinations, it's only a matter of time 'til they cease to be."

Mirth circled Adrian, her messages rushing in echoes about his ears. "Don't listen to my sister. We used you. You heard her. She even admitted it. And that other one was no good either. That high and mighty Miss Middleton. She used you, too."

"I—I thought she cared for me," said Adrian.

"It was all pretend. With her type it always is," Mirth declared. "Observe how quickly the girl ran away. You were merely a pawn to make that idiot beau of hers jealous. It was a lark to that privileged young miss, a pouting brat's game of make-believe. Forget that disgusting little schemer. Forget ill-fated mankind. You deserve far better."

"I wanted to be like them," said Adrian.

"Human? Why?" asked Mirth.

"A human's life is full of irrational whims and doubt and pain," added Sorrow.

"You said so yourself not ten minutes ago," Balefire reminded him. "Do you not recall? You really should do your best to remember the important lessons in life, just as I have. It drives others insane when one is consistently right."

Adrian paused to think and, for the first time, memories fashioned by his own will flooded his brain. He was too new at life to comprehend that it was his determination that erased whatever ugliness was attached to these gossamer visions. He was too naïve to realize that it was he who gave his fanciful recollections more substance than truth. What did that matter when his inner thoughts rang with such beauty? He sensed the force he now held—a faculty with which he could easily drown out reality. Memories, especially those forged from one's own will, were truly powerful weapons.

"What is it?" asked Mirth. "What are you remembering?"

Adrian looked up as if his mind's imagination could project itself there, hovering as real as life before his eager eyes. "Whispers of smoke fading away in the glimmer of the moon," he replied. Adrian reached up to touch something only he could see there.

Balefire groaned. "You are hopeless," he said.

Adrian lowered his hand against the glare of the glass. "I am a common beggar fashioned from dust, and bewitched by a demon. I am cursed. Shut out the light. I want no more of life. All is lost. I am done."

In a glaring flash, Balefire stepped out of the mirror. "There you go, quoting *Paradise Lost*. Just like the rest of this ignorant planet, you'll go on forever blaming forces like me." Balefire paused and sighed. "All right, my boy. Just like our little maid, Phoebe, you've managed to evoke a soft spot in my blackened core. All is not lost. I'm going to grant you one last golden opportunity. Behold."

Balefire took cover in the shadows just as Civette appeared at the door. At the sight of her, the Raven Ladies diminished to their bird forms, and scurried to the crest of a curtained window.

"If you promise that what's in that mirror is nothing more than trickery, I will believe you," said Civette.

Adrian replied nothing. Civette went to him, her gaze fixed on what she prayed was a false reflection. "How wrong I was to judge you in this way. Furthermore, how wrong I was to measure your worth by looks alone. There are many attractive people on this earth. But few are driven by kindness and generosity, such as you. All my life, I've been given whatever I wanted. But what you gave me in one short day was far more precious. You made me see the good that I could make of myself. You made me believe I should try. How foolish of me to run from a parlor game trick. Beauty lives only a short while on one's face. True beauty, such as you have, lives forever in the heart."

Balefire emerged from his shield of darkness. "There now, Jacky Boy. You've been granted the gift of choice. Option one. Remain with this woman. Marry her, if you're so inclined. Grow old and ugly together, and die."

"Such an awful waste," said the Raven Ladies from their perch.

Civette lifted her head at the sound. The Raven

Ladies alighted and stood before Civette. Civette watched as the pair transformed to their astounding visages of beauty. Civette was too fascinated to feel fear. Their darting eyes pinned on the girl, Sorrow and Mirth fanned their glossy, feather-downed capes.

"Growing old is a catastrophe," said Sorrow.

"And ugliness should never be allowed," said Mirth.

"Ignore the girl and inform our prince about option number two," they declared together.

Balefire rendered a swift bow. "The ladies are correct. A creation as transcendent as you, dear Adrian, should never fall prey to disintegration. Besides, there would always be something powerful and mystical inside you, reminding you of what once was, drawing you back to our world."

"Ours is a magical realm of power and spectacle that makes a place like this dull and unimaginative," claimed Sorrow.

"It can be your realm, too," hinted Balefire.

"Where else does the night seem so alive?" added Mirth.

Adrian was instantly surrounded. Balefire and the Raven Ladies barraged him with thoughts—thoughts that jabbed at him like pins. Did he understand the abhorrent thing those humans just did? They ran from a lovely being they, not one hour before, had admired above measure. They condemned him to suffer alone. However, Adrian still had recourse. He could even the score with those distasteful mortals. Not only those, but any the future might stealthily provide. With the help of Captain Balefire, Adrian Bramwell would easily prevail. With his stupendous beauty and charm, Adrian could live on forever, breaking hearts wherever he was destined to go.

"And why should you care about a few lives destroyed?" concluded Balefire. "The sweetest revenge in existence, after all, is success."

The golden light returned to Adrian's eyes.

"What's running through that beautiful head of yours?" asked Sorrow.

Adrian looked at her and smiled. "One for sorrow."

"Two for mirth," said the very lady.

"Three for a wedding, and four for a birth," said Adrian.

Mirth placed her talon-like fingertips under Adrian's chin. "Five for laughing."

"Six for crying," said Sorrow.

The Raven Ladies enjoyed a merry dance as they chanted *seven for sickness, eight for dying, nine for silver, ten for gold!*

Adrian held up his hands. The Raven Ladies paused in breathless anticipation.

"I have decided to remain with Civette," Adrian announced.

The Raven Ladies were dumbfounded. Balefire was not. Her face aglow with happiness, Civette ran to Adrian's waiting arms.

"Eleven for a secret that shall never be told," Balefire concluded. His voice was small but meaningful.

The click of a latch sounded, a side door opened, and Richard Marlow stepped inside. He had followed Civette and the worries of his wounded heart to this very room. The expression on Richard's face was that of a weary man who had witnessed many of the horrors this world could inflict. He had tried to entomb those horrors, but that which is forced to be buried never stays hidden for long.

Civette took a cautious step toward him. Richard was reminded of something he recently said—poetic ramblings about sunlit balconies in distant lands, and dreams of sharing wind and cold and rain. Hearing it now in his head, it made no sense. As lovely as she was, Civette had no place in Richard's future. He calmly realized that she never had. Their story, begun as a fairytale about children long ago—a tale wrought with false dreams and gossamer promises—had reached its desired conclusion. Richard took one last look at the creature standing before the glass.

"Illusion," he said. Richard turned to go. But before he did, he mechanically raised a pistol toward Adrian and fired.

Chapter Thirty: O Wild West Wind

O wild West Wind
thou breath of Autumn's being,
Thou, from whose unseen presence the leaves dead
Are driven, like ghosts from an enchanter fleeing.
~Percy Byshe Shelley, *Ode To The West Wind*

The bullet seared through Adrian's chest of straw and on to the mirror behind him. Where it hit, the glass cracked in fine lines. Pieces began to fall like shattered diamonds to the floor.

"All the bright, pretty things, they break so easily," said Mirth.

"And they never come back," whispered Sorrow. A single tear cascaded to her chest. She rolled the resistant drop between her talon-like fingers, and marveled at the emotions captured within.

Beautiful diamonds that should last forever, Adrian heard in his festered head. He'd said that only today. But now, those words felt like lines from a fairytale recited long ago and since forgotten. His imagined realm, his glittering world of diamonds, was nothing more than perilous shards of glass.

Adrian felt a stab near his makeshift heart. It was small, but forceful. It swept his breath away with the fury of an ocean wave withdrawing from the shore. Adrian wondered if he should be alarmed. His blurred wonderment was brief. Serenity crept through him like a chilled mist. He felt himself flying backward over a golden meadow. Its fragrance filled the air to such a degree that Adrian believed he was being pulled into a rising weight of water. He was not distressed by this.

He saw Bess's cottage. Windswept leaves were rapping at the frail windowpanes. Dying leaves always wanted to fly inside, for they had nothing left to cling to. Bess had grown tired of sweeping them out. He watched from overhead as a blurred vision of Bess welcomed the leaves in to a peaceful passing.

Vines of Dutchman's Pipe wove round the porch rails to smile up at him. Their comical, duck-like faces were beaming. Adrian looked for the clouds. They were not there. The heaviness in his heart lifted. Bess's image vanished from his sight. Reaching out their tendril arms, the Dutchman's Pipe bowed and nodded solemnly to him. Adrian knew what they meant. It was time to return to dust. Adrian tried to raise his hand in farewell, but could not. With a sad but lyrical flutter, the blossoms lowered their heads. There was nothing left to say. Adrian drew in one final breath, rich with the warmth of the melting sun, and surrendered himself, slowly floating up into the hazy abyss of his dreams.

"I am here," he heard Civette say. "I love you."

Adrian smiled. "She does care," he murmured to the souls around him.

And with this, whatever ill intents within him flew, and he was beautiful again. The once spelled and cursed scarecrow transformed into a true man. Kneeling over him, Civette witnessed it all.

"Come back to me, Adrian, come back," she pleaded.

There was never a wish more cherished, yet doomed. With but moments of a genuine life lived, his hand in hers grew cold.

****

Lifting her head, Civette's eyes cried out for understanding.

"'Tis the stuff of life, of dreams, and of twisted endings to tales told about places found deep within the enchanted woods," said Balefire.

There came a deep and menacing groan carried by a great rush of air. A tipped candle in the formal parlor had taken hold at last. Its flame engulfed that room with a diabolical glow. As the blaze inched along, the relics, trinkets, and baubles blackened and burned, their cherished stories searing in smoke. The faces on the family portraits remained unchanged as the gilded frames of their cages sizzled and sparked. Perhaps they'd always sensed that the end was near. Lavish drapes flared, bringing down a close to the act. What had once been a faint scent of decline turned heady. It did not pervade long. This room, along with its proud history, sighed and collapsed into ruin.

Curls of orange light pulsated throughout the ballroom and vanished. With that darkness came a far-off boom.

Chapter Thirty-One: Flight of the Crows

The rumbling was faint at first. It gave the impression that it radiated from the clouds. A heavy silence followed, broken only by the parlor flames feeding on the trim panels, and the sputtering of the storm's final rainfall without.

Hollow zephyrs began to blow, deep and dreary against the very walls of the house. Balefire and the Raven Ladies made their way toward the west-facing windows. The polished floor boards trembled and sighed beneath their feet. Through the windows, far off in the distance, a trail of eleven ravens could be seen flying northward. Their wings rhythmically battled the wrath of the wind. Storm gusts wrenched the onyx streaks from the sky, replacing them with streaks of bitter copper-orange. The colors crept up confident and strong against the churning horizon.

Next came a deafening roar, as full as thunder overhead but far more boundless and foreboding. Through the rainswept windows the three watched as a river of broken fences, small buildings, boulders, and snapped trees raged by them. The Raven Ladies, in fear, were about to take flight, but Balefire stopped them. He pointed uphill. A precipice above served as a barrier, separating the deluge of debris to tumble madly down each side of the great mansion.

Beneath the furious onslaught, lawns became torn

up, flagstones shifted, and ancient stone walls collapsed. Quaint walking trails turned into rolling streams. The bordering autumn blooms did their best to hold on, but the rush of rain water and debris proved mightier. Last to go was the guardian oak at the entrance gate. Its knothole heart was gored by the rails' shiny spires. An indifferent river raced underneath, carrying with it Civette's headband of pearls and the frantic farewells of the great oak's dying leaves.

Next, the cries came, clamors and screeches of agony from those who'd fled the house only to be trapped in this hellish landslide. Richard Marlow, being closest to the house, was the first to be taken. Those below him tried to run away, but their efforts were in vain. Whatever their mortal souls were made of, the good, the bad, the giving, the greedy, the loving, and the hateful all perished together beneath this cascade of destruction. All but the white raven that circled thrice and easily flew away.

John Cairy did his best to escape the landslide. As many do in their final moments, John saw his life as he had lived it. He remembered himself as a child seated in the library at Cairy Hollow. His tutor was pacing the room, reciting a lesson John did not care to hear. Instead, John was sketching the image of a shooting star. When John was older, Bess Dalby claimed that she could hear the jubilant cry of a shooting star as it sailed across the sky. John imagined right then the sheer rapture in that. Despite the tragedy John faced, the feeling was exhilarating.

Bess had always chided John for not dreaming by day. Dreams by day were never cloudy, she assured him. John might have found that magical passageway in his mind when he was young, but such whims and fancies were constantly lectured away from him by his tutor and his cold, unloving mother. Now, in his final moments, John regretted not searching for that magic. Bess claimed that in life, nothing more was needed other than the beauties of Nature, and the reassuring warmth of the sun upon one's face. The memory of Bess, bright with promise, drew up around John's racing heart.

And then, there she was.

Bess Dalby appeared at the foot of the hill. She was enveloped in a glow of heavenly light. John could hear her confessing she'd never loved anyone as much as she loved him. She promised John that once he passed through Nature's fury, they would be together always. John merely needed to believe and let go. There was nothing left upon this butchered earth to bind them. This would be an end to all that was barren and loveless. Bess assured him this as harsh coldness coiled around him. There was no need for fear. Bess would be there, waiting for him on the other side. John trusted Bess. Somehow, he knew he was always meant to, and he called for her as he ran. Her name echoed in the rain. He never felt the impact of the massive rocks that took him.

It was imagined that just before Leona was overthrown with rubble, she recalled the foretelling words: *She'll come like a thief in the night, wrap her agile limbs 'round your ankles, and drag you squirming and screaming to the roots of hell.* In all certainty, Leona saw the images of those she had wronged, elongated faces and accusing hands emerging from the tumbling rocks and the angry debris. She also witnessed her brother and Bess together. Whether or not Leona felt remorse was of no consequence now. The infamous clasp flew from her dress, landing in a ravaging trail of mud. Like many of the others, Leona Cairy Middleton would never be sought out or found.

****

A deep stillness misted the earth. The air was no longer rent with wails and screams. Only the sounds of falling rain remained—a rain which no longer caressed the lush lawns but fell dully on the rocks and the wreckage of Cairy Hollow. It was as if the cherished ground which once supported the great house had, in mere moments, been swallowed whole.

Sorrow turned to Balefire. "You knew this would happen. You predicted it when you said, *Where shall we three meet again in thunder, lightning, or in rain?* You even called it the final hour."

"How clever of me to know in advance the impulses of Lady Nature," said Balefire. "Or maybe she was riled by the notion that your scarecrow was twice as pretty as she. In any event, we can all agree that my passionate theater piece will never see a second curtain. I believe most of my leading players are dead."

Balefire was about to say more, but another low explosion sounded. It was the force of the parlor fire pushing out the heavy wooden door. Reams of black smoke spiraled from its frame.

"We must fly," Mirth exclaimed. Coughing amidst clouds of smoke, Mirth took one last look at Adrian Bramwell's body on the floor next to the terrified and weeping Civette. "I knew this would end badly," was all she ventured to say. Mirth also said it without sympathy, for deep down, she was a scavenger bird without the smallest scrap of feeling.

Sudden dark clouds crept along the floor. Slowly,

the shadows sprawled, oscillating in color until they rose up, revealing the diaphanous figures of those members from the family portraits. There was the judge, swathed in his magisterial robes, followed by his less ambitious brother who was happy to be forever remembered in his red banyan and tassel-edged nightcap. The carefree gentleman in his long, hunter-green country coat, tumbling cravat, and large black hat ambled into the ballroom. He looked toward the sideboard, hopeful for a splash of rum. The severe woman also made her appearance, her gold brocade as stiff as her dour expression. Her husband was there too, attired in his military uniform. He had died somewhere far off in battle, and he seemed surprised to find himself in a house again. A young woman entered, her burgundy velvet gown set off by an Elizabethan collar. She was the first true Cairy bride. A small book lay in her pale and delicate hands. She placed it on a side table. The book immediately flared and burned. All ghostly eyes turned.

Finger-like vapors crept beneath the parlor doorway. Slowly they crawled with a noise, much like bones snapping and cracking. The streams settled into a pool of electric blue. In sparking rolls of power, the opaque silhouette of a woman rose tall. The whirling air about her form reeked of sulfur and crushed roses. The flames beneath her feet restored her color.

Emmeline Cairy made her appearance. She was adorned in her portrait's signature blood-red gown, the very same that Civette was now wearing. Broken, but reborn, Emmeline's beauty shattered silence. Balefire bowed before her presence.

"Emmeline, Emmeline, where have you been? Had you flown off to London to visit the Queen?" he chanted.

Emmeline nodded as if to laugh. From around the back of her skirts appeared the little papillon known as Ismay. Ismay seemed to recognize Balefire and shook her snow-white tail. Gliding above the floor in her slippers the color of a freshly cut ruby, Emmeline joined her family. Even the unhappy woman seemed pleased to see her. Moments later, Emmeline's ancestors disintegrated to ash, one by one. They did not seem afraid to do so. Ismay was the last to go. She offered Balefire a happy but soundless bark as she faded right down to her red bow.

The ethereal Emmeline floated to where Civette knelt with the lifeless Adrian in her arms. Emmeline reached out and touched Adrian's cheek. Her skin was the color of fresh snow under a midnight sky. From her fingertips flew a diamond bright spark that lit up his face. Emmeline looked gently upon Civette.

"I knew you were real," Civette told her. "Ever since I was a little girl, I knew you were here in this house, watching us all. Most of all, you watched over me. I'll be forever grateful."

The smile Emmeline gave Civette was fashioned by fire. It was so bright, Civette had to shield her eyes. With a nod, the phantom Emmeline bowed her head and returned beneath the parlor door in much the same manner as she had appeared. Her light was glorious.

From the splintered skylight came a great fluttering of wings. Ravens by the dozens burst into the room, soaring around the sparks from the flames that floated like tiny blazes of snow. The matriarchal white raven appeared at the crest of the skylight. She watched as, beneath her, the golden tassels on the Glass of Truth caught fire and sizzled away.

Balefire strode over to the lifeless form of his once magnificent puppet. "You had your golden chance. But now it's gone," he said with a shrug. Balefire raised his arms to the havoc around him. " 'Farewell happy fields,' " he quoted, " 'where joy forever dwells. Hail, horrors; hail infernal world! And thou profoundest hell, receive thy new possessor.' "

"Flight of the crows," announced Sorrow and Mirth.

"Tells how the wind blows," they all chanted.

So the ambitious demons of the forest had taken over Cairy Hollow at last. As for Civette, she didn't hear their chants, or notice the wild birds that circled overhead. She remained with her lost love in her arms while the glass in the windows liquified and poured in like rain, and the walls sighed and crumbled from the fire within.

****

The old woman on the stairs smiled a crooked smile. "And that, dear listener, is the end of the story."

" 'Twas a tale brilliantly told, Midwife Corbin," said her listener.

"I am glad you liked it, Captain Balefire," was her even reply.

The two erupted in laughter, their harsh breath extinguishing the spent and solitary candle.

Nature's first green is gold,
Her hardest hue to hold.
Her early leaf's a flower;
But only so an hour.
Then leaf subsides to leaf.
So Eden sank to grief.
So dawn goes down to day.
Nothing gold can stay.

~Robert Frost

A word about the author…

As a child, Mary Carter was devoted to PBS, vintage movies, and classic novels. Many years later, not much has changed. Mary's most rewarding career has been as a youth theater specialist. She has led over 500 art- and history-related programs, and written over a dozen custom-crafted school plays. One such piece was a weaving of Nathaniel Hawthorne's moral legend, "Feathertop" and the 1908 play, *Scarecrow, or The Glass of Truth* by Cornish NH poet Percy MacKaye. From that memorable endeavor, this New England Gothic novel was born.

Mary is the proud author of the 2022 historical rom-com *Rules of Engagement*. *Nothing Gold Can Stay* is her first fantasy creation. You can learn more about Mary at maryjcarterauthor.com or say hello on Twitter @mjcarterauthor or on Facebook.

Thank you for purchasing
this publication of The Wild Rose Press, Inc.

For questions or more information
contact us at
info@thewildrosepress.com.

The Wild Rose Press, Inc.